MW01287088

FOR THE BLESSINGS OF JUPITER AND VENUS

MORE ADVANCE PRAISE FOR VARUN GAURI'S
For the Blessings of Jupiter and Venus

Varun Gauri's debut novel is a funny, surprising book that brings an unexpected and clever twist to immigration-and-assimilation stories. You'll miss it long after you've finished reading.

–Neel Mukherjee, author of *The Lives of Others*,
finalist for the Man Booker Prize

This is an achingly intimate, irreverent novel about trying to find love in a marriage, while failing to fit into an immigrant community filled with social anxieties and unrealistic aspirations.

–Leeya Mehta, Director of the
Alan Cheuse International Writers Center

Funny and serious by turns, this thoughtful novel explores the old and new among Indians in America. A beautiful, open-hearted book, it touches on basic human truths across cultures and ethnicities.

–Suzanne Feldman, winner of the
2022 WWPH Fiction Award for
The Witch Bottle and Other Stories

With picture-perfect detail, crackling dialogue, and charming characters, Varun Gauri has created a wholly original world. With great care and authenticity, this novel renders Indian and American customs, ancient and modern rites and practices, women's and men's hearts and bodies, and all that is involved in the pursuit of true love and a happy marriage, arranged or not.

–Sheila Kohler, author of *Open Secrets*
and the memoir *Once We Were Sisters*

Varun Gauri captures the travails of a modern young Indian couple who find love the old-fashioned way, to the surprise of their families. The couple struggles with scheming relatives. Small-town politics. Real estate deals. Nationalist agendas. What could possibly go wrong? *For the Blessings of Jupiter and Venus* takes us into the heart of the Indian diaspora of suburban Ohio. It is a delightful comedy of manners that poses the question of whether every marriage is, in the final analysis, an arrangement.

–Susan Coll, author of *Real Life and Other Fictions*
and former president of the PEN/Faulkner Foundation

For the Blessings
of Jupiter and Venus

. A NOVEL .

Varun Gauri

Washington Writers' Publishing House
Washington, DC

Copyright © 2024 by Varun Gauri

All rights reserved, including the right to reproduce this book or portions thereof in any form whatsoever without written permission except in the case of brief quotations embodied in critical articles or reviews.

This is a work of fiction. Names, characters, places, and incidents either are the product of the author's imagination or are used fictitiously.

COVER DESIGN by Sequel, NYC
BOOK DESIGN and TYPOGRAPHY by Barbara Shaw
AUTHOR PHOTO by Susan Hale Thomas

ISBN 978-1-941551-42-4

Library of Congress Control Number: 2024941382

Printed in the United States of America

WASHINGTON WRITERS' PUBLISHING HOUSE
2814 5th Street NE, #1301
Washington, DC 20017
More information: www.washingtonwriters.org

Support for Washington Writers' Publishing House comes from the DC Commission on the Arts & Humanities and the Maryland State Arts Council

To my cherished families—
immediate, extended, found—and especially
Ayesha, Yasmeen, Sharif, and Safya

Loneliness is the inability to speak with another in one's private language. That emptiness is filled with public language or romanticized connections.

—Yiyun Li

Love means to learn to look at yourself
The way one looks at distant things
For you are only one thing among many.

—Czesław Miłosz

Chapter One

MEENA PUSHED ASIDE HER VEIL. The gold bangles, heavy on her wrists, slid and clinked. She feared the audience would find the gesture graceless, clumsy, but she had to see his eyes. She would in moments be the wife of this man in the groom's headdress. Maybe she already was his wife. The Vedic ceremony, hours of venerable ritual, had no vows, no exchange of rings, no single moment when choice, her will, exercised its prerogatives.

Perhaps sensing her nervousness, Avi caught her eye and motioned across the temple ballroom. He was offering the wedding finery for reassurance. He pointed up at the beautiful mandap, adorned with white and pink carnations, yellow marigolds, and fragrant red roses. He was smiling warmly, and his expression seemed to say, These old, magnificent powers guard over you. The betel nuts and the bowls of oranges, apples, and coconuts. The sandalwood incense. The ancient incantations of the priest, now pouring ghee into a bowl. The sacred fire burning at their feet. The expectant faces of all the lovely women in the audience, sharp-tongued aunties in embroidered sarees. The silly, sweet nonsense uncles, Avi's father's friends. The communal pride. The coming feast, with buttery spinach and tandoori kabobs.

He was saying their wedding conjured every Bollywood movie ever made, every Indian story ever told. And her husband-to-be was right. Every year, millions of people married this way and went on to have fulfilling relationships and meaningful lives. Or anyway, one had to assume they were fulfilling.

She and Avi hadn't spoken in days, though she had almost called him that morning. Waking up alone in the nondescript hotel, like any of the hundreds of interchangeable rooms she'd passed through for work, had been disorienting. She nearly headed to the gym to run on the treadmill, her habit before board presentations. But this was no business trip. She decided not to call him because she didn't know yet if Avi consoled well, or if talking to him would make her more nervous. Instead, she made herself coffee in the room. She convinced herself that arranged marriage wasn't strange. After all, could any woman say, years later, that on her wedding day she'd really known the man she was marrying?

In the back, children were being children, shouting and darting between empty chairs in the last row. Avi's father was bowing to a man who sported a handlebar mustache, an aspect she and her sister once made fun of, but which now struck Meena as charming. On the other side of the ballroom partition, a waiter engaged his own role in the pageantry, calling for "more rice" and "napkins this table, hurry up!"

The priest, a school director and retired accountant (there turned out to be no full-time Brahmin priests in small-town Ohio), asked them to recite Sanskrit phrases. Avi's voice boomed, prompting Meena's mother to look up, probably thinking, So it will be a loud-talking husband. Meena let Avi's chants fill the ballroom, then spoke herself, at low volume, her voice barely audible over the gas fire humming, the audience falling quiet to hear. She didn't know what she was chanting. Not that it mattered, as her mother might be the only one, other than the priest, who actually understood Sanskrit.

"For the blessings of the sun," the priest said in English, ladling ghee into the fire. The flames fizzled and flashed. Meena saw her toenails, lacquered in gold, gleam reflected fire. "For the blessings of the Moon." The priest invoked remote stars. He called upon the asteroids and Jupiter, Saturn, Venus, Mars. He declared that a wedding is a cosmic event, said it was the same fire and light in the stars and planets that were in the bride and groom—the same atoms vibrating, living and dying and being reborn.

He talked for a while.

"Avinash, Meena, now you lead each other around the fire seven times," the priest said. "This is the Agni Pradakshina. These seven circumambulations sanctify your marriage, by the laws of Manu. As you walk, I will recite the vows of steadfast and lifelong loyalty." The priest instructed Meena to put her right hand into Avi's left. He explained that each step represented one of the great goods in marriage— "prosperity, progeny, perseverance, etcetera, etcetera, you will know the others."

Meena noticed her sister Vishali, in the midst of a selfie, smirk. She was probably asking herself if this priest-cum-accountant was dragging and dropping across his spreadsheets. Or perhaps she was basking in the great goods of her own marriage: passion and being adored. Her husband Andrew was away, unavoidably detained on an important business trip, which undoubtedly made it easier for Vishali to idealize love marriages, especially her own.

Avi rubbed away a piece of dried henna from Meena's palm, then pulled her along, her bare right foot catching heat as they rounded the fire. After three and a half circles, Avi stopped, letting her step by so she could pull him, take his hand, lead. Then he unclasped. He made like he was raising the roof. He gestured at her, encouraging the audience to cheer the symbolism. "Ladies and gentlemen, equality of the sexes!" Avi barked. Someone responded, "Very good, very good." There was murmuring.

She appreciated Avi's enthusiasm and his public endorsement of marital equality, which meant her marriage wouldn't be conservative, but it wasn't clear what the audience made of it. A couple aunties in front were eyeing them suspiciously, as if detecting foreign speech. Probably, neither had daughters like Meena, daughters who'd traveled, earned advanced degrees, excelled in serious careers.

Avi seemed the eager type. At the Sahara Grille, where their families met for the first time, her mother and sister having flown in from Delhi, Avi kept talking over his father, a clammed-up auto mechanic who appeared unsurprised by Avi's interruptions. That was also when Avi announced, to her anyway, that he would be running for township trustee, with an agenda focused on building new schools. Meena was charmed. Avi was renouncing his career in corporate law to return home, and to help children, just as she was giving up the rootless life of business consulting to find a job in a school. They would both be engaged in educational endeavors, fighting on behalf of kids, a couple united in their values. Two minds like one.

But Meena's mother and sister didn't see it that way. They couldn't believe Meena was actually doing it—going through with an arranged marriage, marrying a random Ohioan. That evening, from her hotel room, Vishali sent Meena a link to a documentary about the sadness of traditional Indian brides. She called to tell Meena that she was giving up too soon, running away from her breakup with Peter rather than toward her new husband. True love is worth the wait, Vishali said. She had met Andrew at a raging New Year's Eve party in Chanakyapuri, New Delhi, and Andrew paid for their sumptuous wedding at a five-star hotel, retrieving his wife on a horse.

Meena's mother grabbed the phone and asked how a forward-looking and modern woman could possibly marry a total stranger. Feeling defensive, Meena cited data showing that arranged marriages had higher success rates than love marriages. She said that Avi wasn't a total stranger, that she had looked into him, had done her homework. And she had a great feeling about this. She and Avi had shared that sweet, promising coffee date at Starbucks. There was that moment when he asked with his eyes, and she looked out the window and nodded subtly.

Their mother sighed. "Meena," she said, "you must understand that marriage is never easy, with or without love. I don't care if your husband is sweet when he proposes. I don't care if he is Indian or a white boy going native, like Andrew. It won't matter. Doing this won't spare you pain. Trust me."

That was clearly a dig at Meena's late father, whom Meena had adored, and now had to defend. She said, "Love marriages do not guarantee happiness, as you know full well, Mummy. Why are you even arguing with me? You know what Papa asked me to consider, what he used to say. Arranged marriage is an attitude toward time. Of course I will be happy." Meena, marshaling her arguments, added that her marriage was only semi-arranged, anyway, since she and Avi found each other online, and that it's different in America, where women don't have to live with in-laws, and can have their own lives and careers, even in Ohio.

Avi's ad on YourShaadiInAmerica.com had included photos of him chilling lakeside in a blue flannel, resting against a red maple while sporting a Cleveland Browns jersey, and throwing a football. There had been consistency in those photos. The same confident half-smile, a warm expression, the fashionable grizzle, the broad shoulders, the athletic hips. His proportions beckoned, for sure, but she was more attracted to his solidity, his steadiness. He seemed unpretentious, loyal, rooted, not a slick globe-trotter like Peter. His photo won her over. That and the tongue-in-cheek comment: "My postings and replies are jointly manned by my parents and me, so expect consultative delays (you know what I mean). Let's give this thing a shot."

Meena and Avi finished their circles. The priest had them sprinkle rose water on the fire. He mentioned the sun again, in the context of a digression on the importance of passion in marriage. He called out Polaris, the ever-steady North Star. Grinning like a game-show host, the priest finally said, "Avi, you are a husband. Meena, you are a wife. Be happy, love birds!"

Avi, a foot taller than Meena, was wearing a gold sherwani, turban, and scarf, with a silvery brocade running across his midrib and collar. He pulled her close, draping his arms around her, leaning his body in, resting his cheek on her head. Was he about to kiss her? She would love a kiss. And her mother and sister really should see it. Meena closed her eyes and waited. But he didn't make a move. Was he feeling self-conscious in front of these fussy uncles and aunties? She opened her eyes. He leaned back to look at her, their thighs pressing, and she thought they must look like two irises in a vase, stems together, the heavy headdresses falling in different directions. Finally, the audience started to clap and laugh. Someone shouted, "They think marriage is one long embrace, won't they learn!"

Laughter and applause and feet stomping like running elephants.

He spoke into her ear as the crowd began to approach the stage, "Listen, so during my toast I'll say a few words about why I'm running for township trustee. Just a heads up."

A campaign speech at their wedding?

"Do you think that's appropriate?" she asked.

"It'll make them happy. This wedding isn't just about you and me, Meena. It's for everyone."

Maybe this was how it was done in Southgate, Ohio. Anyway, she believed in Avi's easy confidence, his upraised eyebrows and playful smile, his commitment to family and community, all so unlike her previous life, those empty hopes, and that romance with Peter, such a waste, two burnt-out wicks. She took Avi's arm and descended from the platform as the recessional music began. It was a Bollywood rendition of Beethoven's "Ode to Joy," which Avi had selected, telling her that their wedding, and their lives, would blend East and West, tradition and modernity, the relic and the recent, the stately and the crazy, the choral and the ghazal.

Meena shuffled down the steps in her saree and heavy bangles. Arm in arm, they turned to their families and their two hundred thirty-four guests, plus or minus the last-minute cousin of Avi's who might or might not have arrived from Chandigarh. Rows upon rows of Avi's family friends, relatives, high school buddies, former law firm associates, temple goers, and her few Ann Arbor friends, from graduate school and consulting, came to congratulate them. It was hard to keep track. She wished there were more from her side, that all those junkets around the world with Peter hadn't caused her to lose touch with so many people. More folks seemed to be congratulating Avi and his mother than her, but that was to be expected, of course.

"So, what are your plans?" someone asked Avi. Avi said his solo practice here in Southgate was taking off. Many clients coming in, including some biggies asking for tax advice. He liked that he was working on behalf of the community. He was his own boss. This was so much more interesting than his work in Chicagoland, where his last assignment had been documentation for a wastewater management company outsourcing its IT operations.

Meena overheard Avi's mother say to an indistinct crowd, "I am giving Meena my favorite necklace set. Also, a new apron and vacuum cleaner. Yes, our house blessings puja is coming soon, you see. Meena, come here. These are our friends, the Sharmas. Mrs. Sharma and I watch *All My Children* most days. You would like to join us?"

Avi's mother couldn't be assuming that Meena would be a homemaker, could she? She was probably referring to the first few months, as Meena had just completed her degree in educational social work and would need some time to find a job.

"Nice to meet you, Mrs. Sharma," Meena said, smiling. "I'd be happy to watch with you sometime."

Avi's father, three fingers on his right hand lost to a radiator fan mishap, waved his thumb and forefinger at the crowd, indicating it was time to move to another circle of well-wishers.

Avi introduced her to his "knucklehead" high school friends, Bob and Jim. Jim, tall with blue eyes, congratulated Meena by kissing her on the cheek, very close to her lips, and putting his hand firmly on her back. It was uncomfortable, and Meena turned away. Meanwhile,

Bob took Vishali off to dance, saying, "Yowza, too bad the bride's sister is taken." Vishali was always a magnet for the men.

Avi's father called over his own buddies, "the Punjabi 5," a gang of senior citizens who played cards at the mall on Mondays. They had attended the meeting of the families at the Sahara, announcing, after the baklava, that Meena was a "very well-mannered girl" who was "formidably educated." One of the Punjabi 5, Mr. Verma, now gave Avi a check for $101 and asked Meena to run her finger across his signature. He said, loudly, that he would gladly have given $1,001 if not for this Great Recession and his goddamn broker, who predicted the Dow was about to hit 36,000. The check was made out to Avinash and Meena Sehrawat, though Meena had not changed her name.

Another of the Punjabi 5, Rav Uncle, took Meena by the elbow and led her into a corner, near a gaudy statue of Lakshmi. The goddess wore a bright red dress and sat on a pink lotus, three of her hands holding flowers while the fourth cradled a pot of gold coins. Rav Uncle introduced his son Peeku, who suffered, Avi had explained, from an intellectual disability. Peeku was exceptionally short for a man in his twenties.

"Meena," Rav Uncle said, "please explain to Peeku why arranged marriage is of benefit."

She guessed Rav Uncle considered this a teachable moment for his son. "Peeku, arranged marriage is a wonderful tradition," she said.

"I have a girlfriend," Peeku said. "She works at Kmart. I work at Sears. I'm a team member."

"Still yakking about Kmart girl?" Rav Uncle said. "Meena, you chose to marry Avi despite your past boyfriends. Correct?"

She was no virgin. Avi knew. Everyone knew. But how odd to ask now? She wasn't ashamed of her past, but it seemed tacky, and mortifying, to be put on the spot like this.

"Yes. Why do you ask?"

Rav Uncle was heavyset and squat. He had a thick mustache. He looked like a drinker, with bulbous cheeks and deep grooves that sectioned his fleshy face into intersecting, meaty planes, like a goblin.

"Don't be alarmed, my dear Meena. Let me explain. Your marriage to Avi is VIP example . . . ," he pronounced VIP like wee-eye-pee, and it took Meena a second to understand, ". . . not only for my son but for all young people."

Rav Uncle was a close family friend, and she should probably oblige him. "Yes, getting married this way is amazing," she said.

"You see, Peeku? Look at this bride."

Rav Uncle pointed down the length of her body, head to feet, as if she were on exhibit. This was embarrassing, but maybe it shouldn't have been a surprise. With so many invitees, odds were some lecherous character would be lurking.

"Look, they are moving us toward dinner. It was so nice to see you, Rav Uncle," she said. "Wonderful to meet you, Peeku."

"Have fun, girl!" Peeku said.

Meena found Avi, who put his arm around her waist, his fingers resting, pleasurably, at the top of her hip. He ushered her toward the stage. They sat at the head table, along with their families. Her mother and sister were discussing their favorite restaurants in London while Avi's parents nodded and smiled vacantly. Waiters served the bride and groom first. Shami kebabs, chicken tandoori, chicken korma, saag paneer, yellow rice, daal. A glass of red wine for her. Avi gulped his beer and switched to whiskey.

Rav Uncle announced the toasts. "I am pleased to enjoy the honor of superintending. I will speak one item before turning over to my dear friend, Avi's father Ved Sehrawat, who is like my brother. This arranged marriage of Avinash and Meena is not only their happiness. It is our happiness. It inspires. It imbues. It interpenetrates. Avi, as you know, is running for trustee. Running unopposed! His victory will not only be of benefit, business-wise. That is minor point. The most important aspect is showing the people who currently dominate Southgate, for too many years, that we, also, deserve table seats! Now it is our time, also. Isn't it? Yes, thank you, thank you. I pass baton to father of groom."

Meena's mother and sister were rolling their eyes, and Meena tried to avoid looking at them.

Avi's father turned out to be a mumbler. He thanked fifty people by name. He said leftover campaign contributions would be used for local Hindu charities. He listed all the local weddings of the last year and said his family was proud to add to the record. He was pleased Avi had returned home to help the family, chose traditional marriage, and was now running for honorable office. Avi's father said that when he had been searching for a wife, thirty years ago in Haryana, there were three or four families interested. He could have had his pick of any of those brides. (Avi put his head in his hands.) If he had any wisdom to offer, apart from expertise with both Ford Zetec and Chrysler PowerTech engines, it was this: A husband and wife should share their lives fully, but also keep a few things to themselves, some secrets. Not everything has to be discussed. Avi's mother, for instance, kept her famous okra recipe to herself.

Avi's mother waved bashfully as people applauded.

"One more thing," Avi's father said. "I am very proud of my son." He paused. With his good hand, he appeared to be wiping away a tear. "Avi realizes that life is sacrifice. He knows. Thank you, son. Welcome to our family, Meena."

People clapped and whooped.

It was emotional, seeing this laconic mechanic tear up. At the same time, Meena wondered what Avi's sacrifice consisted of. Giving up his career and coming home? Was his marriage a sacrifice?

Now Meena's mother stood, brandishing a glass of her favorite Bordeaux, which she had furnished for the reception. There were quizzical and embarrassed smiles around the ballroom, as these suburbanites did not appear to have ever seen an elderly Hindu woman raise a glass and give a toast. Meena braced herself.

"I will be brief," Meena's mother began, "as my late husband, who would have delighted in the ancient wisdom Avi and Meena are drawing on, would himself have been. One or two of you, perhaps, will recall Dorothea Brooke from *Middlemarch*, who believed that 'marriage is a state of higher duties.' Such are the current beliefs and aspirations of Meena and, it appears, Avi, in the depths of their consciousnesses. I will not use the term 'souls' here. Avi and Meena, may the gods, should they exist, bless your long lives. May you know happiness and achieve that elusive crown jewel of marriage, a unity of minds. A toast to the unity of minds, ladies and gentlemen!"

The men raised their glasses, but some women smiled at one another sheepishly, probably embarrassed by the bride's mother's wine drinking and forwardness, and identifying her, accurately, as one of those Delhiites who host salons where people read George Eliot and Jane Austen while denouncing the legacy of colonialism.

Someone shouted, "Avi, your turn, come on up, man! And don't forget to tell us where to send the checks!"

Avi stood. "Thank you, wow, what an interesting toast," he began. "Another round of applause, everyone? Thank you, also, to Rav Uncle. Thank you, Dad. Thank you, Mom. Well, my turn. To my wonderful wife Meena, let me say how fortunate I am. You are my queen, my sun, and my moon. And I am the ever-constant North Star."

People clapped politely. Avi paused. He breathed in heavily, his chest rising, then exhaled. He seemed nervous. Meena offered a smile of encouragement, though he wasn't looking her way.

"Again, let me thank my mother and father, who are the very epitome of a mother and father. And let me thank Meena's Mummy for agreeing to let her daughter marry me. I know the marriage of our families is awkward, in some respects. Ours is a modest family. We are not fancy people. In our community, we look for solid and honest investments. We may not be recognized by the rich and famous, those in Wall Street or South Delhi or BKC in the financial district of

Mumbai, but we are good people. Sometimes we are embarrassed, ashamed to be who we are. That must stop! We must be proud. I am an ordinary man, but I will put everything I have into this marriage."

"You get 'em, young man!" someone shouted. Someone else, perhaps Rav Uncle, said, "Continue."

"As you no doubt have heard, I'm running for township trustee. I would be the first Indian and the first Hindu to hold that position in the entire history of Southgate! I have no opposition, but I still need your support. I want to win resoundingly. If I win, I promise you Diwali will become a school holiday, just like Christmas and Rosh Hashanah."

Avi extended his arm toward the family table, then at the Punjabi 5. He nodded and grimaced, appearing very serious.

"And I will do what I can to make sure there is business growth and opportunities for all Indian entrepreneurs! So thank you, everyone, not only for coming today, but for your support. Together, we will bring our community, and Southgate, to the world stage!"

The applause after Avi finished was loud and long. The men gave Avi a standing ovation. Avi's mother, using a napkin dotted green with spinach, wiped the corners of her mouth. Someone shouted "Bharat mata ki jai! Victory to Mother India!" Meena's mother had her hands on her temples, as if suffering a headache.

Avi raised his arms in celebration and then sat down with a flourish. He put his arm around Meena. He had the eager look of a schoolboy, though his breath smelled of alcohol. As he kissed her lightly on the lips, people at nearby tables guffawed and cheered, and he turned and waved at the crowd. She wished their first kiss had been fuller, and more private, and hoped her mother and sister hadn't witnessed that careful little peck.

The rest of the night was a hazy mix of wine, dancing, and small talk. Guest after guest shook Avi's hand, bowed, touched Meena lightly on the back. Aunties in shawls smooched her on the forehead.

Waiters poured yet more drinks. A dermatologist offered his card. Men removed envelopes of cash from the inside pockets of dinner jackets or, in the case of one recently arrived Punjabi farmer, a hidden zipper in his pajama pants. They invited Avi and Meena to dinner, gave out paratha recipes, and dispensed advice on how to get pregnant. There were references to Avi's career and Meena's homemaking skills. There was a mini-crisis when an uncle, styling himself the sound engineer, couldn't get the speakers to work, and another when a different uncle realized how much ghee was in the spinach.

Meena overheard conversations about the state of the economy, a looming and changeable threat, like the winters in the Midwest. Kohli, another of the Punjabi 5, said the auto industry would never be like it was in the '60s and '70s, when he and "the gang" immigrated, along with the engineers and the others, all choosing Southgate for the good jobs and the chance to rise in management. It seemed that for him the memory of the first years in America was yet another nostalgia, amplifying the loss of the homeland, sweet early memories of the relatives and the good food left behind in Delhi and Lahore, memories of when his brothers and sisters were young, parents alive, new friends in America that conjured old friends back home, memories of memories.

When the bhangra music came on and the dancing started, people threw cash and checks at Avi's and Meena's feet. Peeku bashfully asked Meena to dance and, during their clumsy waltz, told her she was the most beautiful bride in the world. Bob and Vishali danced together, yet again, during "Mundian to Bach Ke." Jim, abandoning his wife, whirled Meena around to "Dancing in the Dark." She hoped Avi didn't mind.

Finally, the guests said their goodbyes. The waiters cleared plates and napkins. The catering company started to fold up the tables. Meena went into the bathroom with Vishali to change out of her saree, folding and placing it carefully, along with her bangles, in the

Vuitton bag her sister produced. Vishali suggested Meena keep her makeup on, which "will move things along tonight, trust me," but Meena couldn't wait to wipe it off. Standing over the brass-colored sink, she applied cleansers, oils, moisturizers, and balms until she felt like herself again. Meena slid into a pair of jeans and a soft t-shirt.

When the sisters came out of the bathroom, their mother joined them. "You must be happy, my dear," she said. "Avi seems like a good chap. I hope he is, for your sake."

"Of course he is," Meena said. "I cannot imagine a warmer, more down-to-earth husband."

"I see. You must concede, however," her mother said, "that it is dreadfully tone-deaf to give a campaign speech at a wedding."

"It was fine!" Meena said. She took the bag from Vishali and put it on her shoulder. She wanted to tell her mother to stop being such a killjoy, but that would only provoke another round of argument, and she preferred to remember her wedding as a night of high spirits, celebration, and ease. Her mother couldn't imagine domestic happiness and would be incapable of understanding.

"I also thought it was weird," Vishali said.

"Maybe for you," Meena said, "but it's a big world, Shalu. They loved it. You heard the applause."

The catering staff was waving goodbye, and Meena waved back.

"And the father's toast," her mother said.

"He loves his son," Meena said.

"If he thinks Avi's marriage is a sacrifice, I tremble to consider what that makes you."

Meena had had the same thought, but she now said, "Don't be so literal, Mummy! Would you let it go? It's going to be fine. Have safe flights back. I love you both. Bye, bye." Meena hugged her mother and sister goodbye, then headed out into the warm night, where Avi was waiting.

Chapter Two

AVI FELT A SPHINX MOTH brush against his hair. There were two moths circling, chasing one another. How lovely to move like that. The night was languid and warm, and lemony moonlight glinted off the cars rambling down Richey Road. Behind the temple tower, the hazy moon shimmered like a bowl of yellow lentils.

All night, he had kept refilling his drinks. After his toast, Rav Uncle said, "Good speech! As good as Vajpayee!" His mother whispered, "Such a good boy." Everyone was congratulatory. Some even started calling him Mr. Trustee. They marveled at a young man loyal enough to move home when his parents were in trouble, committed enough to run for office on behalf of his community, humble enough to honor his ancestors with an arranged marriage. This life, here in Southgate, could be his tryst with destiny.

In a tight knit t-shirt, Meena came out with the last of the wedding gifts. It would be divine to slide that shirt off his wife. He might do it after they walked, hand-in-hand, past the threshold of his house. Their house. Alternatively, perhaps in an arranged marriage the modesty of darkness better suited disrobing. He didn't really know.

The black limousine arrived, and the driver loaded the trunk with white garbage bags full of wedding presents, cinched closed. Avi removed his jacket, pockets stuffed with checks and cards, and placed it in the trunk. He held the door for Meena.

His mother and father appeared. "I bought you a new vacuum

cleaner," his mother said, tapping Meena's shoulder through the car window.

"Thank you," Meena said graciously, frowning after they drove off.

"My mother has some preconceptions," he said, "but she'll get over them. Don't worry."

The driver interrupted, asking if the temperature was okay, if they liked soft jazz. "Fine," Meena said, and Avi echoed, "It's so fine." He interlaced his fingers with hers, resting their joined hands on the inside of her thigh. She leaned her head onto his shoulder and closed her eyes, giving him a chance to inspect her medley of curves. She was *by far* the most attractive and accomplished girl he had come across on the matrimonial sites. She was modern and highly educated, yet also taken with tradition and family. How had he gotten so lucky? Fate was smiling.

It was a two-mile drive to the house on Hutton Street, a three-bedroom, white clapboard colonial just off Richey Road. He had purchased it right after deciding to run for trustee. It had needed updating, so, the week after his engagement to Meena, Avi removed the wallpaper with NFL team logos from one of bedrooms, painted the walls off-white, and moved in a desk to create a guest room and home office. He put a four-poster king in the master and started to sleep there, dreaming of his wife's arrival. He put the desk Meena requested into the smallest bedroom, creating her study. He hired a reputable contractor to repair the cracks in the driveway and planted azaleas and hostas, edging the flower bed below the picture window. He had big visions, too, and hired an architect to sketch plans for a screened porch in back and a billiards room in the attic. His father and Rav Uncle were both impressed, and when the Punjabi 5 came over one evening to discuss election strategy over drinks, they pronounced the house "shipshape."

Meena made small talk with the driver as he unloaded the bags.

He said he had launched the limo service after being laid off at the Ford plant, seeing an opportunity to offer rides to the airport, and even to the Cleveland Clinic if elderly clients needed to see an orthopedist or cardiologist or whatnot.

"Time for us to move on," Avi said.

"Sorry to ramble, and you two have a good night," the driver replied, winking.

Avi took Meena's arm as they crossed the flagstones. He opened their front door and flipped on the lights. On cue, she saw the rose petals trailing up the stairs. "Avi, that's lovely," she said. "Thank you."

"I grow red and white roses in the backyard," Avi said. "My father taught me to garden. I believe we might have the best garden in the subdivision."

"Impressive. Overseas, my father always hired gardeners."

A compliment? He wasn't sure. He gave her a thumbs-up.

Avi loaded the white bags onto the dining table as Meena poured herself a glass of water. He saw her gaze land on the tray of yellow rice, oranges, a coconut, and a small brass statuette of Ganesh, which his mother had assembled.

"My mom's idea," he explained, "for good luck."

Meena picked up Ganesh and rubbed his trunk.

"My mummy calls him a fat, entitled brat," she said. "She doesn't like icons."

Bob and Jim would probably say Avi's mother was more Catholic than the Pope. He'd read somewhere that immigrants, like his family, were often more devout than people back home. Due to nostalgia. Maybe Southgate would turn out to be more Hindu than Meena's India.

"Was the wedding too religious for you?" he asked.

"Did I give the impression it was? I hope I didn't insult anyone."

"No, not at all! My mother sometimes, well, in her generation… Want to see the bedroom?"

"Already?"

Her eyes were laughing. He shrugged and pointed at himself, shaking his head in self-mockery, as if to suggest he didn't know what he was saying. He didn't intend to be too forward, though maybe part of him did.

"Can I take in the kitchen, for a moment?" she said. "Maybe we can open a couple presents."

She sat and took off her shoes, exposing henna designs, brown and red runners stretching from toes to shins, like grapevines, organic and edible. His girlfriend in Chicago had tattoos reaching all the way up her legs, her ass a swirl of wolves and flowers.

He opened some cards and read her the checks, some as high as five hundred dollars. He couldn't resist checking to see if she was impressed, but it was hard to tell, and it would be unseemly to ask. She opened a wedding present, a rectangular box wrapped in red tissue. It turned out to be a pink clock with bits of white and green ceramic scattered around its face. How embarrassing. Kohli, one of the Punjabi 5, always shopped at the five-and-dime.

"It looks like mortadella meat," she said, laughing, sounding both appalled and amused. She set the wedding gift on top of the microwave. Avi noticed, perhaps for the first time, the appliance's faux wood frame, those outdated roast and braise dials.

The next gift, flat as a platter, was a framed poster of "The Guru's Ten Principles for Happiness in Marriage," printed on a drawing of a tablet, like the Ten Commandments. Meena read principle No. 4 aloud: "'True intimacy consists in sharing minds, not bodies.' Wow, I wonder if someone is sublimating," she said with a laugh.

What were the odds the first gifts would both be from the Punjabi 5?

"Yeah, so that's from Sharma," Avi said. "My father calls him a man of dignity. They say he's never undertaken an unchaste act in his life."

"Never? How does his wife tolerate that?" She put on a half-smile.

She was flirting. He pointed upstairs. She made a tiny shrug, so he took her arm and led her up the dark staircase.

"Pretty," she said, noting the silk wall hanging directly above the poster bed's headboard. He turned on a small spotlight, so that its sumptuous green and gold threads glimmered.

"I kept it in my office in Chicago," he said, "so people would know where I'm from."

"You're not from Ohio?"

"I mean my family. Before Partition, my grandfather managed a small town for the British Raj. He had a flour mill and a fabric operation. He presented villagers with wall hangings as wedding presents. I'm guessing they looked like this one."

"My sister is interviewing Partition survivors as part of a film project," Meena said. "They've documented ten thousand histories so far. Could she record your mother and father?"

Of course he knew there were untold millions who suffered in Partition, but it was odd to be reminded how commonplace his story might be.

"Sure," he said, though he doubted his parents would appreciate Vishali's questions. "What about you? Where would you say you're from?"

"I don't know, everywhere, nowhere. You know we traveled all over. Now I can say I'm from here," she said, gesturing.

Was she pointing at the bed?

"Should we, um . . .?"

Meena went into the bathroom and locked the door. Avi heard her rummage through a bag. The faucet ran. She emerged in a fitted white top with a small blue pocket at the breast line. She wore red shorts. The henna swirls stopped at her knees.

He held up a finger to indicate he'd be a minute, went into the bathroom, threw off his dress shirt and pants, and put on boxers and a Browns t-shirt. Donning pajamas seemed formal, or quaint, given all that would transpire momentarily. He flipped off the bedroom lights, drew the blinds, and joined her in bed. He reached for her legs.

Her feet started kicking.

"Sorry, it's a nervous tic," she said.

"No worries."

He put his lips against hers.

"Are you drunk?" she asked, pulling away.

"I drank, sure."

She moved farther away, all the way against the post. It was a very big bed he had bought.

"How often do you get shit-faced?" she asked. "I suppose I should have asked before we got married!"

His mother would be confused by "shit-faced." How would you say that in Hindi?

"I don't get drunk often. Tonight was an exception, a celebration," he said. He slid closer.

"Wait, so tell me again what prompted you to come home to Southgate, from Chicago?"

This was easy to talk about.

"After my dad had the accident, and lost his fingers, he couldn't work for months. He had no employees back then, so the shop suffered, and without the revenues my parents couldn't meet the mortgage. I came home, refinanced the shop, put in some of my savings from the law firm. And then, I don't know, it just felt good to help, so I stayed."

"Why township trustee?"

"People like my parents and Rav Uncle, who have been here for decades, don't get enough respect. I want to change that."

"And traditional marriage?"

"I found my calling. I wanted to cement my sense of belonging.

Have a family. Does that make sense? This is embarrassingly whole-some, you know?"

"I love it."

She'd asked him about having children at their coffee date. It was obviously important. Now she asked him again.

"I would abso-fucking-lutely like to have kids with you," he said.

She touched his cheek. "Me, too," she said. She looked fragile, her eyes moist. She kissed his shoulder. After a moment, she turned onto her back and said, "You know, that guy creeped me out."

She probably meant Rav Uncle, who took her into a corner of the temple. But he didn't want to make it seem like Rav Uncle was the obvious guess, so he asked, "Which guy is creepy?"

"Rav Uncle. He asked about my past boyfriends. I think he wanted his son to hear. Or maybe he just wanted the bride to confess her sins. A whore-to-madonna thing."

"A what? He is odd, I'll give you that, but don't prejudge him. He helped refinance my dad's shop and covered the mortgage until I got my paperwork together. My parents are tight with him. You know, he came to the U.S. with nothing yet turned himself into a local ty-coon."

"I have another question for you. How much did you date be-fore?"

"Should we talk about all that, now?"

"Is it a secret?"

"I dated. Not a little, not a lot. Average, I'd say."

"That's all you're going to say?"

He had dated maybe ten girls. Now they embarrassed him, espe-cially Helena, the hippie with the tattoos. Once, in misty rain, the lakeside park smelling of wet earth and beer, he and Helena went out on a pier, stared at the gray lake, and made out for what felt like hours, until he felt itchy and noticed red patches all over his arms and legs.

He hadn't anticipated the mosquitoes lurking, laying eggs, swarming for a blood meal. That date had left him feeling unclean, like a leper.

"Hello, Avi, is that all you're going to say?"

"Sorry. There were some in college and law school. No one in Southgate. No one as impressive as you!"

Her smile was gracious. Or was there a hint of condescension in it?

"How about you? How many guys? Lots, I bet."

"Here and there. None of them mean anything to me, either."

"What about the guy you wrote papers with, the one with tenure. Peter? He had a place in Manhattan. Was he really . . . ?"

"Married. He was. He definitely means nothing to me."

She swallowed and turned her head away. Obviously, he'd hit a nerve. They were quiet for a while.

"Is it okay if I take a shower?" she asked.

Now? His shoulders shrugged involuntarily. She couldn't see the shrug, below the sheets. If she did see it, she'd probably read it as, Sure, if that's what you want. It was really saying, I'm helpless here. She got up and headed to the bathroom.

The shower. Shit. With so much to do for the wedding, he'd forgotten. The diverter valve was supposed to have arrived yesterday, but it hadn't. He'd have to jury-rig a fix.

"I'm going to take care of the shower," he called to her, springing out of bed. How could he have forgotten? He was a mess.

"Hang on a minute, hang on!"

Avi went downstairs, grabbed a toolbox from the garage, and rushed back up. He took out a hammer, though a mallet, if he could find one, would be better. He unscrewed the handle, removed the sleeve, gave the diverter a few taps, and turned on the water. Just a trickle.

She watched for a while, perhaps curious about the mechanics, perhaps appraising his skill set. Then she went out. He poked and checked for sediment buildup. He got up on the rim of the tub and jabbed the showerhead with a screwdriver. Frustrated, he banged the screwdriver against the diverter.

Nothing. He banged a second time and twisted to get more leverage. He was leaning against the wall when he slipped, and suddenly he was falling, sprawling. He landed on his side in the hard, wet tub. He heard the screwdriver clang on the ceramic, and pain inflamed his lower back. He tried to get up but couldn't bend his knees. He couldn't generate power, couldn't lift himself.

"Fuck!"

"What was that?" She was downstairs. "Are you okay?"

"Just slipped. I'm fine, thanks."

His fucking back. After a flare-up a year ago, he couldn't sit for more than an hour and had to take steroids, which made him dotty. Was this going to be as bad? What about the campaign! Voters don't like bathtub bunglers. The Punjabi 5 would snicker. They would chuckle over mango smoothies at the mall, swapping stories about his wedding-night debacle. Who knew if Meena could be trusted to keep this quiet.

Pushing away the shower curtain, he positioned his arms on the edge of the tub and eased himself up. He took one or two slow steps, feeling woozy. Carefully, he slid into the bed as she was coming up the stairs.

"I'm so sorry," he said. "I meant to fix the shower this week, but I was missing a part. I'll get it done tomorrow. Promise. Hey, can we hit a reset?" He sat up and twisted left and right to check the pain. Not terrible. "I'm still up for . . . You? Should we take our clothes off, get into the mood?"

Sighing, she pulled down her shorts and took off her top, folding her clothes and placing them on top of the dresser. She was in a bra and high-cut blue panties.

"What's that?"

A tangle of red and purple discolorations looked as though it wrapped from her thigh to her hamstrings and left cheek.

"My birthmark."

"It goes all the way around."

She grabbed her shorts to cover it.

"Sorry, it's fine. I didn't mean . . ."

"It wasn't in my biodata," she said. "Should it have been?"

"No! You are beautiful, Meena. A little scarring is nothing."

"Actually, maybe I'll cover it up, for now." She started to put her shorts back on.

"You don't have to, really."

The contrast between the henna designs and the birthmark was striking. Immediately, he saw that her birthmark would accompany him, along with her breasts and hips and hazel eyes, to beaches and doctor's appointments, becoming as much a part of their lives as the uncooperative disc in his lower back. He hadn't expected this. But she was probably also adjusting her views, perhaps noting with disappointment the plumpness in his belly, his zero-pack abs.

She was staring into the lamplight, her face expressionless, or maybe she was holding something in. The mood between them, so jaunty moments ago, now seemed weighty. Or so stuffed with meaning as to be lunatic.

She was sitting in the armchair, across the room from him.

"It's unexpected, isn't it?" she said. "I mentioned it in one email draft, but it ended up sounding like a livestock ad. Men don't disclose physical flaws. Why should women?"

He motioned for her to come to bed. "This man doesn't have any physical flaws!" he said.

She got onto her back, pulled the sheet up to her neck, and looked away, her mouth still and her eyes twinkling. She was play-acting the iconic shy bride. Or maybe that's who she was, under all the vogue.

In one motion, he forced himself on top of her. I have a demure, sweet, glamorous wife, he thought. He could both imagine and feel the shapes beneath the taut sheet, her plump breasts ready for the unbosoming. He caressed her shoulders and chest, felt along her narrow waist and shapely hips.

Then his own hips lit up. Lower back. Searing pain.

He coiled off her, twisting to take the pressure off. As he landed, his arm extended onto the side table and knocked over the table lamp, which fell onto the floor, ceramic cracking, the light bulb shattering.

"Oh my god! Are you okay?"

He lay still on his back, trying to manage the pain. He could feel her gaze.

"Maybe we shouldn't do it, right away," he said.

"What? What just happened? Are you upset?"

He slowly turned to face her, giving himself a moment.

"Not upset. Kind of confused?" he said. "A couple friends said it's better to wait, when it's arranged. It just kind of hit me when . . . Sorry, I should've focused on this before. This is awkward, isn't it? I don't totally know what I'm doing."

"It's okay. It's just . . . are you sure you're not disappointed in my . . . in me?"

"No way, not at all. You're beautiful, Meena."

She was at the far side of the bed now, examining the lamp debris on the floor. Was she worrying she was sold a bill of goods? If she might one day suffer the fate of the lamp?

"I don't have a temper, Meena, if that's what you're wondering. If I had a temper, which I don't, would you have wanted me to list that in my biodata, along with the fact that I live in a house with a broken showerhead?"

A small smile. She could sense his good intentions. Thank goodness.

They lay quietly. "I saw some funny ads," she said. "One guy said he was a Deputy Manager and an about-towner. He wanted a girl who was not a party animal."

"That's disappointingly plausible," he said. "I saw an ad where the woman said it's okay if the man has long hairs, but he shouldn't have animals in the house."

"My sister wrote me an ad like that. As a joke."

He turned to face her, carefully, and said, "One woman wrote that if she met a good clean-shaven man, she would show him her beauty spots. Her guru said she had lots of beauty spots. Another asked for a husband who lives near the Metro, does not eat onions, and is an all-around hero."

"One guy said, 'My body is filled with hardness because I am working hardly. I am playing, also hardly.'"

He chortled. She did, too. It hurt to laugh. It also felt good.

"When we talked before the wedding, I got the sense you didn't want us to know too much about each other," she said.

"I liked the idea of a traditional engagement," he said. "Like my parents had. And their parents."

"Your grandparents barely had a say, I'd imagine. We had lots of choices online."

"I think of ours as traditional, maybe semi-arranged. We didn't date first."

"I don't trust romance, either," she said. "Sorry, I don't mean to sound unappreciative, I loved the roses." She leaned and picked up some petals off the floor. "I mean romance before you get married. Decisions are better when you're not drunk on love."

What a good way to capture his outlook. She was articulate, smart, perceptive. He really had lucked out.

"So tell me more about what our marriage represents for you. I know you just sort of said it," she said.

"You're the kind of girl who likes to hear things more than once?"

"The kind of woman. Yes, I am."

"I was ready. It seems like the important part of marriage is the readiness."

"And why me?"

"You had a great ad. Your picture was cute."

She was staring, expecting more.

"And you seemed like someone who appreciates contradictions. The spicy stew. The crazy kitchari. The motley mixture. The absurd in the spiritual. The humor in the melodrama. The blotted in the beautiful."

He was talking nonsense, probably because he couldn't really explain it. But it felt good to wax lyrical, and his answer seemed to relax her. She lay back, seemingly more comfortable now than downstairs, when they first walked in.

"Yeah, maybe it's a silly question," she said. "Why does anyone marry anyone? Your father had choices. Why your mother? Not sure why we believe it has to be a special someone. Did I tell you I chose you alone?"

"What do you mean, you didn't ask for your mother's approval...?" He almost added *of me.*

"No way in hell my mother would approve of any arranged marriage. Mummy considers herself a modern woman, a proud opponent of the tradition. To be honest, I think she's cynical because her marriage to my father was terrible. And my sister is *in love*, as she will tell anyone, and doesn't endorse arranged marriage, either. What about your parents?"

"They're really proud of me. That was an interesting moment, your mother's toast."

"Your father's, too. He's so proud of you. Coming home. Running for office."

"I'm an only child. I'm not doing all this just for them, though.

I really believe in our community. All the Hindus in this town, and there are a lot of us, deserve representation. I want Diwali celebrated in the municipal offices and in schools." He paused. "In your mother's toast, she made a kind of sideways comment about your dad. Did you hear it?"

"I was my father's favorite. It complicates things."

She had pulled a pillow between them. It felt precarious to say any more about her family.

"I was wondering . . . Do you see me as a traditional bride?"

Perhaps she was thinking of his mother's purchases, the apron and the vacuum cleaner. Her soap opera invitation. His mother's expectations would have to be addressed at some point.

"I see you as modern and respectful."

"I'm going to get a job."

"Of course. Can I ask you a question?" he said. "What about Peter, the married guy?"

"What about him?"

"Was he a lot older than you?"

She shook her arms, stretched out her legs. It looked as though she might be deciding how much to reveal.

"Ten years."

"A professor?"

"At Stanford, but he was visiting at Michigan. I met him at a conference of CEOs in Detroit."

"Which CEOs?"

She looked out the window at the lamplight. He took the opportunity to slide a pillow under his knees.

"Ford, GM, Bosch, Beaumont Health. Why?"

"Those are big companies. How much money did he make?"

"Peter? I don't know."

"You said he worked on competitive business strategies? This was a couple years ago, before the crash?"

"Back then, everyone was seeking an edge."

"Was Peter a ladies' man?"

"What are you asking?"

"How did you meet?"

"During his lecture he had trouble with his mic. I was in the front. I jumped on stage to help. He called me afterwards."

"Wait. You jumped on stage?"

He imagined jumping, and his lumbar region flared.

"It was a TED talk kind of event, with huge screens of his talking head. Everyone was waiting for the AV guys, but no one came. He asked the people in the front row to help him out. I jumped."

"Why?"

"I don't know. I ask myself that. Something about the moment."

"You thought he was cute."

"Maybe."

"And rich."

"You talk a lot about money, Avi. I liked Peter's mind. Leaders need to know themselves, know their own biases, that line of thinking."

What was wrong with talking about money? Money was important.

"So then what happened?"

"I reset the audio input. He smiled and waved at the crowd. Then he muted the microphone, asked for my name and number."

"He called you?"

"The same night. We had dinner at an Italian restaurant. We started to write papers together. We went to conferences. Really nice places. Davos, Bellagio, Bariloche. But it started to feel empty. There was this tree, in Patagonia, with thick boughs. The winds forced it to grow sideways off a cliff. It seemed like no place on earth. That's what I felt like."

"You felt like what?"

"Like I wasn't on the earth. Like it was a vacation from life."

"Sounds great. Did he get tired of you and find someone else?"

Meena stared at him. He had put his foot in his mouth. He did that. It could be a problem. With her. In the election.

"I asked if he would ever leave his wife. He said no."

His back was stiffening. Pain was starting to run from his hips down through his right leg. A car's headlights shone through the window.

"My father said to me, in his last months, that it's a mistake to expect much from romance," Meena said. "The highs and lows are too much to bear, for some people."

She sounded sad.

"Your father sounds like a wise man," he said. "I wish I had known him."

"He was always on my side."

"Now we're always going to be on each other's side," he said. "Deal?" He extended his hand, and she took it. "So let's use the shower downstairs, for now. I'll get this one fixed ASAP."

"Should we get some sleep?" she asked. "You're not one of those guys who needs to conquer on his wedding night, are you?"

"Not at all," he said. But he felt disappointed.

After a pause, she said, "My father said love takes practice. Good night, my husband."

She gave him a kiss on the forehead, turned onto her side, away from him, and in a few minutes was out.

A blow job might have calmed him, he supposed, but it wouldn't have been right to ask for one. It was a strange situation, being in bed with a girl he barely knew, and not just some girl from a bar but one he was supposed to love.

Was this confusion why he'd forgotten to fix the shower? The wedding was great, it had gone well, but there were stretches when he'd felt like an observer.

The bluish streetlight, peeking in through the blinds, never looked as lurid.

Still, there would be another way to remember this wedding night. He hadn't thrown in the towel. He tried to fix things. Even after the shower fiasco, he'd kept trying. Tonight illustrated, to any fair-minded observer, even to the blinking Punjabi 5, that he would be a good husband, an honorable official, an exceptional man.

Chapter Three

AVI'S MOTHER had left Meena a brand-new can of Folger's, along with a sticky note, "Especially For You, Dear Daughter, Enjoy!" Meena would've preferred her Brazilian blend. Avi was still upstairs, maybe hung over from all that scotch.

Why had Avi abruptly ended the sexual exchange? Had he really decided, all of a sudden, that it was better to wait? She supposed it was possible. Sunita, one of her Ann Arbor classmates, had an arranged marriage, and she and her husband did wait months to make love. She pretended to be bashful, patient, and innocent. She said it was cathartic to let the institution impose its forms. This, despite being, in her words, a "grown-ass woman." Then, when they finally did make love, it was spectacular, seismic. Is that what Avi was thinking? Maybe he was an especially sensitive man. Maybe this was a good thing. Most of her exes, perhaps all, had been narcissists.

Or had her birthmark startled Avi and taken the wind out of his sails?

It was a blustery spring day. Outside the kitchen window, a cloud wandered, exposing the countertops to beams of sunlight, as in the old Dutch compositions she loved, until the currents buffeted another slate cloud, darkening the room again.

Avi came down wearing khakis, tan loafers, a white oxford shirt, and a blue blazer. He was clutching a briefcase.

"Meena, I have to run," he said. "Breakfast meetings at the Au Bon Pain. Do you forgive me for running out on our first morning?"

He leaned in to kiss her on the cheek but seemed to lose his balance, his lips grazing her ear. He was stiff.

"Have a good day, Avi," she said, giving him her biggest smile.

"You, too, babe!"

With the campaign underway and Avi's solo practice still new, the plan was to honeymoon after the election, in Cambodia and the Maldives, stopping in Delhi to visit with Vishali and Andrew en route. It was hard to object to Avi's dedication, giving up a vacation on behalf of his campaign and community. Still, it would be sumptuous to be sunning on a beach in Malé.

Watching Avi through the picture window as he opened the door of his sedan, she started to think an Asian honeymoon might be too exotic for him. His friends at the wedding, the Jim Bobs, appeared insular. All the foreigners he was close to were Indian, it seemed. All Punjabi, in fact. His parents and the Punjabi 5, in their polyester pants and oversized eyeglasses, seemed hidebound, cut off from the hustle and bustle of Indian cities yet ill at ease, still, in contemporary America. The style codes, even in a small town like Southgate, confused them. She wondered if Avi's fashion choices had been as colorless in Chicago. She could hear her sister calling him "Stodgy Avi."

This traditional marriage was never going to be a fairy tale, some prince-charming-and-his-damsel affair, but she hadn't anticipated today's letdown. Her husband looked like a fuddy-duddy, a typical suburbanite, plain vanilla, no flair, no masala.

Well, keep your eye upon the doughnut and not upon the hole, her father would have said. He was always repeating sensible proverbs.

Avi honked three times as he backed down the driveway. Meena stepped out to say goodbye, though she felt self-conscious waving from the flagstones. Doing the housewife pose.

She had promised Avi's mother that she would prepare for the housewarming party. Did it mean anything that Avi wasn't here to help, and had left the domestic chores to her? Maybe not. Couples divide tasks depending on who's available, even in love marriages. Still, this situation would undoubtedly prompt I-told-you-so's from her mother and sister, if they knew. In response, her mind rose to Avi's defense: He had raised the roof on behalf of marital equality at the wedding, hadn't he?

Meena located the brand-new vacuum cleaner in the coat closet. She ran it over the frumpy rug in the foyer. Upstairs, she threw away the remainders of the bedside lamp and vacuumed up the shards. The kitchen, outfitted with beige linoleum floors and builder's standard appliances, needed a scrubbing. Meena wiped clean the utensil drawers and the tacky cathedral-style faux-wood laminate cabinets. Wiping the kitchen surfaces, she noticed muck on the grout separating the countertop's white tiles. Why put that much grout between kitchen tiles? She gouged out the muck with a knife. Hoping Avi, rather than his mother, had purchased the garish plastic placemats, she buried them at the bottom of the trash can and ordered replacements made of woven hyacinth. She tidied the pantry, stocked with salt and spices, sugar, Meijer's vegetable oil, baking soda, white flour, curry pastes, and coconut cookies.

Late morning, needing a break, she wandered out to the back garden, where Avi was growing tomatoes, cucumbers, and hot peppers, as well as roses and forget-me-nots. She cut three white rose stems and placed them in vases on the kitchen table. Avi's interest in gardening had attracted her to his profile because her father used to garden, too. He proudly grew impala lilies and bougainvillea in their back lawn at the house in Thailand. Once, after a fight with her husband, Meena's mother got so angry she cut off the heads of the lilies. When Meena and Vishali then found their mother crying in the kitchen, she advised them to date and meet as many men as possible, which was a freedom women of her generation didn't enjoy. Now, Meena wondered if her mother's buried desires were why she fell for Peter in that illicit, glamorous affair. She'd seen Peter through her mother's eyes. Maybe their mother's desires were also responsible for turning Vishali into a romantic.

Meena started to dust the living room, which consisted of a stark white couch, love seat, and chair set. She made a plan to replace it all with modern furniture. She would also repaint the living room gold and the dining room deep red, like a house she and Peter saw in Crete. Wiping down the glass coffee table required working around various brass statuettes of Hindu deities. On the table's bottom shelf were picture books of the holy cities of India and the Cleveland Browns' 1964 championship. She stumbled on Avi's high school yearbook. Reading it felt like spying. Jottings from his classmates included the usual promises to stay in touch and allusions to "you know what." For his senior photo, Avi had put on a blue suit, a bright green shirt, and a broad grin. Under it, someone wrote, "You shoulda won most likely to succeed." Mr. Zappa, a teacher, wrote, "Thank you for your outstanding contributions in world history. I'm confident you will make us immigrants proud. You might well be the next Dr. Henry Kissinger." People had ambitions for her husband.

Her father would have liked that. He admired men who worked hard and were committed to public service, and he would have appreciated Avi's loyalty to his family and hometown. Her father prided himself on being no-nonsense, disciplined, faithful. He was more laconic than Avi, though. When Meena would call him in Delhi, from Ann Arbor, sometimes all he could think to ask was, "So, is it cold in Michigan?" Vishali, like her mother, couldn't stand their father's reticence. They said he was like a sphinx, but Meena thought his reserve was an essential part of his rectitude, his dignity. She knew how to reach him, and they were close.

If it weren't for him, she probably wouldn't even be here, in Avi's house. After her father's second heart attack, he implored her not to waste her life. In his office overlooking Firoz Shah's tomb in New Delhi, he said the relationship she was having with this Peter fellow concerned him. It was a dead end. What was she doing? He worried about her judgment regarding men. Few women find a Romeo. She needed to be realistic. The main thing was having a good life, not a good day. He asked if she had considered an arranged marriage. He said that arranged marriages had lower divorce rates. He pointed out that every marriage, sooner or later, becomes an arrangement. He interlaced their fingers and asked, as perhaps his last and final request, since his time was coming to an end, that she at least think about it, and that in any case she look for a solid young man. That she start a family. Having children was the best thing he ever did, and Meena was the best person he ever knew.

From one of her suitcases in Avi's bedroom, Meena retrieved the vase she had purchased at a gallery in Ann Arbor, on a drizzly evening in eastern Michigan, right after returning from her father's cremation. The vase was misty black and lacquered in gold, designed to look like a treasured Chinese antiquity beaten down with age, possibly priceless. But the artist had smashed it when it was half fired, gashing a large hole in its heart, leaving two shards of uneven porcelain that folded inward but didn't touch.

The night she bought it, she set it on the mantle, as if it contained her father's ashes. Then she tried to work, as she had a deadline, but she couldn't focus. She had so much more grieving to do. She started to hear a sighing, a whispering, as though someone else mourned, too. Her little-girl self? The child her father wished her to have? To distract herself, she started out for a walk, planning to wander the empty streets, but as she put on a green windbreaker, her favorite coat, the desire to walk vanished. She stared vacantly into the open refrigerator, unable to decide what to eat. Maybe her father was right. She wrote Peter a letter, then crumpled it. She started to throw it into the wastebasket, but what if it landed on the floor, ending up as a lonely wad? Should she toss it into the bin, or walk over and drop it in? She couldn't decide anything. Her pilot light was going out. She went coatless into the wet night. There was an old beech outside her apartment. She wanted to hug it, but would hugging the tree soothe and comfort, or would she be unable to wrap her arms around it? She bent forward, leaning into the cold, watery bark.

The email she finally sent, at 4 am, was simple: "Peter, could we be together one day? Tell me if there's a chance." His reply was curt. He would never leave his wife.

Later, Meena thought that in addition to her father's plea and Peter's reply, and also perhaps the fact that her younger sister and her friends were all married or in long-term relationships, it was the beech tree that led her to arranged marriage. Something tall, solid, rooted. The tree didn't jockey, fight, contend, push, charge, exaggerate. It simply stood. It had integrity. That's what she needed, rather than excessive striving, fantasy and self-romance, wanderlust and the absence of loyalty, which Peter represented for her. When she came across Avi's profile, he seemed an anti-Peter, down to earth, concerned with local issues, devoted to his hometown and football team, someone to start a family with.

Now, Meena climbed upstairs to her and Avi's bedroom. She went through her jewelry box, which sat atop the walnut dresser. She found the necklace her father bought for her on a business trip to Kabul, consisting of a set of polished turquoise stones attached to a bronze Afghani pendant. She fastened it on and stepped back to get a better view in the mirror. The oval stones rested solidly on her neck, creating the effect of a choker. The turquoise highlighted the hint of blue in her copper eyes, but the pendant rested, awkwardly, on her breastbone. It had never fit. She could rip out a stone or two to raise the height of the pendant, but the spider webbings of copper filament were fragile. If broken, they might not reattach. What can you do, she thought, life is life.

Her father had used that phrase all the time, along with the typically Indian wrist motion in which he flipped his hand and let his fingers fly, as if opening a door in midair. When his wife complained about the poor quality of the bitter gourds he brought home, when the monsoon was late, when his wife went on and on about the supposed horrors of Indian nationalism, when he confessed to Meena that her mother always slept with her back to him, when his daughters, each in her own way, made bad choices: What can you do?

"You would like him, Papa," Meena said aloud as she removed the elegant, fragile strand from around her neck. "I'm going to have a family now."

She should be feeling excited. But she felt sad. Maybe it was inevitable. Genuine beginnings were often built upon sorrowful endings.

IN THE AFTERNOON, as she swept the back patio, a neighbor, a shirtless man with a beer belly, was trying to start his lawn mower. The engine kept cutting out. Frustrated, the man uttered profanities at modern factories, the mayor of Southgate, the governor of Ohio, the president of the United States, the coach of the Michigan football team, and everyone in China.

Meena's phone buzzed. It was Vishali.

"Flight delay, my dear," her sister said. "Mummy and I have a moment. So, how was the first night? I want every, tiny detail, what time you went to bed, how you felt during the big moment, how it was waking up next to Mr. Avi Sehrawat. Tell me, tell me."

"It was fine," Meena said, her mind half-occupied with her neighbor's toil. "All good, nothing out of the ordinary."

"No report, then? With lime, please? Sorry. We're in the business lounge. Thank you so much. Your name is Robert? Yes, it's Chanel. Thank you."

Vishali was a hopeless flirt. At that New Year's Eve party at the Australian High Commission in Chanakyapuri, she had danced with six or seven guys before zeroing in on Andrew. Robert the bartender would now be smiling at his tall, thin customer, with her silky black hair, fair skin, doe eyes.

"By the way, Andrew sends his warmest regards," Vishali said. "If it was anything but the Resona contract, he would have moved heaven and earth to come to your wedding. You do understand, don't you, dear? So you were saying, what, there is nothing to report? There was no hanky-panky? Is that what you're saying? Mummy, she's saying there is nothing to report."

Meena heard her mother laugh ruefully and say something that sounded like, "Why am I not surprised?"

"He's a good man," Meena said. She was again feeling defensive, and feared she sounded that way. "He's sweet."

"Mummy is asking if he inquired about your relationship with Peter, your past and all that. Some others were asking, at the wedding."

"Avi's becoming a businessman, so he asked which CEOs Peter and I worked with." It was hard to lie, flat out, to her mother.

"Mummy, she says he asked which CEOs Meena worked with. Status conscious, then? That's understandable, though it is widely known to be rather bad taste to inquire into previous lovers on the wedding night." Vishali laughed.

"It wasn't like that," Meena said. "More like one businessman's curiosity about another."

Vishali was silent, perhaps noting Meena's pique. Maybe it was necessary to give up a few morsels to satisfy her mother's and sister's hunger. "There was a funny moment," Meena said, "when we were comparing marriage ads we came across. He showed me a silk wall hanging from the Handicrafts Emporium in Delhi. He's so loyal. He said it reminded him of his grandfather."

Meena heard their mother say, "That old place?" Visiting the Southgate Mall, her mother and sister had pointed out the chunky team logo waist belts, the frumpy tracksuits, and the honey-baked ham shops. Such a kitschy little town, they both agreed.

"Did he talk about his campaign plans, what he's going to do in office?" Vishali asked.

"Rezoning, something. I'm not interested, to be honest." She didn't want to get into his proposal to make Diwali a school holiday.

"Shalu, give me the phone," Meena heard her mother say. "Munu, listen to your mother. Ask Avi about his plans. Find out about his investments, and how his career will affect yours. Will he make you stay home, put on a pretty face and campaign for him? He must treat you like your own person. Any equity position in any partnership, which is what a marriage is, after all, must include voting rights. You must insist. Maintain your own bank account. Set up the expectations, now."

"If it were me," Meena heard her sister say, "I'd undress him, give him my severe profile, and say, 'Status quo means no go.'" Laughing, Vishali said to Robert that no, she wasn't talking to him, and asked for some pretzels and the check. "We're just teasing you, dear!" Vishali said, having grabbed the phone back. "Also, if things don't develop in bed, Munu, consider porn. Guys love that."

"That Rav fellow, he is definitely into porn, trust me," Meena heard their mother say.

"Rav Uncle into porn?" Vishali said. "High drama in little Southgate, who knew? Munu, my advice is don't wait too long. I've heard that happens in arranged marriage. You don't want to start thinking of each other as brother and sister. Buy some lacy bras. Let him know you're waiting in bed."

"Shalu, that's your my style, not mine," Meena said.

"True enough, I admit it. Andrew brings me lingerie when he returns from his trips. And perfume and scarves and shoes. It's amazing to have a husband who adores you. He doesn't understand how he was able to live before he met me! But to each his own, my dear. Uh oh, the flight. Bye, Meena. We have to run. Mummy sends her love, dear."

Meena went inside and stretched out on the white couch. They were probably talking about her touchiness right now, on the way to the gate, poking fun at her, grinning as they boarded the plane. They were jealous of her relationship to her father. They needed to knock her down a peg. Her mother and sister were proudly secular, anti-traditional, and she was now an object of curiosity, the arranged-marriage bride.

Actually, they were probably just drunk.

None of this mattered, anyway. The important question was not what they thought of her but how she felt about Avi and her new life. The problem was that she didn't know, right now.

She decided to go for a walk, heading two streets east where, Avi said, there was a path in Linden Park. The houses on Avi's street were brick colonials and Tudors, the lawns green and even. It was quiet and empty, not a soul on the streets. A visitor from rural India or South Africa, or one of the other countries where she and Vishali spent their childhoods, would wonder if these houses were inhabited at all, or if they were evacuated owing to rumors of disease, or witchcraft.

On the path, she came across a few people walking. There was an elderly couple, South Asian, out for an afternoon constitutional. The man was in mom jeans and half-sleeves. He walked several steps in front of his woman, who wore a salwar kameez, one end of the scarf draped over her head. They seemed the type to have had a traditional marriage, too, but back when chatting with your spouse wasn't a thing. She tried to say a friendly hello, but the couple looked past her, as if she was a threat. Perhaps they had learned in their home villages to ignore strangers. Or maybe long marriage in a foreign land narrowed their vision. Or perhaps hiding secrets from one another made reticence habitual.

When she returned home, she couldn't help but notice how unimaginative Avi's living room looked: cheap Indian miniatures on the walls, a big peacock-feather fan suspended from a nail, so many brass deities, unpolished and discolored. She checked her phone to see if Avi had texted. Nothing. His business meetings were probably keeping him hard at work. It was instinctive, it didn't mean anything, just a habit rather than a conscious desire, she told herself, as she started to swipe through Peter's social media. There was a picture of Peter, his wife, and their three kids biking past a chateau in the Loire Valley. He'd just released two new working papers on Southeast Asian growth. Meena recognized one of his new coauthors, Nicolette, a pretty research assistant Meena once met. Her successor, in more ways than one? Meena read the abstracts of the papers. Notably, he'd changed his views on value-chain economics.

A professional-sounding text wouldn't mean anything, and she wrote: *I saw your new value-chain estimates. So you agree with me now??*

She tossed the phone toward her feet, since it was a throwaway line and she didn't expect a reply. She certainly didn't need an answer. To her surprise, though, there came a quick buzz: *Right you are, Meena! I can now see what you were arguing.* She answered: *I knew I was right!* He said: *I know, I know, don't rub it in, you should let a guy down easy. Talk about it sometime?*

She hesitated, uncertain. Peter might not know she was married. She got up to see if Avi was back. The driveway was empty, and she was alone. She made herself tea. It wasn't like she was always thinking about him, and she didn't want Peter to get the wrong impression, so she waited half an hour, sipping her tea, eating a biscuit, then wrote: *Super busy, but yeah sometime.*

Chapter Four

AVI TOOK ADVIL around the clock. It was the only way to take the trash out, weed his vegetable garden, and even tie his shoes without pain. When the soreness didn't subside, he switched to steroids, which made him jittery, like several shots of espresso, but at least they allowed him to meet clients in his office, where he gave tax advice and revised wills and estates. He also resumed campaigning, scheduling speeches at the business associations, working the social media, and coordinating his volunteers. He called his parents daily to ask if they needed groceries or whatever, and took trips to the Meijer's or the Indian grocery store for his father's papayas and his mother's okra.

He let Meena move furniture around and pick the best layout for the housewarming party. He let her dust and vacuum. She cooked, and her meals, especially her cactus flower salad, chicken vindaloo, and shrimp Tampico, were delicious (though his mother would probably find them chichi). Meena took on the job of watering the plants, indoors and out. She seemed the very model of a supportive, yet modern, wife. Falling into traditional roles, her around the house, him bringing home the bacon, was unexpected, given their outlooks and friends, but it also seemed understandable, in light of his injury. Meena didn't seem to mind.

In the evenings, they played Scrabble or watched TV. One night, as they were lying side-by-side in the big bed and watching a rom-com on his laptop, Meena rested a hand at his waist, which seemed like a hint. Uncertain his back was up for it, apprehensive, he brought her hand to his cheek and said, "I am so, so lucky to have you, Meena."

She gave him a warm look, then returned her attention to the show. He wasn't sure if she heard the implicit rain check in his comment, or if she actually liked this way of being together, the assumed sweetness, steady mutual support, no words needed, like an old couple. He asked himself why she didn't reciprocate and say she was lucky, too. Did she interpret his lack of passion as principled chastity, as in Sharma's Commandments for Happiness in Marriage? Fearful of betraying his confusion and disappointment with these early days, he grew increasingly guarded and quiet, like his father.

He thought meditation might help. He'd never been trained. Instead, he'd learned his techniques from various websites, cycling through Om and Hong-Sau mantras, kriya yoga, pranayama breathing, and a Born Again/Hindu mash-up that interpreted Jesus as Vishnu's reincarnation and the Lord's Prayer as a sloka. Now he went into his study closet and sat on a blanketed folding chair, partly because he didn't know what Meena would think if she saw him meditating, partly because someone said blankets and closets insulate you from impure currents. He exhaled aloud several times, his pitch going high-to-low, like a vacuum cleaner unplugged. He tried bare attention, focusing on his breath. But he couldn't corral his monkey mind, literally on steroids, and, after ten minutes, caught himself anxiously considering whether he was now Indian enough, or still between paths. He ought to be in it, now, with the quasi-arranged marriage, having returned home to take care of his parents, embracing and soon-to-be leading the local Indian community. Still, he felt the same unease, in the pit of his stomach, as he'd felt in Chicago. Maybe this was about anticipating election day. Maybe his worries would evaporate once he accomplished the community's goals—placing Hindu diya candles in front of the town's municipal offices, successfully lob-

bying to make Diwali a school holiday, rezoning the disputed real estate parcel, in Washington Woods, for Rav Uncle's development project. Maybe this unease was about campaigning, which didn't come
naturally, and would eventually subside.

Plus, he wasn't used to all this attention. Everyone was abuzz. The
Punjabi 5, the entrepreneurs styling themselves "young tigers," and
the elders at the temple were all saying Avi's imminent election sig-
naled the community's arrival. Southgate Indians would be players.
Indian diaspora businesses, like the Indian economy itself, would be
leavened in yeasty mutuality, rising everywhere you turned. Tamil entrepreneurs were building radiant temples. Rav Uncle was bestowing
convenience store franchises to community members like a bon vivant
throwing candy from a parade float. Sharma was flying back from
Delhi with tens of thousands in black money strapped to his body, if
anyone's relatives needed to stash some cash. Even Avi's father's shop
was in the game, offering discount oil changes on Hindu holidays. It
could be carried to excess, but Avi enjoyed the mutual pride. It felt
personal, as if some essence of his being, some animating principle,
which he had always hoped for and ardently believed in but never experienced, was now manifesting.

Maybe Meena could share in this collective honor. If he could
get her to experience it, too, their unease about having married this
way might dissolve in the sea of communal passions. He folded his
meditation chair, put the towel on the top shelf, and stretched out
his back. He found Meena in the kitchen.

"I'd love for you to see me in action," he said. "There's a Memorial Day potluck, with constituent Q&A."

"I'd love to hear you talk about your education plans," Meena
said. "We haven't had a chance to discuss them." She paused. "Do I
need to bring a dish?"

He didn't want her to feel compelled to cook, like one of the
church ladies, but he hadn't made other plans.

"Only if you want," he said. "I could order something, too."

Avi also invited the Punjabi 5, who were eager to join, saying that before they died, they needed to see a local Indian candidate campaign and win. It was obvious they were pursuing spectacle, that sitting in the audience would feel like mixing a spoonful of pickled mango into otherwise bland holiday picnic food.

The venue was the Ticonderoga Grille, across the street from Richey Road First Baptist and next to Sylvan Public Golf Course. Avi took some Advil, then drove with Meena straight out Richey Road, cruising past Southgate's landmarks, the billboards. One, a scantily clad couple holding hands at a beach resort, was captioned "Take Time Off for Bad Behavior." It indicated where cars exited the Basilica of the Most Blessed Sacrament, complicating left turns for opposing drivers. Another billboard, next to the Fifth Third bank branch, pictured a setting sun, orange wake on blue water, and promoted "Petoskey by the Bay, Where Summer Comes Alive."

"Hilarious, aren't they?" Avi said, hoping she would soon share his affection for Southgate. He liked to think his feelings mixed ironic bemusement with an appreciation for small-town dreams.

"Sounds like people around here don't know how to enjoy themselves," she said.

The Punjabi 5 greeted Avi and Meena with enthusiastic handshakes, shepherding them over to inspect the food. The Grille had put out burgers, hot dogs, beer, and soft drinks, while attendees had contributed coleslaw, beans, cornbread, and condiments. Avi's mother brought masala potato salad. Meena set her endive, blue cheese, and walnut arrangement on the table. There was dark wood and leather throughout the restaurant, chandeliers in the shape of deer antlers, mounted stuffed elk heads.

"Not an agreeable atmosphere for Hindus," Kohli said.

"The air con is very good," Verma replied.

Avi started to glad-hand, making small talk about the hot

weather, the Indians and the Reds, Ohio State football, and real estate prices. His father and the rest of the Punjabi 5, along with Meena, took seats up front. Avi's buddy Jim Vinson, sitting in back, mock saluted with a Pabst Blue Ribbon bottle. The Richey Road First Baptist pastor, in a suit and tie, functioning as emcee, introduced Avi as the next Southgate township trustee. "He is running unopposed, you know," the pastor said. People applauded politely.

Avi's introductory remarks concerned technology, a topic he was comfortable with, given his background in IT outsourcing law. Avi said the key to economic revival was productivity, as well as the right mix of technical expertise, financing, and low-cost labor. He said Southgate could do tele-medicine, tele-banking, even legal e-discovery. He argued that rezoning the Washington Woods parcel was the first step in making Southgate dynamic again, at which point Rav Uncle shouted, "Hear, hear!" Having satisfied his backers, Avi pivoted to education and school construction, making eye contact with Meena, who appeared to be listening with interest.

Q&A focused on what the Washington Woods strip mall development would do to traffic flow, weekend hours for business licensing, and bulk trash pickup. Someone asked whether the Taco John in the strip mall would serve cinnamon sugar crisps. No one asked about the schools.

Jim, putting down his beer, sidled up to the mic. He wore an American flag pin in his lapel. People applauded, as the Vinsons were a prominent family of farmers and local leaders, including generations of mayors and sheriffs.

"Avi, man," Jim said. "You and I go way back."

"Go ahead and ask your question, Jim," Avi said, dropping half an octave in response to the hint of harassment in Jim's voice. There had always been undertones. In the period when Avi and Jim used to hang out, throughout elementary and middle school, Jim's family would invite Avi to their Sunday School to teach him about Jesus. It was disorienting because, back then, Avi only knew Jesus as a humorless and robed figure with a long beard, probably a follower of Shiva. They'd managed to stay friendly over the years, though Avi did well in law school and Jim became an unsuccessful real estate agent, wedding band performer, and friendly drunk, the black sheep of his distinguished family.

"Don't you people own land near Washington Woods?" Jim asked, gesturing in the direction of Meena and the Punjabi 5, noticeably the only pack of brown-skinned people in the audience.

"My uncles do," Avi said. "I mean, they're family friends, not really uncles. But you know that." Rav Uncle, Verma, and Kohli looked tense in their seats.

"Why rezone in a way that benefits you people? Why not zone it agricultural? Lots of farmers in Southgate."

"Actually, I'm glad to clear this up," Avi said. "That adjacent land was purchased over a dozen years ago because we believed, they believed," he looked at Rav Uncle, "in the future of Southgate. The belief came first, when zoning plans weren't even imagined. You've seen the economic studies. All of us will benefit from rezoning. And we can use the revenues for school improvement. We all benefit."

"Some of us will benefit more than others," Jim said, again studying the Punjabi 5.

"That's incorrect, Mr. Jim!" Rav Uncle shouted, standing up. "As Mr. Avi is saying, you have it arsy-warsy!"

A man in a VFW hat turned, squinted, and laughed. An old lady in a purple smock tsk-tsked. The pastor requested that people remain quiet and respectful. Meena looked out the window.

Turning toward Rav Uncle, Jim said, "At Avi's wedding, you said you people plan to dominate Southgate. You said it's your turn now. We all heard it. Don't think I didn't. My family has ancestors buried in this soil. We're not going to let you take over."

"Not going to let us?" Avi said. "What's that supposed to mean?"

"I'm running for township trustee," Jim said. "This is my announcement. I'll file my papers this week."

"Will the papers be on time, Jim? Are you sure?" Avi asked, though he knew it wasn't too late.

"Show me the papers!" Rav Uncle demanded. "Transparency! We will inspect your signatures!"

There was murmuring and commotion. The pastor raised his palms, trying to keep things under control. Meena covered her mouth.

"Transparency? What about those campaign contributions at the wedding?" Jim said. "They were throwing checks while Avinash danced. Was every one of those contributions from an American citizen?"

Shit, they hadn't broken campaign finance laws, had they? Avi started to feel panicky. Everything he thought of to say sounded stupid, or weak.

"Nothing personal, Avi," Jim said. "Business is business. And values are values. Bottom line is you people are too clannish for Southgate. Here we let people make their own choices. Like what you like, love who you love. We don't force anybody. Avinash had an arranged marriage, just so y'all know the facts. My wife Julie stands beside me as an equal. Julie, come on up here."

Julie, in a bright red minidress, walked to the front and waved.

"We are not male chauvinists!" Rav Uncle shouted. "You are chauvinist! Look at her legs. Put on some decent clothing!"

People hollered. Someone said it was always like this when "these people" came. Avi had to do something and thought of Meena. Next to his wife's cultured intelligence, her beauty, Julie would look like a crone.

"Meena," Avi said, "would you stand up for a second, so we can acknowledge you? My lovely wife is here supporting me today."

Meena sat still as a mannequin. Avi gestured, encouraging her to stand. Seemingly flustered, she shook her head. Avi gritted his teeth. Finally, slowly, she stood. There was tepid applause. Meena sat down quickly.

The pastor took the podium, thanked everyone for coming, said it was certainly going to be an interesting election, and encouraged all people, men and women, husbands and wives, to vote their own conscience. He would pray for the best man to win. People shook both men's hands as they filed out.

"Ambush," Rav Uncle said when they convened in the parking lot to debrief. "These people use dirty tricks. When I ran for mayor fifteen years ago, that was 1996, they made candidates read the bylaws out loud. They knew I didn't attend English medium school! It was good you mentioned those economic studies, Avi, but don't talk like a socialist. Nobody likes those people."

"Uncle," Avi said, "should we have shouted like that? Should we be stooping and playing Jim's game, mudslinging?"

"Are you calling your uncles muddy?" Rav Uncle said. He glared and got into his black Mercedes, along with Verma, Sharma, and Kohli. Avi's father shrugged, patted his son on the shoulder, and drove off in his used Lexus. Avi and Meena got into the Oldsmobile. Avi stole a few glances at Meena as they backed out of the parking spot, but she was avoiding eye contact. They drove in silence.

Thank goodness he'd invited her. Otherwise, people might have assumed he kept her home, under lock and key. But she didn't seem to enjoy being a campaign wife. He'd wanted a modern woman, and of course she would have her own ideas about politics and campaigning.

They drove past new home construction, a large pit and two gravel mounds, next to which a shirtless man, wearing a stars and stripes bandana, cigarette in his mouth, was digging out the foundation with a spade, one shovelful at a time. They passed Round Lake, a putt-putt course on one side, King's Cemetery on the other. He wanted to point out these landmarks to Meena, but it wasn't clear how to break through the silence enveloping them. There was a slight upward incline as they cruised by his old high school, and he wished he could tell her how special it was to live in a place where you noticed these slight changes in elevation.

From where did Jim develop the confidence to run for office, despite being a drunk? The question answered itself. From his family, obviously, from being slapped on the back by people like that construction worker, guys who could say their forebears fought in wars with his, were all buried in the same cemetery. Meanwhile, Avi barely knew his own grandparents, let alone his great-grandparents. His ancestors were gloomy ghosts lost in the pre-Partition darkness. But didn't they deserve respect, too? Didn't they also have a right to be known, venerated, honored, right here in Southgate, where their descendants, including Avi, lived?

"Meena, I'm glad you came," he said. "I thought the campaign was going to be a cakewalk, kind of fun. I didn't expect an opponent."

"What Jim said was awful. Simply awful."

"I'm so glad you stood up, too, defending our values, defending our marriage."

"I didn't like being put on display, like an exhibit."

"I'm sorry. But you understand, right?"

"I don't, actually."

"I thought there was no one better to defend our honor than someone as cultured and attractive as you."

"Our honor? Whose?"

He wasn't sure what she meant, but she *would* come around to appreciating his point of view, understanding the community's goals, sympathizing with this campaign.

"I told you," she said, "not to give a campaign speech at our wedding."

"What? That's not what you said. Today's events had nothing to do with the wedding. We didn't deserve those slurs. It was like he declared war on us today."

"At the wedding, you said you're running for the local Indian community. You didn't mention anyone else. So when did the chauvinism start?"

"My community is my priority, but I wasn't attacking anyone."

"Watch it, Avi!" she said. He thought she was angry. But he hadn't noticed the car in front had stopped. He slammed on the brakes.

DATE NIGHT. Maybe that would help them get out of the emotional quicksand. He picked an exciting movie (not too serious, with a romantic angle) and made a bouquet of roses and peonies from the garden. The plan was to buy lots of candy at the concession stand (to create that carefree feeling), take her hand in the midst of a scary scene, heighten the intimacy during the drive home (when he would point out local landmarks and the sites of his own special memories), then share a drink, maybe champagne.

It was Friday. He sprinkled rose petals on the bed. The late evening sky was azure and vermilion. There was no need to dream of Caribbean beaches when the Midwest felt like this. He found her on the love seat reading a psychology textbook, gorgeous in her green kurta-style dress.

"Hey, Meena, I was thinking we could see the *Mission: Impossible* rerun at the Odeon Max?" he said, presenting her with the bouquet.

"They're beautiful. Wow, thanks. A date?"

"A date."

He held the car door for her. They chitchatted about her job search and his campaign during the drive over. At the concession stand, he bought Junior Mints, Sno-Caps, Reese's Pieces, Whoppers, two Diet Cokes, and two large popcorns. She laughed, said it was extravagantly sweet. He offered it all to her during the car chase scene, whispering that he believed in snacking during car chase scenes. During a close-up of Tom Cruise's fiancée, an ingenue with full lips, he could see the starlet's milky skin reflected in his wife's glistening eyes. He reached for Meena's hand, which she gave without hesitation. They were like a sweet, innocent couple, communicating their hopes with slight adjustments of the clasp. A finger brushing the palm. The tautening grip when the villain lurked.

She wanted to drive home to learn the city streets. The stars' desperate kisses were still dancing in his head. Saturn was shining brightly, next to Vega, in the summer triangle above. He was feeling adventurous, daring, open to any angle, real or imagined. He was married to a beautiful woman. He was going to win an election, infiltrate local politics the way Tom Cruise had just penetrated Vatican City. His spirit was soaring, his heart at peace, having transcended its usual cleavages.

"I love this town, Meena. Knowing where I belong, where we belong. Isn't it amazing?"

She didn't reply, at first, concentrating on a left turn.

"I'm wondering . . . ," she said, having settled into the lane, "why do you think we haven't had sex? Should we be worried?"

That was not easy banter. Not the lightheartedness he was going for.

"I'm not worried," he said, kicking out his legs and checking the flexibility in his hips and lumbar muscles.

"We should talk more," she said, "about our needs, as individuals. I think we're making assumptions about each other. It feels familial. I don't know, maybe it's normal in a traditional marriage, but it feels weird."

"You're saying we don't talk enough?"

Meena looked at her phone. She was using an app for navigation but somehow still missed the turn onto Maple. She drove slower so as not to miss the next turn, so slow that the truck behind honked angrily.

"Where the fuck is he going? What's the rush?" she said.

"Global commerce, you know, we're not a backwater," he said. His own tone surprised him. It sounded defensive, and dismissive, like his father brushing back his mother when she asked him to come home sooner, yet he didn't know what else to say. Something was wrong. Had this been a mistake? Why had they passed weeks and weeks without sex?

They drove by a huge, shuttered mall with empty parking lots the size of football fields. There were just a handful of cars in the lots, far from the stores.

"What are those cars doing there?" she asked, sounding irritated.

Was that an indirect reference, maybe a dig? Or did she really not know what happened in deserted parking lots?

"Teens and parking lots," he said, "prescription drug deals, police busts, blow jobs."

She looked at him, then refocused on the road. They were quiet for a while.

"I still can't get over Rav Uncle asking me, at our wedding, about my past boyfriends," she said.

Still focused on Rav Uncle?

"He can be tactless," Avi said, "but give him his due. When he came to America, he got a job picking corn in Iowa. He owned just three shirts that whole year. He somehow got documentation. Then he started a convenience store chain. Now he has multiple successful business ventures. He's worth millions."

"I didn't like being some kind of model wife for his son."

"Peeku is interested in this girl, he's crazy about her, obsessed to the point of harassing her. Our marriage is an alternative approach, to get him out of his pickle."

"I think Rav Uncle doesn't like me."

"Of course he likes you. Who doesn't like you, girl?"

"I wish you'd stop calling me a girl."

When they got home, Avi went into the kitchen and poured two glasses of champagne. She gulped hers quickly, then headed upstairs. When he went up, she was already in bed, her clothes strewn on the floor. Usually, she folded her clothes carefully.

He went into the bathroom and brushed his teeth. He should not have made that crack about blow jobs. He'd been half-thinking of the election, how the community had to clean up all the activity in deserted parking lots, how he could address it. But why had he said it with such edge? Just hours ago he was feeling good about his new life. Now his heart felt like a junkyard.

When he got in bed, she was asleep, her chest rising and falling. Should he wake her? He stared out the open windows. It was hot. The cars were throttling down Richey in seemingly random patterns, maybe one car or two, then five or six together, then long silences.

Meena flipped onto her stomach, turned her head away, and threw off the sheet. In the pale, fluorescent light of the streetlamp, her birthmark looked alive, a colony of red and blue unicellular organisms. He slid slowly down the bed, his feet dangling off the edge, to look more closely. There was a mole, a small cluster of hair. Meena's legs were the color of a brown pear, the birthmark like a giant bruise. It wasn't a big deal. It would look fine, in normal light. It was unfortunate that it embarrassed her. He was no *GQ* model himself.

Love takes practice, she had said. She was his lovely wife, even if he didn't know her. He kissed her on the shoulder.

"What are you doing?" she said, half-turning.

"I was thinking that maybe tonight . . ."

"Not tonight. Things don't feel right, Avi."

"I'm sorry. I don't know what's happening to us."

"Do you think it's because . . . ," she said, pausing, covering her face. "Is it my birthmark?"

"No. It's just life. Nothing's perfect."

"I'm thinking of getting it treated. I'd planned to, but one thing or another got in the way."

"Don't spend too much time worrying about it."

He ran his fingers down her arm.

"What if we never make love?" she asked.

"What? Of course we will, I know we will," he said.

"But just suppose. Would you be open to adopting?"

"Let's not go there, Meena."

"I don't know what I'd do if we can't . . . I want a family, Avi."

"Meena, it's too soon to talk like this. It's like you're jinxing things."

"I know, I know. I'm sorry. Good night."

She kissed his fingers, then pulled the sheet over her head.

What was going on? He was aiming at humility, humble dedication to his parents, his community, and his wife. It was as though selflessness was creating a wall, closing her out.

Chapter Five

MEENA KNEW she had to get along with her mother-in-law. To Avi, it wasn't only important, it was indispensable. She could read it on his face, the way he breathlessly said, "So, Mom thinks we should . . . ," and from his repeated reminders that she go watch *All My Children* with his mother and Mrs. Sharma.

Worried she might inadvertently say something offensive or provocative, Meena kept putting off the soap opera date. Surprisingly, however, when she finally did go over to Avi's parents' town house to watch, it actually went well. Without expecting that Meena serve her or even asking her daughter-in-law to help, Avi's mother Kamla had put together a tray of onion pakoras, vegetable samosas, and boondi. The women sipped tea, snacked, and watched in silence. After the episode was over, Mrs. Sharma talked so much that Meena barely had to say anything. Kamla reported, through Avi, that it had been a very nice afternoon, and that Meena seemed a nice, humble girl.

So when Kamla called to invite Meena to go shopping with her, as they needed a few items for the housewarming ceremony, Meena thought she knew exactly how to behave. When Kamla said she'd already arranged the catering, then recited their shopping list (betel leaf, sandalwood paste, marigolds, ghee, turmeric powder for making handprints, and a "Prayer Pack" of grains and seeds to be used as offerings), Meena replied, "Yes, Mummy."

Avi's mother arrived in her own run-down luxury car. She wore a blue saree and little old lady tennis shoes. "By the way, I am taking charge because you're new in town, and Avi's father doesn't care what I do," she said, mixing a dollop of martyrdom into her assertion of authority.

As Kamla drove them past the deli on Richey, she talked up the community's wealth and success: "Rav Bhai, *his* house is like a palace." And, "Somanathan, just twenty-five years old, came to America last year only, he *already* has a good job, and a Mercedes." And, "Kohli looks simple, but he is clever with *words*."

It was obvious that the point of these comments was Avi's father's shortcomings as a provider and Kamla's own extraordinary, long-suffering devotion. Plainly, Meena couldn't say that. When Kamla's complaints became more explicit ("Avi's father, of course, knows none of these things"), Meena did everything she could to avoid taking sides in her mother-in-law's marital problems, and listened quietly as they wandered through the aisles of Patel Brothers, loading snacks and prayer items into their cart. To signal comprehension, not sympathy, Meena delayed her smiles until a few seconds after her mother-in-law finished speaking.

"Avi's father loves cars," Kamla said. "Any kind of car. Honda, Toyota, Chevy. He's good at fixing. He could fix our town house, if he wanted. He doesn't talk. All day together and not a single word. He sticks his nose into the car magazines. Fortunately, Avi calls me almost every day."

"Fortunately," Meena said, after a moment.

Every day? Could that be true, or was Kamla exaggerating to feed her pride? Meena sympathized with Avi's father, thinking she would keep to herself, too, if she lived with Kamla.

"When we were young, Avi's father kept his shop open late," said Avi's mother. "Nine, ten, eleven o'clock. Avi would come into the bed. So what? He told me funny stories about his friends. I don't know what would have happened to me without him."

"I see," Meena said.

Was Avi's intimacy with his mother, her longing for a stand-in husband, the source of his insecurities, of his awkwardness and reticence in bed?

"Avi went shopping with me. He went to the doctor with me. Once it was so late and his father wasn't home, past 2 a.m., and I was worried. New wife, new country, you know. But Avi was there. He took my hand and said, 'Don't worry, Mummy, Daddy is coming.' He was just six. I don't know what I would have done without him. Such a good boy."

Meena had read in her cross-cultural psychology class that Hindu boys separate from their mothers not by individuating, the slammed doors and the fuck you's, like American teenagers, but by bonding with their wider extended family, watering down the mother brew with splashes of aunty, cousin, and grandma. But Avi had no extended family nearby, just the nutty Punjabi 5. Did that explain why he craved public recognition, and needed to run for office?

"You were lucky to match with Avi," Kamla said.

"I didn't realize he calls you every day," Meena said.

"Of course. Mothers and sons are always close," Kamla said. "When Avi was a baby, I used to go with all the new brides to the park, you know, the one where people go running. We wore our best jewelry, stood near the flowers, and poured water into silver bowls. After seeing the full moon reflected in the bowls, we sprinkled water on each other and broke our fasts with sweets. The other ladies were praying for their husbands' health. I was also praying for Avi's. Why not? Listen, why don't you and I fast together? For our good fortune, and for Avi's election."

"Fast together? Okay," Meena said.

"Good girl!" said Avi's mother.

Meena could see now that Avi wasn't merely a stand-in for his mother's distant, laconic husband. Modern laws forbade dowry, so

Avi was her half of the bargain, her gold, her riches. Avi's mother would continue to offer up her son's luminous virtues, over and over. From the way Kamla's eyes were glistening, Meena suspected her mother-in-law's early years in America had been desperate days of abandonment. Arranged marriage to a sullen husband, parents and sisters faraway. Kamla couldn't directly face her husband, cold as the moon. She needed a looking glass, so she used her one son.

They were in the checkout line behind a man with a hairy chest, chunky necklace, shirt unbuttoned halfway to his waist. Avi's mother waited for him to bag his goods and exit before saying, "Let me ask you one thing, Meena. Must you look for a job? Maybe you can stay home, take care of the house, be homely? Good campaign wife. It's more attractive."

More attractive? Maybe to you.

Meena decided to pretend she hadn't heard the question. They had finished loading grocery bags into the trunk and were buckling in. She turned on the radio and hummed to the idiotic pop song playing. Kamla was glancing in the rear-view mirror but also peering at Meena, expecting a response.

"So I heard it's going to rain," Meena said.

"Ohio weather is not to your liking, then? My attitude is to be sunny on inside, no matter circumstances on outside. Keep trying. No matter the complications."

Keep trying no matter the complications? What did that mean? Had Avi, on one of his daily phone calls, told his mother about their sexual difficulties? He couldn't have. Could he? Meena didn't think Kamla, unlike Rav Uncle, was interested in prurient details. She seemed an idealizer, but who could say? Some people thirst for exactly what degrades them.

After she dropped off Avi's mother and unloaded the groceries, Meena ran up the stairs to her study and slammed the door. She paced back and forth in the small room. It was a good thing Avi wasn't home. She needed to figure out how to put it. She'd moved to Ohio. She had acted deferential to his mother. She pretended to like soap operas. She agreed to host and was preparing the house for a Hindu ceremony she didn't much care for. She was waiting for him to be ready for sex. She could even put up with campaign events. But not work? What were a PhD in economics and a degree in social work even for? Vacuuming, aprons, and afternoon naps?

Avi had better speak up for her and resist his mother's request.

Irately, mindlessly, Meena picked up her phone. Trying to make herself feel better, she navigated to her list of academic papers, most easily seen on Peter's homepage. He had a new picture. He was standing in front of a bookcase in his office in the Manhattan apartment, arms crossed. Bright blue eyes. Always the perfect haircut. There was his list of accolades. Still the special mention, in large print, of the one international political economy paper they had coauthored, the one with the cheeky and suggestive title they came up with while laughing and drinking caipirinhas in Rio, "Advocating Plucky Dualism: Trade, Gender, and the Foreign Invader."

She texted him: *Hey, what's the research agenda these days?* Peter responded in a moment: *Inflation as distributional conflict. Also, FYI, going to be in Delhi, on and off, in case you're ever passing through, would love to pick your brain.* She debated what to say, then replied: *You, interested in conflict?? Yeah, would be good to catch up sometime.*

AFTER THE DATE NIGHT, things between them seemed to grow even more awkward. Avi was acting nonchalant, giving her hasty hugs goodbye in the morning, often with a bromide: *Gotta hit the road. Take it easy. Have a great day.* As if they were friends, not lovers.

She hadn't intended to sabotage their date night. During the movie, she had felt ready for love, but by the time they got home, it hadn't seemed right. Maybe she was more self-conscious about her birthmark than she knew. The birthmark hadn't been an issue with

Peter, or any other boyfriend. Then again, she hadn't had a traditional marriage, or any kind of marriage, with anyone else.

Or was the problem Avi? What if he just wasn't attracted to women like her? When deciding to marry him, the possibility hadn't even occurred to her. What a fucking disaster that would be. Then what? Divorce, already? Adopting a child in a loveless marriage? She was getting ahead of herself, she knew, jumping to conclusions. Still, she was now worrying all the time.

After saying goodbye to him on the stoop, she would try to calm herself by making tea and toast with butter and blackberry jam. She sliced an apple. She ate outside on the back patio early, before the mayflies and gnats circled. She threw apple bits to the koi swimming in Avi's little pond. The fish crowded the surface, gulping hungrily. Then, to distract herself from the state of her marriage, she took a second cup of tea upstairs to her study and scanned the job listings.

The public-school positions required a certificate, which she didn't yet have. An Ann Arbor classmate suggested the Woodmont Academy or another of the prep schools. Parents there would expect their counselors to arrange internship opportunities, really poverty tours, to places like Sierra Leone or Flint. If she sought that kind of vanity, she could have stayed in strategic consulting. She couldn't be anywhere near that world anymore, the peacocking conference panelists, the self-satisfied citation counts, name-dropping and grandstanding. Plus, everyone knew about her and Peter. It was humiliating to be pitied.

After scanning the job listings, she would sometimes check her phone for texts from Peter. Not because she wanted to be in his circle but to know she still could. In order to reject it, she thought. She knew she shouldn't be texting him, now that she was married, but they were innocuous, professional exchanges. Avi was probably in touch with his exes, too. Then she would go into the bathroom and lock the door. She started taking pills and applying a steroid cream to shrink her birthmark. She had considered treating it in the past but always stopped short because she couldn't reconcile the treatments, whether creams or pills or expensive lasers, with her politics. She had been committed to resisting the male gaze, overcoming the normativities. Now those viewpoints seemed simplistic. If the birthmark bothered Avi, why not treat it? A chaste marriage was unbearable.

Meena was washing steroid cream from her fingers when Vishali called, their mother patched in.

"Happy news, Munu!" Vishali said. "Remember that actor? He's coming to my yoga classes! My studio is going to be successful! He likes incense and waterfall sounds, Western-style yoga. They were Andrew's idea. My husband has so many good ideas!"

"Good to hear, Shalu," Meena said. She didn't feel like praising Andrew's ideas.

"And you? How is the job search?"

"I'm optimistic. I will find something. Hopefully."

"What is meant by this hopefully?" their mother said, pouncing.

"We have a lot going on, housewarming party, election," Meena said. "Avi's family needs my support at the moment."

"I warned you, Meena. Do not let them railroad you."

"I'm not being railroaded, Mummy! I will get a job soon. I have to. I will get antsy otherwise."

"Of course you'll get antsy," Vishali said. "I'd go crazy in a town like that. On the subject of antsiness, any news, dear? Have you two succeeded in doing the necessaries?"

"I'm not worried about that, either."

"No man wants to wait, whatever he's saying, Munu," Vishali said. "On the inside, he must be suffering. No doubt. Make it happen, Munu, for the sake of your marriage."

"I'm trying." Meena didn't want to share too much, but their approval felt like sunlight after a gloomy week. They'd long recommended she do something about the needless discoloration. "You will be happy to hear I'm treating my birthmark," she said.

"Some benefit to arranged marriage, after all," their mother said.

"You know what I think?" Vishali said. "I was thinking you could put a tattoo over it. A tattoo of something Avi and his family would like. Put a tattoo of Ganesh on your butt! His mother would be so proud."

"Shut up!" Meena said, laughing. Vishali, exasperating as she could be, was also funny. Like their mother, she deployed learnedness alongside social sarcasm, a combination that made them desirable in New Delhi circles, where party conversations involved inflating and popping people's reputations in the same breath.

"Come, think, what else would make your husband happy, Munu?" Vishali asked.

Rose petals up the stairs, or lines of Junior Mints and Reese's Pieces leading to the marriage bed?

"What else would make her husband happy?" their mother said. "You're sounding like a silly goose, Shalu. Husband this, husband that. A woman must focus on her own happiness."

"What do I care how it sounds to you?" Vishali said.

"We are waiting until we're comfortable," Meena said. "It's different in a traditional marriage."

"Oh dear. Such fatalism," their mother said.

"Andrew is coming back from Tokyo in an hour," Vishali said. "I'm putting on that purple cocktail dress. So cute. I'll send you a photo. Bye-bye, dear."

Vishali probably wasn't intending to make Meena jealous. But with Meena settled into the land of bowling alleys and dollar stores, and their father's influence on the family fading, it was obvious Vishali now considered herself the lucky sister. Madly in love with her rich husband. Jetting to Balinese beaches for the holidays. Yoga stardom.

Bollywood actors. Vishali's perfect marriage, her peerless talent for love, it all must feel like wispy, spun sugar deliquescing on the tongue.

AVI'S MOTHER asked her to push the living room furniture to one side and lay out white bedsheets for the guests to sit on. Meena took upstairs the vase she bought in memory of her father, carried the foyer table into the living room, and dutifully set up an altar with Kamla's favorites: Ganesh, the remover of obstacles; Laxmi, the goddess of wealth; Shiva for protection. Meena laid out a bowl of fruit, a plate of marigolds, and incense in cups.

In the kitchen, she lowered votive candles into shot glasses filled with coconut water. The trick was to drop the candles gently and evenly, else a lick of water splashed onto the wicks, turning them into duds. But her fingers wouldn't fit, and she kept plunging the candles in at odd angles.

"Use these," said the priest, holding a pair of tiny tongs. She hadn't heard him enter. He stood in the kitchen entryway, watching. He wore a turban, a white kurta, and a blue Nehru jacket, more festive attire than at their wedding.

"My hands shake, so I carry them in my coat pocket. Concealed carry!" He cackled.

He was short, Meena's height. She detected a faint smell of garlic on his breath.

The tongs worked. She inserted the remaining candles. Together, they lit the wicks.

"I once attended your mother's Victorian literature salon, many years ago," he said. "You were a girl."

"One of the salons in Delhi? At the flat in Lajpat Nagar?"

"Yes. There was a display, on a side table, of a wristwatch collection."

"Oh, my father's! My mother thought she might have recognized you at the wedding. What a coincidence. Why didn't you tell us, Pandit Mohan Ji?"

"Don't stand on ceremony, call me Mo! Your mother is rather formidable, so I kept quiet. In Lajpat Nagar, your father and I had a most interesting conversation about turnkey construction projects."

Mohan Ji asked her to help him distribute the votives around the living room. She arranged candles on the altar, along the floor beneath the picture window, and in the open doorways.

"You have a good eye," he said.

He sat down cross-legged in front of the altar and started to light the incense.

"Let me tell you a story. When I was growing up near Lahore," he said, his back to her, "the British fired the teacher at my secondary school. For supposed insubordination. They replaced him with a ruffian, a man who hunted white tigers with a musket and engaged in dacoity, who couldn't be bothered to teach. My father was furious."

He laughed again, nearly knocking over a stick of incense.

"My father took revenge by conducting an experiment. He had three sons. He would pay the school fees for two of them but withdraw the third. That way, one could determine if English school was valuable or worthless. My father was using English empiricism, you see. Hoisted by their own petards!"

"You?"

"I taught myself. I played in the streets with servants and children of servants. Now, although I am a happily retired accountant, as all accountants are happy to retire, I run two charter schools. One is in Pittsburgh. The other is nearby. The students are mostly immigrants. The schools run year-round. No summers off for me! Anyway, let's cut to the chase, as they say. I hear you have degrees in social work and economics. The local school needs a counselor who can also teach."

Could this be true? This tale seemed like a personal myth. Authenticity forming in the crevices between facts and self-creation. And a job falling into her lap? For real? Exactly what she was searching for, and from a family friend? Her mother-in-law could not complain if she accepted a job from the priest.

"You barely know me. Are you offering me a job?"

"Reading résumés is part of the officiant's job these days. Linked-In!"

"I would love to work at your school!" she said, then realized she hadn't asked about the salary, benefits, anything. Who cared. She needed something to do, a diversion from the smallness of this town, from her confusing marriage. She recalled that married people discuss jobs with their spouses before accepting. "Actually, can I chat with Avi and confirm tomorrow?"

"Yes, yes, talk to Avi," he said. "Due diligence."

She wanted to thank him for his generosity, and bent to touch his feet, as one does with elders, but he chortled, pushed her up, and gave her a fist bump.

Avi's mother came in with samosas, paneer tikka, vegetable biryani, malai kofta, saag paneer, and sweet rice pudding. She had said there was no need for Meena to cook, as Kamla had it under control. Now she told Meena where to place the trays. Kamla ushered the guests, as they arrived, to specific locations on the bedsheets. She directed Meena to fulfill guests' requests for water or mango lassi. Meena did as she was told. She had a job offer, so what did she care about her mother-in-law's imperiousness?

Avi, who was picking up Rav Uncle's wife Chrissy and Peeku because Rav Uncle was running late, now came in, waved from the door, and started to help his mother. Peeku, his hair neatly combed, wearing a suit and bright orange tie, said, "Do you like my outfit, Meena? I dressed up for your party. Orange tie for the Browns. You look beautiful."

"Thank you. And what a nice tie, Peeku," Meena said. "You like the Browns?"

"I love everything about my town. And it's more awesome since you moved here."

"Aw, that's sweet, thanks."

It turned out to be a more exacting ceremony than the wedding, Sanskrit without translation. The priest invited Meena to offer halwa to the gods, then patted the top of her head, like she was his daughter. People recited chants, made their own offerings. Avi's father held a pot of coconut water into which Avi dropped grains from the Prayer Pack. The priest announced the names of the several seeds in a beguiling tone that seemed to join festivity and parody: "Barley! Sesame! Whole wheat! White rice! Mustard seed! Moong!" Dipping hands into red paste, guests left so many handprints on the walls that the dining room started to look like a kindergarten.

Rav Uncle arrived in slacks and a dress shirt, the top buttons undone, displaying chest hair and a gold necklace. So predictable. He bowed and gave namastes to the priest, Avi's parents, and others of his generation. "Running late, yes, so sorry," he said. "My salesclerk didn't show up. Hispanics!"

Meena cringed, though no one else seemed to react. Perhaps they were used to it. Avi's father announced, "Rav Bhai's wedding announcement story is published. Please share, Rav Bhai."

Rav Uncle stood so everyone could see him. He coughed and cleared his throat. He unfolded a paper from his shirt pocket.

"Wedding announcement will appear in *Indians Abroad*, which you people, no doubt, are familiar with, and also," he said, pausing for dramatic effect, "in *Saffron Sun*."

How mortifying. The paper was a vehicle for nationalist propaganda, and Meena hoped her mother and sister wouldn't come across it.

"We are becoming big politicians now!" someone said, punching Avi on the arm.

"Avinash and Meena Sehrawat," Rav began to read, "children of

Mr. and Mrs. Ved Sehrawat and Mrs. Paromita Mehra, loving and devoted wife of the late Mr. Rahul Mehra, were married at the Southgate Hindu Temple."

"Loving and devoted! Okay, okay," Kohli shouted, puckering at his wife. Meena closed her eyes and felt like keeping them closed for a long time.

"Having sampled Western-style dating, this modern couple nevertheless settled on arranged marriage. Disappointed with lovey-dovey activities, they chose devotion, humility, and ancient traditions. These are keys to lifelong happiness. Peeku, are you listening? Okay. Now the couple have inserted the key into the ignition and are driving. They are satisfied how engine hums. It has smooth rotating crankshaft. It spirals like a spiraling football pass. The couple sees that past experiences are no bar to arranged marriage. All young people everywhere, whomever they supposedly love, whomever they have touched, can achieve happiness through arranged marriage."

"Whomever touched, oh ho!" Sharma shouted.

"Figure of speech, only!" said Rav Uncle, smiling and pleased with himself. "Avi says, wisely according to this columnist, that what matters is not whom one loves but how. Meena believes that Avi's devotion to his family is his best quality. We send our best wishes to this young couple, who report satisfaction in all aspects."

Rav Uncle dropped the paper onto the floor and raised his arms, a smug expression flattening his mustache. People responded, "Great piece, Rav Bhai! Congratulations, Avi and Meena!" Avi acknowledged the praise. Rav Uncle bowed. Peeku looked upset, punching a fist into his palm.

Meena felt like crawling under the bedsheet. That was so badly written it seemed like satire. It couldn't possibly be sincere praise, could it? Maybe she didn't have an ear for this kind of discourse.

Sharma announced that Avi was now, by unanimous acclamation, the new head of the Southgate Punjabi Association. Time for young blood, he said. We are going to win! The money is going to roll in. Business opportunities! Global recognition! Diwali holidays!

Were they delusional? Meena's own mother would find this event small-minded, provincial. Big cheers over small stakes. Neurotic chauvinism, as if Southgate, a town in the sticks, were part of the Indian grand narrative. Would there be a single soul in Delhi who had even heard of the Southgate Punjabi Association?

Avi stood, looking sheepish and smiling nervously, put a palm on his heart and said, "Thank you, Uncle. With the greatest humility, I accept."

Rav Uncle raised his arms, indicating that people should take it easy. "Remember, it is difficult to defeat Vinsons. There will be dirty tricks, like they used on me when I ran for mayor. Stay one step ahead. You must be willing to fight!"

Avi said, "Of course," though it sounded tentative.

If Avi needed the backing of these reactionaries, not to mention his mother, would he feel pressured to make his marriage appear even more traditional?

Guests were splitting into little clusters, some wandering outside. Meena thought of asking Avi about the priest's job offer, but hesitated, worried he might brush her aside, or, with his family friends milling about, answer her the way they expected him to. She told him she was stepping out for fresh air.

It was a cool and pleasant evening, the big summer sun setting behind distant thunder clouds. She smelled clean air, sparked ozone. Kids were running on the front lawn, playing tag and jumping over Avi's goldenrods. People sat along the flagstones, snacking on samosas and drinking beer. Giggling women in bright salwars strolled carelessly down the sidewalk. A cavalcade of guests' cars lined the street.

The priest (she couldn't call him Mo) was standing next to a white Cadillac SUV. He threw a coconut, smashing it on the asphalt driveway. It cracked into large, jagged hemispheres. A boy in a baseball hat picked up a piece and licked coconut water. The priest mut-tered Sanskrit over a lemon, a pomegranate, and another coconut and placed them at the base of the Cadillac's front wheel. He threw henna coloring over the hood. The car owner interlaced a few marigolds on the front grille and got into the driver's seat.

"Go," said the priest.

The driver ran over the sacred fruit.

"Who is next for new car blessings? Who else has a new car?" asked the priest. "So many of you? It's like rush hour out here!"

He giggled when he saw Meena.

"These young tigers want me to bless their fancy new cars. Your house, their cars. I'm catching two pigeons with one bean! A retiree has to pay the bills, you see. By the way, I should have said, we can cover your salary at a level commensurate with your education, on the state pay scale. One-year contract, renewable."

Incredible. She returned his fist bump and said, "Thank you, um, Mo. I'm so, so grateful!" He grinned, bowed, dabbed, and wandered over to talk to Sharma.

The evening sky was brilliant, the orange hour transforming into blues. People were sitting on cars, swapping jokes and laughing. Kids were hooting and howling. If things went well, she would have mean-ingful work at a school, just as she had planned. Maybe life in South-gate would be okay. Maybe she and Avi would have a kid, resembling one of these on the lawn, someday. Maybe she could be happy here. Actually happy.

Avi came out. He looked worried, she could tell, already possess-ing a radar for her husband's distress. "What's wrong?" she asked.

"Nothing's wrong. Just had a talk with Rav Uncle. This election is not going to be a cakewalk. Rav Uncle said I need to go after Jim personally. There are some rumors he's having an affair. Rav Uncle wants me to take on his marriage. Because he made fun of ours."

"That sounds ugly."

"It's okay. Rav Uncle pushes me in a good way, actually. I'm learning what it takes to succeed. It'll be okay." He seemed to be talking to himself.

He hugged her. It felt good. She wondered if he sensed her anxiety about the job offer and was offering reassurance. Or maybe he was seeking hers, reaching for support. He slid his hands down to her waist. Lower still. Fingers reaching down her legs, he seemed aroused. His head tilted. She tilted too, ready for a kiss. But he released. He seemed to be waving at someone.

He was so self-conscious. She wanted his thoughts, not only about this curious exchange, but also about the priest's offer. It didn't seem the right moment, though. Rav Uncle's voice was probably still in his head, and all his parents' friends were hovering. Who knew what he might say.

Chapter Six

IT WAS HOT. Avi peeled off his t-shirt. Tonight had potential. But Meena had her back to him and might be too tired. He flipped over to sip some water, taking care not to yank the sheets, and there was slack, all of a sudden. Did she generously release a bit of bedding? Perhaps she was alert to him. She turned. Perhaps she was feeling restless, too. Their movements, a shift of the pillow after a pull on the sheet, seemed like the exchange of tense hopes. He was going to turn and face her, speak, but she sighed, reached for her eye mask, and turned away from him, signaling the end of their quiet dealings.

Her breathing deepened. In the blue streetlight, her ample chest rose and fell, her wide hips like parabolas. He studied the curvature of her breasts and, leaning over, the angles of her jawline, which created her intelligent, oval face. So many curves and lines to check out, to trace and bisect.

Maybe their marriage wasn't fated to be sterile. Perhaps it was the circumstances. Throwing out his back on his wedding night. Hiding that he threw out his back. Guilt that he hid throwing out his back. His mother's constant presence. The nosiness of the Punjab 5. Meena's worldliness. Her mother's sophistication, in contrast to his parents' lack of refinement. Arranged marriages occasioned too many points of view. There were all these rules he was supposed to know, but didn't.

All of a sudden, he hated Sharma's wedding present. He had to get rid of it. He quietly got up and went downstairs. Rummaging through the boxes of gifts they left in the basement, he found the framed poster, the guru's "Ten Principles for Happiness in Marriage." He drove it to the basilica parking lot and dropped it in the dumpster, the glass shattering with a satisfying crack.

He hoped throwing away that annoying gift, and adopting a more determined mindset, would turn things around, and reawaken the hope and promise he had felt at the wedding. It did coincide with big news. When he got home, he saw a message from Kohli: *Army brothers want live interview. Fifteen-minute segment. You only! Mr. Jim not invited.*

This would be complicated, but also a big opportunity. The local cable access news show, which aired Saturdays at 9 a.m., was run by two brothers, former Indian army, now joint owners of a Chevy dealership. For years, it had been suffering from declining viewership. Hardly a surprise, as the brothers reviewed current events in administrative tones, then pivoted to music videos, mixing Lata Mangeshkar, Adele, and other warblers with Panjabi MC, Jay-Z, and hip-hop artists. It was a head-spinning combo that gave Avi's father headaches. He had to take two Advil to watch. Bending to complaints, the brothers recently had made the inspired decision to move to a live interview format and hire a new host, Monica, a fair-skinned, blue-eyed Kashmiri girl who had grown up with Avi, Jim, and Bob. She was stunning. Everyone knew she was headed for a glamorous TV career in Los Angeles or New York.

The thorny part was that Avi had asked Monica out in twelfth-grade English, in the middle of a discussion of Ophelia's madness in *Hamlet*. She refused him, saying her parents didn't want her dating a non-Muslim boy. Somehow, though, Jim managed to go out with her that spring. Perhaps Monica had been curious to date a white dude from a celebrity family, and hid their relationship from her parents. Irritatingly, she taught him a handful of Urdu words, and Jim would strut down the crowded hallway dispensing *as-salamu alaykum* for "hello" and *phir milenge* for "see you next time."

See you next time. Yeah, at your concession speech.

Avi texted Kohli that yes, of course he would do this. He went to work in his office and stayed up most of the night preparing. He studied the joint ambulance agreement with Springfield Township, the proposed sales tax hike to pay for the new county jail, and the possibility of sheriff patrol car coverage for roads in unincorporated areas. He considered how to advocate making Diwali a school holiday, which could be dicey to discuss, as Monica and her family could feel excluded. Maybe he would argue for Eid and Diwali both. Then again, that would aggravate Rav Uncle, who thought Hindus were primary.

He needed to ask Rav Uncle for advice. The man gave unsolicited opinions in an aggressive manner, but he was also influential, the undisputed community leader. He knew how the world worked. Avi's family had relied on him ever since Avi's middle school graduation party, when he saved their reputation, maybe the whole community's.

That event had been Avi's mother's idea. She had wanted to celebrate Avi graduating with a perfect GPA (the achievement was listed on the party program) and also recognize Avi's father's repair shop clearing a hundred grand. A "two-for-one" shindig, as she put it. Avi wore his favorite t-shirt, plain yellow with a "Cool Jazz" decal whose letters were filled in with sparkly photos of Bourbon Street. His mother pinned a carnation to the C in Cool Jazz, matching the pink carnation in his dad's "Auto Doctor" polo.

Jim Vinson's band, headlining the party, started with a set of rock standards, then transitioned to headbangers. Jim wore sunglasses. For protection against Avi's shiny shirt, he joked. The Punjabi 5 were at first put off by the music, but they wanted to show everyone they weren't party poopers and eventually started to dance, doing incongruous bhangra moves. They began to hop up and down. Soon they were doing the Chicken Dance, mooing like cows. The band started playing "Old MacDonald" as the old guys went from one barnyard animal to the next, having fun. Avi's dad, who never danced, was crowing like a rooster.

Teenagers notice the potential for humiliation the way dogs detect the aroma of meat. Soon kids were pointing, jeering, imitating the old men, taking videos and passing them around. It was horrible. His father's dance moves would be recorded for eternity, watch parties of his father's menagerie shared in basements, becoming legend, people crowing like his dad at high school prom. Avi was mortified. He froze.

Rav Uncle handled it. He approached the stage, glowering, and made that gesture, finger across the throat, suggesting decapitation. When the band kept playing, he pulled the plug on the amplifiers, and the singing stopped. He politely thanked the band for their performance and asked the two kids with video cameras to turn them over. When they hesitated, he took out a roll of hundreds and gave each kid five crisp hundred-dollar bills in exchange for the cameras.

Rav Uncle made sure Avi understood the moral of the story. After everyone left, he took Avi into a corner and explained that Americans don't like weird people. No one does. Think of Europeans and gypsies. The good thing about America, though, is that there is an equalizer. Money. Did Avi think his friends would give a crap about his cheap t-shirt (Rav Uncle ran a finger across the glitter on Avi's chest), even notice it, if Avi walked around with rolls of hundreds? Think of Mitt Romney, Rav Uncle said. How could that man, wearing magic underwear, be taken seriously as a presidential candidate? Obviously, it was due to Romney's wealth and business acumen. Rav Uncle said consulting, or even corporate law, could be a good field for someone like Avi, with a weak personality, someone who requires money yet is not entrepreneurial enough to start his own businesses. He said if Punjabis have money, we can dance, dress, talk, as we wish.

Even run for and win office. But if we don't, he said, our young people will choose more shiny paths, and our values will be lost.

Avi expected Rav Uncle to push that same agenda, money and status leading to community recognition, when he came by later that week to discuss talking points for the TV interview with Monica. Instead, Rav Uncle brought over a bottle of Johnnie Walker. He was in a mischievous mood, maybe half-drunk. He gave himself and Avi a large pour, on the rocks, and asked Avi to cut a plate of sliced tomatoes and onions, his preferred snack with scotch.

"Will you make the township rich? Yes or no? That's it," Rav Uncle said, taking a big sip of his drink.

"But Uncle, doesn't that depend on the regional economy," Avi asked, "and whether township policies can attract new businesses? And then there's the question of spreading the wealth . . ."

"This thing, that thing," Rav Uncle said, proving his point by nibbling at a tomato slice like a mouse. "Talk like a master, not like a servant. Clear voice! Let's hear it."

"Like this?" Avi said. It felt like he was yelling.

"Louder! Project confidence! Success is willpower!"

On Saturday, Avi arrived at the TV studio, third floor of an office park building on Maple, at exactly 8:15 a.m. The "green room" consisted of particle-board desks, office chairs, a table with Dunkin' Donuts coffee and muffins, and a pair of full-length wall mirrors. Avi sat down at a desk and watched as Monica finished her foundation, applied blush and light coral lipstick, and lined her eyes in deep kohl. She wore a pink saree, exposing her fair and smooth abdomen. "This will be interesting, Avi, see you in a few," she said, tapping him on the arm and heading out for the first segment.

Avi had considered bringing Meena onstage to join him for the interview. She had such an engaging presence. But he decided the erotic tension of being on camera with Monica *and* Meena could be overwhelming. Stupefying.

In the green room, Avi reviewed his notes. He did forward bends and jumping jacks to get his blood flowing. He tucked in his shirt, straightened his red tie. Tuning in today would be hundreds, maybe thousands, of viewers interested in his positions on the issues. He had to sound authoritative. He touched his cheeks and chin, double-checking that he had shaved.

When he entered the studio, Monica greeted him with kisses on both cheeks, like they do in France, as if to demonstrate she was going places. The temperature was chilly, probably to compensate for the hot quartz lamps. Two glasses of ice water rested on the marble table between them. His parents, the Punjabi 5, Peeku, and Meena, all seated in front, looked to be nervous on his behalf, or maybe they were angry about Monica's convoluted kisses.

The cameraman said they were live.

"Avinash Sehrawat," Monica said, "welcome to the show. First off, congratulations on your recent wedding. Your wife Meena Mehra is in the audience, I believe."

Avi's father motioned for Meena to stand, and she did, tentatively. The Punjabi 5 clapped, Monica joining in. Avi, uncertain if the applause was intended for Meena or his marriage, balked. The lights were bright, but he could see that Meena, in her green salwar kameez, had a wary expression.

"Let's get right to it," Monica said. "What are your views on subsidies for biodigesters?"

What the hell? He stretched his toes against his loafers. He took a sip of water.

"Well, subsidies are definitely part of my plan. Many hard-working Ohioans can't make ends meet, and cash assistance can . . ."

"Sorry, Avi. Township trustees have no role in social assistance programs," Monica said.

"No direct role, you're right. But there is the bully pulpit. Anyway, subsidies can also spur entrepreneurship. They can make the township rich. That's the main thing. I believe in the global economy, where we will shine. I have a vision. I call it Make in Southgate . . ."

"Sorry to interrupt, Avi. I asked you about biodigesters. What are your views on our poultry processing capacity?"

Two questions on agriculture? Was she still in the tank for Jim?

"As we all know," Avi said, "farming is important in Southgate, and my opponent's family runs a large agricultural concern that wants to expand operations. That's fine. I like chicken and sausage as much as the next guy. Well, I just remembered you don't eat pork sausage, Monica, sorry if that offends! But I mean, everyone needs an opportunity; it's not all about farming . . ."

"Are you insinuating that Southgate farmers have too much clout?"

"Oh, no! I'm not insinuating. The Vinsons are well respected, but we have to work together. We all share the same values . . ."

"Actually, Jim Vinson says you don't embody Southgate values. How do you respond?"

Why was Monica being so aggressive? Like she was auditioning for *60 Minutes*. If they'd gone out, stayed in touch during college, maybe one of her high-flying contacts in LA would've hired him as a lawyer to the stars.

"I believe in my community," he said. "My campaign is about determination and dignity for Southgate, and for America. By the way, Jim's been saying my traditional marriage to my lovely wife, Meena, sitting right there in the green, in case the cameraman wants the shot, is strange and un-American. I want to tell you that's nonsense. My marriage is totally American."

"That's interesting. What do you mean? Perhaps you could share more about that topic, Avi," Monica said, lighting up. The army brothers probably told her a debate about marriage was good for ratings.

"Immigrants provide new ideas," Avi said. "Think of yoga or what Ravi Shankar did for the Beatles. Or taco trucks. You want to hear my raincoat theory? Life is hard, and sometimes it rains. We all get wet, muddy even. Everyone needs some protection, something to help during life's downpours. Arranged marriage is like that. You instantly have people to turn to, not just a bride but a whole community. Everyone needs raincoats, not just old-fashioned Asians."

He hoped the Punjabi 5 didn't mind being called old-fashioned.

"But raincoats are more or less interchangeable," Monica said. "I think that's the issue. Don't you have to be compatible with your partner? Suppose you have different ideas about money, or religion, whether you want kids. What if you aren't physically compatible?"

Not physically compatible? Was that why Monica had chosen Jim, years ago, because he was attractive to her, and Avi wasn't? Or was she referring to his marriage remaining unconsummated? She couldn't possibly know that, could she?

"I mean, most men and women can make it work physically, you know?" Avi said.

"Ha, good one. Obviously!" Rav Uncle shouted from his seat.

"Please, people," Monica said.

"Physically, ha ha! Meena, he needs your help now," Rav Uncle shouted, laughing again.

"That's a thought," Monica said. "Meena, would you be comfortable joining us up here? It's your marriage, too."

Oh boy. He'd have to stay composed, with them both on stage.

Meena looked reluctant, but after his mother pulled her elbow, she stepped past Sharma and Rav Uncle. One of the cameramen set out an extra folding chair, and Monica pointed. Too late, Avi realized she was indicating for him to offer his own comfy armchair to his wife. To act chivalrous. But he'd missed it. Conscious of the perspiration suddenly forming in his armpits, Avi folded his arms.

Meena settled into the collapsible chair, crossed her legs, and threw back her hair.

"Meena, you look lovely!" said Monica. "So, are you also anti-romance? What do you say to those of us who live for a candlelit dinner, a love letter passed between classmates, boxes of chocolates? What's wrong with those things?"

"Nothing wrong," Meena said. "There are chocolates and nice dinners in traditional marriages, too. It's just about which comes first, the romance or the marriage."

"Interesting. So why did you choose Avi? You must have had plenty of options, someone with your talents and elegance."

In case the camera was interested, Avi extended his arms and pointed at himself, making a joke, trying to say, What's not to like?

Peeku yelled, "You the man, Avi!"

Avi quickly refolded his arms. Rings of sweat wouldn't be visible through his jacket, but still.

"I don't know if I can answer why it was Avi," Meena said. "We felt it was time. We thought the other person was good, and good enough. I suspect there is a kind of love that comes after commitment, not necessarily before. I know most people think there must be a reason they fall in love, that the other person completes them, the other half of the jigsaw puzzle. But maybe that's an illusion. Maybe we need to believe in destiny because otherwise the roller coaster of romantic love is too intense."

Wow, Meena was good. As polished as Monica, in her own way. He was lucky to be up here, with her, with them both, in fact. But also unlucky, as he, his candidacy, was supposed to get the spotlight?

"But you must have had other options, and looked at many profiles, right?" asked Monica.

"That's true," said Meena. "Well, I liked Avi's bio and photographs. I was searching for a straightforward man, down-to-earth."

Avi was watching the two women. It was weird how he ended up with one rather than the other. Rather than any other. Was he supposed to feel something special, unique, for one woman? He wasn't sure he did. He could've been happy with Monica. How, then, had he ended up with Meena? Was marriage choice basically random? He inspected the two women sharing the stage with him, scanning for any specialness in their smiles, figures, energies, values, careers. Some clue to orient him. Help him decide. As if he was still deciding. Monica's blue eyes versus Meena's hazel eyes. Monica's sleek legs, Meena's ample figure. Monica's elegance, Meena's intelligence. Their features were merging, as if he had married one multifaceted woman. Might he have both, somehow, in his mind? Urdu and Hindi. A smooth, fair abdomen. Sipping coffee at Starbucks. Ophelia throwing flowers. A body tattooed with kohl. Wolves and roses. Shrimp Tampico. Hot quartz lights. Wads of hundreds. Carnations and marigolds. Indian values. Los Angeles glitz. Gandhi's wisdom. Churchill's power. Full contact. He wanted it all.

"I want full contact, and the price is eternal vigilance!"

He had blurted it out.

Monica and Meena both stared, considering his words. On the camera monitor, Avi saw a close-up of himself, his brow moistening.

"Avi, what are you talking about?" Monica asked.

"That Monica and I are happily married," Avi said.

"I think you mean that you and *Meena* are happily married," Monica said. She gave Meena a commiserative look.

"Yes. Of course. Sorry, dear!" he said, fixing his gaze on his wife.

How mortifying. Meena was smiling tightly, nodding, signaling that he needed to keep it together. They were still on the air.

"Sorry to say that we have to end on that note," Monica said. "I would love to keep talking, but our time is up. Avi Sehrawat and Meena Mehra, ladies and gentlemen."

What a disaster. Total. Un. Mit. Igated. Disaster. Yet somehow, people were still clapping. The audience was offering a standing ovation. Monica gave Meena a little hug, whispered a few words in her ear, and sent her off with kisses on each cheek. Thinking he now knew the drill, Avi leaned in close for the double kisses. But Monica pulled back and offered a handshake.

In the parking lot, Avi's parents patted him on the back and said they were proud. Sharma said Avi had sounded learned, like a guru. Verma told Avi not to worry, he couldn't remember his own wife's name half the time, and often confused his daughter Bittoo with his cat Ritu. Kohli said vigilance was the watchword, now. Rav Uncle, in an oddly suggestive tone, said Avi and Meena looked like they needed some wine. He had a pricey bottle of cabernet from his new liquor store in the trunk of his car, and he gave it to Avi.

Everyone was pretending he did well, and that just made everything feel worse.

"Why are we celebrating?" Avi asked.

Rav Uncle said, "Good comments on wealth. In the end, we will shine!" He spanked Avi on the back.

"Southgate shining!" Verma said.

"India shining!" Rav Uncle said.

Without speaking, Avi and Meena got into the Oldsmobile. Towering rainclouds gathered overhead. As they passed the debauched couple in the "Take Time Off" sign and turned onto Richey, large raindrops thumped on the windshield. He lowered the window to let the rain blow on his face. Distant lightning flashed, the beginnings of a summer storm, the thunderclouds releasing themselves to condensation and free-roaming electrons.

"You did okay, Avi. Don't beat yourself up," Meena said.

"It wasn't okay."

"The first time on camera isn't easy. You have to learn to be yourself on stage."

"I wasn't myself, was I?"

"Avi, to be honest, I really hope not."

When they pulled into the driveway, the storm had mostly blown over, and Meena said she wanted to clear her head by going out for a run in the light rain. He stood on the flagstones. The breeze was cool and refreshing, his suit's woolen sleeves and pants wet with perspiration and rain. It was almost a surprise to be in clothes, as though he and Meena had been naked on camera, their marital intimacies, or lack thereof, on display.

He changed and drove to the gym. There was a Saturday spin class, and he really needed to work out. The instructor started the class at 70 rpm, then had the students stand and sit, stand and sit, steadily cranking up the pace. The girl biking next to him, ivory-skinned, wearing a glittering diamond ring, stretched her long, supple arms to retie her ponytail. The questions wouldn't go away. What if, instead of Meena or Monica, he had chosen this lovely woman?

After class, he showered in the locker room. The water was cold and invigorating, like a waterfall in a state park where he once hiked. The sun had reflected off dappled green maples, there were birds, a hawk overhead, and maybe some girl was there, too, watching, and she smiled and waded into the waterfall to join him. Who?

Maybe she was all the girls he ever had a crush on. Maybe arranged marriage was an amalgam. You married one woman, but possibilities remained alive, the way it was for Lord Krishna, the ever playful one, who bestowed love on sixteen thousand cowherd girls, his eternal consorts.

HIS BACK HEALED, and in the end, it was straightforward. They were eating Thai takeout at the kitchen table, chicken satay and papaya salad. They had finished Rav Uncle's pricey bottle of cabernet. He was thinking Rav Uncle could be right. Maybe success was about willpower.

"Meena, please come over here," he said. "Sit."

She sat in the chair next to him. She gave off an impression of helplessness, her gaze unfocused, but he didn't dwell on it. He ran his fingers along her jawline. He put her hand in his lap. He kissed her on the lips. Her mouth responded. She moved her hand to his crotch. They fondled. He hurriedly took off his clothes, throwing his t-shirt, shorts, and underwear toward the dishwasher. She removed and folded her blouse and bra, placing them on the kitchen table beside the foam container of fried rice. She shimmied off her jeans and slid off her panties, draping both over a chair.

They were naked, his erection complete.

"Should we go up to the bedroom?" she asked.

"Why?" he said.

Perhaps Peter, plump from expense-account meals, older, preferred dim bedrooms that masked his flabbiness. Not Avi. No more running from his desires. They could make love on these cold kitchen tiles, under bright lights, or in front of the picture window, as far as he was concerned.

She shrugged and got down onto the floor, her fleshy, pineapple-shaped breasts flattening. He fell beside her. He caressed her waist. He cupped her breasts. His fingers traced the arcs between her hips and chest. He rolled on top of her. Brown-on-brown felt primal, familiar. He slid off her, got on top, slid off again. He kissed her thighs, put his tongue into her. He kissed her birthmark, so she knew it meant nothing.

This was the moment. At last. He found his way inside her. It felt tight, secure. He didn't want his greed to overwhelm her, so he moved slowly. After a few moments, her breathing quickened, and she put her hands on his ass. He could no longer hold back. He gave in. He thrusted. He pounded. He was thinking only of Meena. His wonderful wife, no one else. He wanted her to know this marriage was about her alone.

"Meena! Meena!"

"Wow, you're loud." She laughed.

After he came and pulled himself out, she kissed him on the lips, then on the forehead. She turned, reached for a brown Thai Orchid napkin, and wiped herself. She started toward her clothes.

"Wait," he said.

He didn't want her to leave. Dusky light was shining through the patio doors, a tawny owl whistling. He saw her for what seemed the first time. Her jawline curved like a pear. There was a swoosh in her eyebrow. How had he not noticed?

"This swirl," he said, tracing her brow, "it's lovely."

She halfway turned, covering her face. "I didn't know if . . . I thought it was my . . . Oh, God." A tear fell through her fingers. "I thought you weren't attracted to me." She was trying to hold back.

"No, Meena, no," he said, reaching for her hair, "it's not you, it's me."

He took a moment, playing with her hair. He needed to tell her.

"When I slipped in the shower, our first night, I threw out my back. That's why I couldn't do it on our wedding night. I've been on painkillers ever since. They're messing with me, or something. This whole situation . . . Not knowing you and yet married . . ."

"You threw out your back?"

"Fixing the showerhead."

"Why didn't you tell me?"

He ran his tongue across his teeth.

"I wanted to make a good impression. I didn't want to come across as inept and weak. Then I didn't help with the housework, or getting ready for the housewarming. After my back got better, I felt like a liar for hiding it in the first place. It was stupid. Sometimes I don't know what's going on in here." He pointed at his head. "I'm sorry, Meena."

She took his hand, rested it on her abdomen. "Avi, remember when I said I was relieved you aren't one of those guys who has to conquer? I meant it."

He hugged her. The evening light was soft. Her skin was so smooth. Things between them suddenly felt tender.

She pulled away, her lips tightening. She was about to say something difficult. He steeled himself.

"The priest, Mohan Ji, offered me a position at the school he runs. It's a good salary, a one-year renewable contract. I was thinking . . ."

"Are you actually asking me? Of course you should take it."

"Even if your mom asked me to stay home? Do you know about that? I didn't know what to tell her."

"My mom has hang-ups, but they're my problem, Meena, not yours. I'll explain how important working is. For you. For us."

She rested her head on his chest, wet eyelashes fluttering on his skin like moist butterflies.

It was almost too much to bear, this soft being-togetherness. He felt the urge to say something cheeky. "Now I have a question for you," he said, putting on an impish look. "Were you thinking of me when we . . . ?"

She matched his roguish cast. "Maybe it takes a while to get into each other's fantasies, you know? In our situation? Maybe I was, and maybe I wasn't."

He wished she had said she was fantasizing about him, even if it wasn't true. Maybe she wasn't the type who required delicacies, half-truths, white lies. He wasn't used to people like her.

They stayed on the kitchen floor a while, touching. Her body responded to the lightest brush of his fingers. His chest tingled as she stroked it. Night was falling, the patio lights glowing brightly.

Sex for him wasn't like dousing thirst, the calm after a tall glass of cool water. Sex awakened rather than quenched. He wanted more. Her body was a door opening up his marriage.

Chapter Seven

THEIR SEXUAL CHOREOGRAPHY was becoming intuitive. Meena knew what she liked, and he was understanding her. After devouring her feijoada, he asked her to sit in his lap, then softly kissed her ears and neck. It felt feathery. Another night, they went into the living room for dessert, berries and chocolate, and he bit a strawberry as she put it in her mouth.

They were learning each other's moods, body preferences, firmness or lightness of touch, the moment for a wink, a sly smile. The confidence growing from being skin-to-skin, the body-knowledge, the fullness in the chest, undeniable intimacy. She remembered an Egyptian boyfriend who watched her like a dog considering a squirrel, and it felt like that, Avi always eyeing her and aware of her presence, though with the reassuring knowledge that he was her husband, the man who would watch, care for, and support her forever.

One day, after making love midafternoon, lying face-to-face inches apart, he said he loved her.

"I love you, too," she replied.

It was a partial truth, though. Her intense passion wasn't just for him. It was for this life, the shape of her days, her quiet toast and tea on the patio in the mornings, anticipating a fulfilling job, the prospect of working with kids. And then evenings of devoted intimacy. Soon there might be a little one in her arms, then the little one would be running between her legs, playing on the front lawn. Her love wasn't for Avi alone. It was about the script, the storyline, the whole arrangement. Her father was right. It wasn't just the identity of her spouse but the practice of loving that conjured this exquisite spirit, this hallowing.

She wrote her sister, mother, and friends, telling them how happy she now was. She told Vishali not to worry, as "the necessaries" were now being completed, and that she was excited to start her job. She purchased teaching and counseling accessories, including a sensory spike ball for kids to fidget with, drawing paper, Monopoly money and candy for incentives, and yoga mats. Vishali ordered a sign for her office door: *Meena Mehra, Counselor. Whenever possible, be kind. (It's always possible.)*

When Peter wrote, she didn't reply. She deleted his texts. She removed the entire text chain from her phone. She would never again correspond with him.

One summer evening she was chopping vegetables for a biryani and listening to music. A blues singer was serenading a new day dawning. The lyrics and the rhythms hit home. She skipped in place as she sliced the carrots. She swayed around the kitchen table as she sectioned cauliflower and cut potatoes. She put down her knife and pirouetted.

She sat at the table with her glass of cabernet. Her father had been right. Arranged marriage was good, it was better. This way, sensuality was a gift. Not something you earned, supposedly, through courtship, through seduction, high heels and perfume. Not something you supposedly deserved for who you were, so pretty and so smart. That was a vanity. This, on the other hand, was unexpected, a gift, a blessing.

TWO LINES. As solid and bold as those running down Richey Road. No doubt. Meena wiped herself and wrapped the test stick in tissue. Her period was late, so the result wasn't a total shock. Still.

She was going to have a baby, a family. Her mother, despite her indifferent and hard-boiled veneer, never failed to relay the news when one of her bridge partners became a grandmother and would now have to concede the wisdom of Meena's choice. Her father would have been thrilled. He would have kissed her forehead and embraced her. Her shoulders still remembered his hard grip. One day, she would take her baby, maybe a toddler by then, to the banks of Yamuna, where they had scattered his ashes.

After all the disappointment, the confusions, she was at last going to have a family. A real home. In a close-knit town where relatives and friends could provide support. Now she could genuinely let down her guard. Give in to this life in Southgate. Commit. It had worked out. She could trust not only the man she was with but herself, her judgments and decisions. And believe in this child's nascent life, which was also her and Avi's burgeoning life. All made possible by her choice, and the magnificent powers she had surrendered to.

Who would the girl (she imagined a girl) look like? Avi, herself, maybe a combination? Meena hoped the girl would have his long legs, his handsome wide face. But her lips, fuller than his. Once, when she and Peter were enjoying cocktails on a quiet beach in Northeast Brazil, she saw a little girl with peanut butter skin chasing a beach ball and laughing. Pointing her out, Meena remarked how beautiful mixed-race kids could be. It was obviously a suggestion, though oblique, about how their skin tones might combine. Peter looked at her severely, as if to say, Don't go there.

Avi would be thrilled. His parents, too. Probably even Rav Uncle would be pleased, as Avi and Meena were now exemplary newlyweds. It bothered her that she cared what Rav Uncle thought. Then again, he would probably be proud of a new community member. He might buy their girl handsome birthday presents. He, and all of the Punjabi 5, would be the goofy great-uncles, people to laugh with and, sometimes, when she and her little girl were snuggling in bed at the end of the day, tell silly stories about. It would be good to have family friends nearby. Doting grandparents. She never had that, having grown up rootless. She wouldn't tell the girl about Peter, but she would certainly share her arc, it was probably the most valuable wisdom she possessed, how going from pointless nomadism to a structured, enclosed life had brought her meaning, had brought her love. *It brought me you, my beautiful daughter.*

Avi would be a good father. He might be unduly solicitous about what people thought. He might defer to his mother's notions about how to dress the girl, pinks and yellows, hair ribbons. Barbie dolls. Toy ovens. And yield to his mother's Hindu rituals, like shaving off the little girl's hair in order to cleanse her bald scalp with holy water and turmeric. Fortunately, the little girl would also have her mother, aunt, and grandmother to travel with, have conversations with about careers and social justice, visit the Louvre with. They would explore all of India, not just the rituals and ancient splendor but the pluralism, Muslims and Hindus, tribals and castes, the arguments. Meena could teach the girl Hindi. Meena could teach her how to be a modern woman.

Avi would care deeply for his daughter. He would be a far better father than any of her previous boyfriends, egotists all. She and Avi had had to make their share of needful adjustments, but he would come through as a father.

SHE CALLED, but he didn't answer. So she went shopping at the mall. She bought bibs, a body pillow, nursing bras, maternity pants, and prenatal vitamins. Too soon for all that, she knew, but she couldn't resist. She purchased an outward-facing carrier to show off their baby while taking walks in Linden Park. She bought Avi a backpack stuffed with diapers (to signal her expectations), a coffee-of-the-month subscription for mornings after sleepless nights, and matching Papa and baby t-shirts.

When Avi did call back, she was driving, half in a daydream about nursing. "Avi, Avi, I have some amazing news. Are you ready?"

"Me, too," he said.

"Can I go first?" When he didn't reply, she said, "I'm pregnant."

"Wow, wow, wow. Are you sure? I mean, we've been drinking a lot, and I don't know if that would interfere with test results."

Amazing he didn't know how urine pregnancy tests worked! Maybe most guys didn't.

"False positives are rare. And my period is late. It's irregular, sometimes, but this is really late."

"So you'd be due in the spring? Right around the time Rav Uncle will have me do the ribbon-cutting for the strip mall. No chance of pushing back the timing, right?" He laughed. "Joking, of course. This is good news."

That joke fell flat. He didn't sound particularly excited. Then again, it wouldn't be his body changing, maybe he couldn't quite imagine it, pregnancy being an abstraction. He would get there, with time. In eight months.

"What were you going to tell me?" she asked.

"Remember my friend Bob? His friend Gwen, who works at Vinson Family Farms, got her hands on, don't ask me how, she got her hands on photos of Jim making googly eyes at some businesswoman. I'm told there's even a shot of him with a hand on her crotch. Rav Uncle says this is going to hit like a grenade. It's going to be huge. The only thing is, we have to give Gwen, along with Bob, an ice cream franchise in the strip mall. But we're keeping it quiet, obviously, Bob and Rav Uncle and I are all keeping it quiet, no fingerprints. Gwen's going to release the pictures next week. Don't tell anyone, okay? To be honest, I'm a little nervous telling you. But I thought I should in case Jim feels he has to hit back."

"What do you mean, hit back?"

"I don't know, something about us, about arranged marriage, who knows."

"This is a terrible idea, Avi. And it feels so . . . sordid."

Moments ago, she was feeling transcendence, and now they were talking about . . . what?

"It's not easy to beat a Vinson, as Rav Uncle says. Remember, Jim is impugning all of us. I wish I didn't have to do this. Listen, I've got to talk to Bob . . . Oops, there he is calling. Love you. I'm really happy."

This was crazy. What if Avi's scheme backfired? He would scramble to defend himself, erase his fingerprints from the ice cream transaction. He would probably blunder, as he had on TV. He wasn't made for political combat, despite all that talk about community. He didn't get that the threads of the community were money and power, which were Rav Uncle's domain. Power and money made Avi uncomfortable. Perhaps they bored him, too. He'd grow confused and demoralized. He wouldn't be able to focus on fatherhood. She might have to manage parenting alone. She could do it. She was more competent than him, in some ways. Maybe most ways. She might have to lean on his mother, go shopping with Kamla instead of him. She'd hire someone to turn her study into a nursery.

This was disappointing, though. Perhaps what she had interpreted as dedication, in his marital ad and his outlook more generally, was worry. A fear that he was insufficient. The fantasy of the collective shoring him up. But it was too soon to say. Why get ahead of herself? What she was feeling now was probably an inherited moodiness, the skein of her mother's and father's arduous marriage, not hers.

THE SCHOOL was a twenty-mile drive south. She usually left early, though she didn't need to. There was hardly any traffic, perhaps because it was summer, the regular schools closed and people gone camping or fishing in the state park. Parking was also easy, as the school's lot was large and always half-empty. A vinyl banner that read *NoMad Charter School, K–12* hung over old signage carved in the stone archway: *Low-Volume Metal Stamping and Die Co., Inc.* Air-conditioning units, many of them nonfunctional, protruded here and there. It was hot. Mayflies flitted about.

A sign from the state education department took credit for playground renovations. There was a new rubber surface, red and yellow pizza slices, and a row of polar bear statues. On a climbing wall, an artist had rendered *The Great Wave*, the blue crest about to submerge the three fragile fishing boats. The shiny equipment and allegorical art, an affair of primary colors, were supposed to be playful and bright, like childhood itself, she supposed. But it contrasted with the crumbling brick, the threadbare grass and scruffy trees in the adjacent field. The fine line between encouragement and compulsory happiness. As at weddings.

Ironies everywhere. She imagined that Mohan Ji, the priest/accountant/headmaster, appreciated them. He probably came up with "NoMad" himself. She could hear him quip, "It's less alarming than Low-Volume Dying School, I'd say," speaking the way he had at their wedding, simultaneously sacred and preposterous. She'd had to suppress a laugh when he called out the marital duties—"prosperity, progeny, perseverance, etcetera, etcetera." One of these days, she'd tell him one of the "etceteras" was fixing broken showerheads.

The priest had requested that she teach today, filling in for a social studies teacher who had fallen off a ladder cleaning his gutters. Her abdomen felt tight. Perhaps it was nervousness, the stress of her first class. Maybe it was the pregnancy advancing, her baby expanding. Just before class, she went to the bathroom, removed a vial from her bag, and rubbed essential oils into her midsection, breathing in whiffs of cinnamon and cloves. She wore a yellow sundress. The window was open. A warm breeze brushed her legs.

The teacher's lesson plan was ad hoc, vague generalities about "economic globalization." As she wrote out economics terms on the blackboard, a lawn mower droned outside. There were several immigrants in this class, including a handful of South and West Asian girls, some in headscarves. She decided to start by describing her family's journeys, thinking that would show the students that she, too, was a migrant, and had to pause before answering where she was from, assess how many ambiguities the questioner could tolerate.

"I was born in Bombay," Meena began, "but we moved around. I attended an otherwise all-white kindergarten in Cape Town. I spent the rest of elementary school in Delhi. My parents are Indian, so we should have fit in there, but we didn't. Middle school and high school in São Paulo and Mexico City. Then Phuket in southern Thailand, with its go-go bars. All before I was eighteen years old."

A girl in front, with a long black ponytail, nodded.

"My father's company kept moving him to new sites," Meena said. "It didn't matter if his kids had to change schools or leave friends. Any guesses why my father agreed to move?"

"Life with your mum was boring?"

"Maybe," she said with a grin, as the guess wasn't far off.

The remark came from a boy in back with a flat-top haircut. He high-fived his buddy. The class laughed, a sign the students were becoming alert to one another, the classroom unity forming. That was good. She had been speaking too directly, and teenagers thrive on misdirection.

"Boredom doesn't cover airfare, though," she said. "Or some of you would be frequent fliers, am I right?"

More laughter.

"He didn't have many choices," Meena said. "There weren't enough jobs in India. Now, why are there more jobs in some countries than others?"

Head shakes. Shrugs.

"Productivity. Some places have more capital, more money, also more education, and people are healthier, and the governments better. That's where the jobs are going to be."

"My dad says there ain't enough jobs in Southgate," a boy said.

"True. Productivity varies among regions in the same country, too, depending on those same factors. In theory, we would all just pick up and move to the cities with more jobs. Easier said than done, right? Most of us don't like leaving our friends and relatives, our memories. If only our world didn't require so much dislocation."

Vacant stares. She was speaking with excessive authority, as if she knew where hope came from. Still, they needed to understand the remote actors and impersonal structures that influenced their lives, restricting their possibilities, limiting their imaginations. They needn't blame themselves for feelings of marginality, insignificance, emptiness. Beads of perspiration formed on her abdomen.

"All that was solid melts into air. Have you heard that?" she asked.

More blank looks, though one boy, in back, in a button-down shirt, gave a thumbs-up.

All of a sudden, she was breathless. The enormity of the world, the powerful and unknowable forces flowing, like plasma filaments sparking the innards of a transparent, high-voltage ball, were exhausting. She breathed in, out. She massaged her abdomen.

These poor souls. This girl in front in jeans and blue eyeliner, whose mother had MS. That boy touching up his moussed hair, his father in prison in Ethiopia. That slender kid from Sudan who came into her office last week and told her he couldn't sleep.

Poor, poor souls.

"Can I tell you guys something? You guys mean the world to me," she said. "I love you."

Nervous giggles. A girl in pink nail polish and lipstick mouthed, "Oh, that's sweet," perhaps mockingly. A boy in a Pistons t-shirt put on a shit-eating grin. The girl in front, with a headscarf, looked at her skeptically, pen twirling in her hand.

Why on earth had she said that? She felt hot, her face flushing, though she didn't think the students could tell. Her knees were wobbly. She sat down in the teacher's chair. It was rickety, unbalanced, and didn't steady her. She took a series of short, quick breaths. She inhaled more slowly, more deeply. Then she was nauseous, her stomach starting to heave. Now she was feeling cold, goose bumps on her bare legs. She was shivering.

She looked down. There was a blood smear on the chair, between her legs. She could feel blood pooling in her panties.

A Mexican girl pointed. The tall kid next to her turned his head. The classroom hushed.

"I'll be back," Meena said. She stood slowly and, with one hand under her crotch, so nothing would drop, the other holding onto the desk, the doorknob, the wall, walked out into the hallway. When she reached the girls' room, she grabbed a handful of paper towels and wiped her hands, legs, panties, dress.

She walked out of the building slowly. In the half-empty parking lot, near her car, she found a trash can and disposed of the paper towels, hiding them beneath Miller Lite cardboard packaging. Mistake. The act of bending shot pain across her midsection and down into her legs. She took a stack of lesson plans and paperwork from the pile in the backseat and scattered them on the driver's seat. As she sat and switched on the ignition, staples and paper edges cut into her thighs.

Driving steadied her nerves, helped her think. She didn't have fibroids, as far as she knew. Was this an ectopic pregnancy, or a miscarriage? Her mother, who had two miscarriages, talked about spotting, not bleeding. Could it be cervical cancer? Why was this happening? Just days ago, maybe even this morning, she had everything she hoped for—a good husband, an encouraging community, a family of her own, a settled life. Did a person's story change that fast? Was happiness a shimmering soap bubble?

St. Luke's was closest, but she drove toward Beauville Hospital because Avi's mother praised it, usually when informing people that

Avi could have been a doctor. Meena turned on the radio. There was a chance of thunderstorms, a crash on the southbound lanes, delays heading north. As she passed the crash site, she saw a police officer help a dazed man back to his car. Seeing that made her dizzy. Was the bleeding getting worse? The hospital parking lot was packed, but she found a space on the far side, near Boulder Ridge. As she hurried across the rows of cars, ignoring the accumulating wetness between her thighs, she noticed the storm coming, gusty winds breaking off wispy sections from low, slate clouds, a mountain-like cumulus approaching from the west.

To the receptionist in Emergency, Meena explained she was having heavy vaginal bleeding. The receptionist immediately arranged for a wheelchair to take her back. A Filipino nurse helped her out of her dress and panties and into a hospital gown. She asked for Meena's personal details and medications as she took vitals. Meena's blood pressure was alarmingly low. The nurse called in a doctor, tall and smiley, who ordered an IV and a drug. Another doctor arrived and asked questions. Did Meena know if she was pregnant? Yes, she was. Did she have fibroids? Not that she knew. Did her family have a history of cancer? Not that she was aware. Which medications was she on? Prenatal vitamins, steroids and beta-blockers for her birthmark. The doctor touched Meena's shoulder, called her a "poor dear," and asked if they could examine her cervix. The nurse returned. They did an ultrasound.

Fetal tissue fragments were causing the bleeding. They would remove them.

The doctor returned and again asked for the names of the medications she was taking, and Meena repeated the names of the beta-blocker and the steroids. The doctor frowned. "Studies are inconclusive," she said, "but those have been linked to miscarriage risk."

The doctor was talking about fetal fragments, studies and risks, like Meena wasn't even there. This was happening to her. This was her life. Her choices. What had she done? What had she done to her baby? What had she done because Avi couldn't handle a birthmark?

Meena asked the nurse for her phone. She called the priest and left a voicemail apologizing for running out on the class. She called Avi. He didn't pick up. She messaged him: *At Beauville Hospital. Miscarriage.* She waited. When there was no response, she called him again, leaving a voicemail this time: "Avi, I'm at the hospital, having a miscarriage, going in for surgery, would you call me already?"

They took her out of the ER, admitted her into the hospital, wheeled her down hallways to a new room. A new doctor arrived, a woman in blue scrubs, a blue surgical mask, and a matching turquoise bindi on her forehead. Could this woman have been at their wedding? The doctor explained that the main risks of a dilation and curettage were infection, scarring, and infertility, plus the usual risks of anesthesia. A nurse asked Meena to confirm her emergency contacts.

I've lost my baby, Meena thought. She'd had so much loss. The world was indifferent to intentions and plans. What can you do?

Outside the hospital room window, the leaves on the trees were drying, yellowing, stems wilting, about to yield to the seasonal winds. She saw a brown cardinal, a female, in a tree. Its sharp crest, with red accents, wobbled up and down. A scream resounded inside her abdomen. A private scream. She felt hollow. Then a cramp shot down her abdomen to her foot, and she screamed aloud. An attendant came in and added something to the IV drip. They would start soon, she said. After a while, the anesthesiologist arrived. He administered a new pack of fluid. He asked her to count backwards from one hundred.

Once she had been in the hospital with her father. It was a minor heart attack, his first, and at the time they didn't think his condition would grow serious. As they waited in the fancy, high-end hospital room in São Paulo, she sat in a wingback chair and read him his favorite children's books—*Moss Pillows*, *Where the Wild Things Are*, *Goodnight Moon*.

Meena now felt woozy. Oblivion was gathering. This chapter of her life might be ending. She was sailing in and out of weeks and almost over a year. Goodnight hospital room, goodnight beeping, goodnight fluorescent light. Goodbye, child.

A machine was beeping. A white steel equipment cabinet directly in front of her. How did it get here? Was she in a new room? A male nurse dreamily checked her vitals. Actually, he was working efficiently. She must be the delirious one. He told her to wake up. She tried to sharpen her attention but remained dazed, disoriented. She waited, it seemed hours, for someone to tell her what happened, where her baby had gone.

Her embryo might already be in a biohazard bin, commingling among the amniotic fluids, saliva specimens, semen, vaginal secretions, pleural fluids, and organ biopsies of dozens of human beings. Biodebris. Soon to be incinerated beyond recognition. The embryo, the fetus, the baby, the little girl, if she ever existed, even in the way a promise exists, a presence no less present for being a possibility, a state of hopefulness, would never be fulfilled, never walk, never talk, never know her mother's love.

Meena asked a nurse for her phone. Avi had texted, called, texted again. He had been trying to explain that he was in a sensitive meeting and had turned off his phone. He was on his way.

The doctor returned. She said it all went fine. Meena could go home in two hours if she remained stable. Meena would likely bleed for a few days. Over-the-counter pain medicine should suffice, but the doctor wrote an order for a prescription painkiller, just in case. She told Meena to avoid vaginal sex. Until she was comfortable. At least six to eight weeks. The doctor said there was another issue, though. Meena had a slightly deformed uterus, bicornuate, or heart shaped. Meena said she knew that. But she hadn't known what the doctor said next. The deformity raised the risk of miscarriage between two and forty percent, though the miscarriage rate could be higher, or lower, no one knew for sure. It wasn't clear if Meena could have carried the baby to term, anyway. The doctor said she was sorry to be the bearer of bad news and gave Meena the names of a few specialists.

A deformed uterus? She might never have her own child? She was suddenly furious. Avi's mother and the Punjabi 5 would overinterpret the news, spout mind-body mysticism, suggesting that an inhospitable womb explained her personality, her wish for a career, her unmotherly tendencies. They would inspect Meena's abdomen with their clinical-spiritual gaze, evaluate her against the maternal archetype.

Fools.

Why had Avi referred to her birthmark as "scarring"? Why hadn't he discouraged her from treating the birthmark? Because removing it would make her more desirable. Actually, he had been appraising her this whole time. Assessing her value to him and his family. Arranged marriage had turned him into a buyer, an online purchaser of women. He worried over the implicit dowry, whether his marriage had been a good trade.

It was also his character. He was preoccupied with appearances. Seeming manly, appearing tough, like when he hid his back injury. He was always telling Meena to do things for appearance's sake. Help his mother get the house spic-and-span for the housewarming ceremony. Be nice to Rav Uncle. Make them look good. Say this. Don't say that. Campaigning was completely about appearances. Coming off strong. Pure, perfect. A smooth unruffled veneer, clothes like a uniform, like some boring dignitary. All his talks, his campaign speeches, were tantamount to hiding weaknesses, covering up the blemishes. Turning his eyes from reality. She should've known. His pictures on the wedding website had been too good, probably photoshopped.

Meena saw her stained yellow dress and bloody underwear in a sealed plastic bag on the nightstand. A nurse, sounding carefree, said that when patients needed new clothes, they looted the hospital's collection of articles donated for the homeless. She gave Meena hospital underwear and heavy pads, as well as an oversize blue blouse and a pair of baggy jeans. Meena put on vagrant's clothing. She signed her discharge papers. She texted Avi, telling him not to park. They would bring her to the front entrance. A candy striper helped Meena into a wheelchair and escorted her down the hallways, through several sets of double doors. It was early evening. The sun was blasting into the hospital atrium. It looked like the storm had come and gone. The waiting area was packed: an obese woman breathing from an oxygen tank, a family holding a baby with a bandaged head, old men staring at nothing.

Avi pulled up in his father's old Lexus. "Meena, I'm so, so sorry. Here, let me help you get in."

He took her bag, opened the door for her, made sure she was buckled in. He thanked the candy striper. It was annoying, him pretending to be gallant, treating her like a helpless woman after she'd just gone through a vaginal evacuation alone, woke up alone, dealt with the loss alone. He started to drive slowly through the parking lot, pausing at the crossing lanes and checking for traffic. Maybe he was turning over what to say. Apparently, sympathy for his wife was hard work.

"Meena, I'm sorry I missed your calls," he began. "Rav Uncle set up a meeting with a major newspaper that is about to run a story about the election and Jim's affair, they're actually calling it an 'affair,' so I was in a meeting with the editors, and I was worried I'd let slip something about the deal with Gwen, and I disabled notifications so I could concentrate."

"I needed you, Avi."

She looked at him, then defiantly turned away.

"I know, and I'm really sorry," he said. She could feel him starting to take her in, his gaze moving between her and the parking-lot traffic. "I'm so sorry. As soon as this election is over, it'll be different. I promise. I wish it weren't the case, but I have to be available . . ."

What was he talking about? Why was he *always* talking like this?

"I hate this," she said.

"I'm sorry, I feel awful, I wish I had more time," he said. "I feel bad. We'll try again. In some ways, it's actually better this way, to wait until I can really focus."

"Did you just say it's good I had a miscarriage?"

"No, no, that's not what I meant. I'm sad. Really. I want to be a father. It's just that it's easier for a guy when he has a clean slate. This was a misfortune. But we didn't cause this, it's not like we get to choose when . . ."

"The treatments for my birthmark caused the miscarriage. That's what the doctor said."

"For real?"

They were at a stop sign. He lifted his hands off the steering wheel, gesturing helplessness.

"That's it?" she demanded. "That's all you have to say? Don't you want to explain why you were fixated, why you didn't tell me not to treat it? Are you going to apologize?"

"Fixated? Meena, Meena. I didn't need you to treat it. I'm so sorry, but I didn't ask you to do that."

Such a liar. She had to get away from him, from all this. What was the point of this marriage if she couldn't have a family? They came to the row with Avi's car.

"There's the Oldsmobile. Drop me off here."

"You don't have to. I can come back in a car service to drive it home."

"I said drop me off."

His mouth hung open, like someone pretending to be an innocent victim.

She didn't turn back to wave or acknowledge him. She drove to Speedy Car Wash, a few hundred yards down Maple. There was no blood on the seats, as far as she could tell, but she wanted this car wiped clean. As the Oldsmobile traveled down the conveyor through the suds and spinning brushes, she sat, exhausted and uncomfortable, in one of the plastic chairs in the waiting room, the anesthesia wearing off and the pain returning. Once the car was outside, a group of Hispanic men vacuumed and scrubbed its interior. There were hot dogs, pretzels, and baked goods for sale. The smells made her nauseous.

When she got back into the Oldsmobile, she noticed that the car-wash employees had left protective paper covers on the seat cushions and floors. Undoubtedly, this was to satisfy Southgate drivers, who appreciated a barrier between the workers' bodies and the newly sanitized surfaces, the car owners so fussy and superficial, obsessed with appearances and proprieties, like everyone else in this town.

AT HOME, Meena changed out of her homeless clothes into pajamas. Tired and lightheaded, probably from the anesthesia, she rested in the king bed. Avi brought her chicken soup and a heaping bowl of warm rice. She told him to leave it on the dresser, and to leave her alone.

She couldn't sleep. She kicked and turned. Dozens of questions slithered along the surface of her mind, like earthworms after a soaking rain. What kind of husband makes himself unavailable when his wife is pregnant? Avi said he had a meeting with the editors and turned off his phone to concentrate, to avoid mentioning that tawdry scheme involving Gwen and Bob. Why did he get involved in that dirty business, ignoring her advice? Had he always been comfortable with sleaze? There might be more to him than she knew. Behavior like this didn't come out of nowhere. There was probably some foul or embarrassing incident in his past. Perhaps that's what had ended his career in Chicago. Sex with a coworker? With a secretary? A financial impropriety? Who takes campaign contributions at a wedding, anyway?

She couldn't stop remembering that moment, on their wedding night, when he saw her birthmark. The shocked look. Eyebrows raised, open mouth. He pretended not to care, but she had noticed him, more than once, inspecting it. Of course he wanted her to treat it. Even if he hadn't said so directly. Why deny the plain truth? The answer came to her quickly. Avi wasn't strong enough. He leaned on people around him—Rav Uncle, his parents, his volunteers and frat brothers—to feel good about who he was.

How had she been so wrong about him? Or maybe she hadn't been wrong, and she was getting carried away now. Maybe all these changes, the marriage and the stress of the campaign, were disorienting him. Maybe he'd return to being the kind, decent man she saw online, and met at Starbucks, once all this was over.

There was a way to see who he really was, inside. She once saw him write in a small green book, his journal, then leave it in a dresser drawer. She'd noticed it, but didn't remark. Maybe she had, through some spider sense, anticipated this moment. Millions of wives, particularly the women assigned to a husband by their families, averted their eyes. They had to, to get by. That wouldn't work, not for her. She had vowed to accept her husband, to be patient, but now, after the miscarriage, she couldn't look away anymore. If she didn't look, she wouldn't see, and if she didn't see him, how was she ever supposed to trust him?

He was gabbing on the phone downstairs. She started going through his dresser drawers, sorting through socks and underwear and t-shirts. She searched inside the closet. She fell to all fours and pushed aside his shoes, which Avi had arranged in orderly stacks, the laces all facing the same direction. She looked under and between his loafers, oxfords, tennis shoes, wingtips. Still nothing. She looked in the corners, behind the baskets of socks. She searched on the shelves above, through his sweaters. She even looked through the hangers. Nothing but his tangy body odor.

No evidence. Still, the fact that she was searching through his belongings made it clear. She didn't trust her husband anymore, and she had to get away. She would go to Delhi, she instantly decided. She wanted to see where they had scattered her father's ashes. She wanted to tell her father she'd done her best, really tried, but this wasn't meant to be. She might not be able to have a child, so what was the point of traditional marriage, all those empty platitudes about family and generations? Her mother and sister were helpful in crises. They would console her. She could meet up with friends, former colleagues. Peter said he might be passing through.

She restacked Avi's shoes just as she'd found them, laces across the tongues.

SHE DREAMED she was being carried past twin foam nozzles in a car wash, the top and bottom rinses shooting water, the brushes scrubbing her skin, a group of men wiping and drying her body.

It was a relief to wake to a dark room, the streetlamp off, velvety night peeking through the windows. She imagined the wide sky outside, a purple bowl of soupy stars, the first bits of red and yellow appearing in the trees in Linden Park. It was surprising to feel nostalgia for the American Midwest, already. For the clean crisp air of autumn. In Delhi, the skies would be hazy with dust and smoke.

Her mother had warned her. After that meeting at the Sahara, she had pointed out the bluster, the lack of curiosity, among these people. She observed how Rav Uncle posed complex questions as if they were rhetorical, and everyone took that to be normal. At the wedding, her mother said these people were cleaving to simplifications and public rituals—the henna, the garlands, the tikka, the steps around the fire, the rites and rules, all the hoariness they could muster—because they were isolated, cut off from their homeland. They had no mooring, no family lore. Avi's mother's okra recipe would appear to be their principal heirloom.

She could see now that arranged marriage had been a mistake. The bride and groom were supposed to have faith in the clan, the wedding pageantry, the wisdom of the elders, all the old formulas, but she and her family were too secular, and Avi had no idea what they meant. Her father, who understood these things, was gone. Alone, what chance had she against the ancient roles, the social equations in which wives acquiesced to the in-laws' dominion?

Avi entered the bedroom quietly. He whispered her name. She pretended to be asleep. She heard the closet door open. Clothes rustled. He probably had an event tomorrow, was sorting through his khakis and oxfords. The uniform. That task required no brainpower, but he would still be squinting, the self-important look of the big decision maker.

Peter had his problems, but at least he was in touch with his own desires. Once, at a ball in Rio de Janeiro, he wore a linen suit, and she was in a gown and heels. She felt his eyes flicker at her from across the ballroom as she returned with the caipirinhas. At a noisy beachside bar, Peter downed a mussel stew and shrimp risotto and codfish balls, throwing seafood shells onto the floor, grunting in delight with each cracking of a lobster claw. It had been a mistake to ask Peter to commit, that's not who he was. But had there been anything wrong with those moments?

"Meena," Avi said again. "Are you awake? How are you feeling?"

"Fine."

"Can we talk?"

She didn't answer. After a moment, he flipped on the light. The effect of the glare was to make him look small, much smaller than the image in her mind. "I'm really sorry about what happened, Meena."

He sounded earnest, but what did sincerity have to do with self-deception?

"Meena, I want to tell you . . . I've really come to rely on you. I don't know where I'd be without you in my life, my wife at the wheel."

He sounded worried, but it was also funny, this addendum to his so-called raincoat theory. The wife not only as a raincoat but a tugboat, guiding the husband to safe harbor.

"You'll be fine, Avi. You have lots of people here."

When rehearsing the next lines, she hadn't paused, but now she waited, aware of the looming loss, the pain, disappointment. He would get over it. He was one of the Southgaters. His mother would probably have him back on the matrimonial websites, searching for a replacement, within a month. The Punjabi 5 would shake their heads, chuckle into their broccoli cheddar soup. These people didn't do tragedy. No inner depth. It was all comedy or melodrama, like in the Bollywood films.

"I'm going to New Delhi," Meena said.

"You're going?"

"To be with my family. And to take some space."

"For how long?"

The words in her mind were, It's over, Avi. But she wasn't ready to say it aloud.

"I don't know."

"Are you giving up, then? Already? Are we done?"

Pain flared in her abdomen. She turned over slowly, inhaled, exhaled. This was just a cramp, her uterus shrinking to its normal dimensions. That of a small heart.

"Avi, I'm cramping. Would you leave me alone now? We can talk logistics later."

She was dying for sleep, for darkness, for a different life.

Chapter Eight

HIS MARRIAGE already a failure? Avi could still smell the sandalwood, feel the sacred fire's heat. The beautiful ceremony, the marigolds, the roses, the ancient chants, it felt like yesterday. And making love to her, that dip in her eyebrow, the owl hooting. Did that evening in the kitchen mean nothing? A beautiful marriage, a promising campaign, a life in his community, all so glorious, glittering. Was it ending so fast?

Meena was spending most of her time in bed, uncommunicative. She was recovering from the miscarriage, but maybe she was just in there planning a life without him. He poked his head in to ask how she was doing. She was polite, but it was clear she wanted him to go away. He didn't know what to do. Some nights he took a scotch to the back patio and stared vacantly at the koi rising and diving in the pond.

He actually felt sick. Meena's impending departure felt like a lump, a malignancy. He had a burning sensation, a hot skin-stain. The ache ate at him, a sac of sadness enveloping him, a painful patina. He kept up his work schedule and campaigning, but his meetings all seemed to peter out in a puddle of pity, as if his sickness was blindingly obvious to colleagues. He had the unmistakable mark of a loser, a man cast aside.

He kept going over his decision making. Was the idea of mixing East and West, acting simultaneously modern and traditional, a mistake? Maybe he should've let his parents take full control of picking his wife, like in the old days, or else he should've stayed in Chicago and married Helena, his hippie girlfriend, or if not married her, taken her up on the invitation to rent a camper and travel across the country with her guitar. What he was attempting was too confusing, too much mixing of identities, too many impurities.

Somehow, though, Rav Uncle managed to be both modern and Indian. He married a white woman after his first wife died and yet remained the local Hindu champion. Maybe leadership wasn't about symbols but domination and willpower, as Rav Uncle said, and Avi was just too nice. Too weak, to put it plainly.

He couldn't stop ruminating, though it was making him feel worse. He remembered how, a couple years before, after a radiologist had noticed an "incidentaloma" on Avi's kidney during an MRI scan targeting his lower back, he'd feared he had cancer. For seventy-two hours, he was a wreck. But then, when it was confirmed to be a harmless cyst, a nothing burger, his hard scaly self snapped back into place triumphantly. What had he been afraid of? What was he thinking? Why had he been so fearful and foolish? He wasn't going to die, not right then, of course not, he was too young, too healthy, thriving, full of spirit.

In the same way, after a little while Avi started to believe that Meena couldn't possibly be leaving him, at least not for good. He was too alive, too zestful, to suffer the fate of a rejected man. It was true he had been too preoccupied with the campaign and had neglected her, had in fact failed her when she needed him most. He could imagine how bad she must have felt during the miscarriage, alone and vulnerable. Had losing a child reminded her of the loss of her father? And traditional marriage couldn't have felt natural to her, either. She was educated, modern. They'd had bad luck, and the misunderstandings. But did she really think he told her to erase the birthmark? He hadn't said that. She couldn't possibly believe it, not deep down. She must be acting out of shock, blaming him because everyone needs someone to blame when things go wrong. On some level, this marriage was a rebound relationship for her, after Peter, so maybe she still needed time to work things through. He hoped, even began to expect, that after a few weeks in Delhi she'd see their marriage more clearly, see him more clearly, and return.

Of course, her decision to return, like her choice to leave him, would be hers, not his. What was in his control was his attitude. What he could do was recover his confidence, let go of the loser's aura, drop-kick the sac of sadness. Wouldn't she be more likely to return if he was attractive? And wouldn't he be more attractive if he was confident, which meant continuing with the campaign and winning the election, making people proud?

That was his mindset when he conveyed Meena's departure to his parents. His father was sympathetic, saying it would be okay, that it wasn't a surprise, as every marriage needed a tune-up now and again. His mother said, "Leaving us?" After a moment she added, "Of course." After another pause, she said, "Actually, this doesn't surprise me at all. Meena's mother is the haughty type, the kind who would summon her daughter selfishly. These mothers cause trouble for new-lyweds. Meena's mother is probably sick and needs her to come home. It's typical. I'm not surprised." His mother had a facility with cover stories, which was both gratifying and depressing.

Rav Uncle, however, said Meena's departure was a significant issue, and Avi better come up with a plan for explaining his wife's absence at campaign events. Rav Uncle scheduled a brainstorming session, summoning Avi, his parents, and the Punjabi 5 to a meeting at his house. Topics of discussion: firstly, campaign updates; secondly, managing the crisis in Avi's marriage and its impact on the community. This was going to be dreadful, but Avi felt he had no choice but to attend.

Rav Uncle's house, situated atop a hillock on six acres, with two double-car garages, a two-story portico, and eight Corinthian columns, was widely known as the "Taj Mahal of East Central Ohio." Community members called Rav Uncle, who built the edifice after his first wife suddenly passed, the "Shah Jahan of Southgate." Everyone loved parties at the Taj, where Rav Uncle's new wife Chrissy and the women would lay out roasted eggplant and dhaba-style chicken, while Rav Uncle and the men drank whiskey and sat cross-legged on white bedsheets to play cards, and Avi, Peeku, and the other Punjabi 5 kids threw a football under the stars.

Avi took a chair next to his parents. On the other side of Rav Uncle's dining table sat Kohli, Sharma, Verma, and Chrissy. Rav Uncle, leaning on his elbows, glowered at the head. Chrissy's silver tray of tea and biscuits gleamed under two brass chandeliers.

"First item, election updates," Rav Uncle said, staring at Kohli.

Kohli reported that the hand-on-the-crotch photograph, involving Jim and the heiress from Ohio Cattle, was just the tip of the iceberg. There were eyewitnesses who'd seen them checking into a hotel. There might be a photo of them leaving an adult video store together. The *Central Buckeye* was exploring an exposé on Jim's marital improprieties.

"Excellent," Rav Uncle said. "Wonderful news! Now we will see who supports family values." He banged the table and clapped, encouraging others to join. Avi felt for Jim's marital trouble, but it would be disrespectful not to clap when so directed.

Verma asked, now that Avi's victory appeared likely, if Avi could spearhead a repeal of the $35 fine for watering lawns during droughts, which he found annoying. Kohli said he wanted the township to do something about the deer herd that congregated in his backyard at dusk, eating from his bird feeder and leaving droppings.

Avi shrugged his shoulders and said he didn't know how much influence the trustee had on those matters, legally speaking.

Rav Uncle tsk-tsked. "Don't laugh off such requests, Avinash.

Take what is ours. Remember, this will be Asian century! You must make connections. You must use connections. Flex!"

Avi pursed his lips.

"Second item, Meena's departure," Rav Uncle said. "This must remain hush-hush. Or people will say if man cannot manage own household, how will he manage township?"

"Why was she surprised the election kept you busy?" Avi's mother said. "You must help your own family, your community. What else? Arranged marriage is always for family's needs. His mother"—she gestured at her husband—"chose me because she had arthritis and needed a good cook. So what?"

"Avi," Rav Uncle said, "because Meena left you, Peeku is now saying arranged marriage is bunk. He is calling his Kmart girl many times every day. He walked five miles to Kmart girl's house and stood outside waiting. The girl's father is telling us to keep our son away from his daughter, even threatening legal action. An embarrassment."

"My son is such a sweet boy," Chrissy said, "so much hope, ready to love anybody, like a child."

"Then what are you saying, that Avi is not sweet, that he is to blame?" Avi's mother said.

"Again, you women bickering?" said Rav Uncle. "My points are the following. As I said, keep quiet about Meena's departure. Also, Peeku will get married. I am putting foot down. Hard. No more pussyfeet. Avi, I am delegating to you task of going on computer and finding good bride for Peeku. I will give you checklist. You will place Peeku's ad on one of these internets."

"I'd like to help," Chrissy said.

"No, no, you fuss too much over the boy," Rav Uncle said to his wife.

"Avi is very good with computers, and he can relate to anybody, like a secretary of state!" Avi's mother bragged.

It was maddening to hear people discuss his marriage. He

clenched his fists under the table. It didn't seem right to push Peeku into a marriage, even if he was misbehaving or pestering a girl, but Rav Uncle might be right that Peeku, with his limited faculties, could get out of control. Maybe arranged marriage would be natural for Peeku, even if it had proved challenging for Avi and Meena.

"Are you sure it's right for him?" Avi asked Rav Uncle.

"Obviously, I am sure. Why else am I asking you?"

Chrissy said, "Thank you, Avi. Would you help me bring Peeku his tea? Maybe you can cheer him up."

"And tell the boy he must go with you for morning training," Rav Uncle said.

When Avi had first returned to Southgate, Rav Uncle had him take Peeku out to a football field for morning training exercises, which were scripted to resemble those early-morning nationalist gatherings in India. Avi and Peeku wore khaki shorts and polos. They did salutations. They prayed. They did forward bends and yoga push-ups. Jumping jacks, sit-ups, and one-legged hops. Fencing with sticks. Rav Uncle was still pushing these exercises, though Peeku often resisted.

"No tea," said Peeku, hiding under the covers when Avi, holding Chrissy's tray, opened the door.

Peeku's room had barely changed since Avi was last there, a year ago. Posters of Browns players, a calendar of NFL cheerleaders beside the bed, laundry strewn everywhere.

"Come on, Peeku, man," Avi said. "Have some cookies."

"No cookies."

"How about throwing the ball and doing some exercises tomorrow morning? Red Right 88?"

"The exercises are stupid!"

"The training can toughen you up, dude. Peeku, come on. Let's talk, man."

Peeku pulled his head out from under the covers. "Where did Meena go?"

"She went to Delhi, but she'll be back soon." Avi added, "Her mother wasn't feeling well."

"My dad didn't have an arranged marriage. Why do I have to?"

"They want what's best for you. They're worried about you, that's all."

"I want to marry Sheela."

"Peeku, her parents won't allow it. They're angry, dude."

"I talked to her. She said I'm nice."

"Peeku, man, it's one thing to get married. It's another to find a match that works. I'm going to find a few girls for you, then we can talk again. Let's see how it goes, okay?"

"Leave me alone so I can watch a wee-deo," Peeku said, turning on the TV with his remote and navigating to a replay of a Browns playoff game.

Wee-deo. It was depressing to be surrounded by so much mispronunciation. Avi's mother said *re-zoom* when boasting about her son's CV. His parents went to dinner at *rest-o-rons* and worried about the *mortt-gauge* rates on their town house. Then there was the time in third grade when, on Avi's first and only trip to India, they'd stopped over in Paris and Avi's mom, confused, pooped in the bidet.

All so embarrassing. And yet, they were his people and community, the ground of his character, the heart of his vision, the core of who he was. His constituents and his axioms. Or maybe his *con-stee-two-ants* and his *ax-yums*.

MEENA WAS FINISHING her packing. Four large suitcases. Her Chinese vase, wrapped in towels, was stuffed into her carry-on. The framed picture of her family, taken from the foyer table, was shrouded in sweaters. If she was taking that stuff, her trip to India, which he thought would be fairly short, might be very long.

"You don't want to leave that stuff here?" he asked.

"Those things mean a lot to me," she replied.

She wasn't clarifying her plans, not giving him even that, apparently.

She had planned to use a car service, but he'd convinced her to let him drive. When he reached for her carry-on, she grabbed it from him, adding, "Don't stress your back."

Maybe she was being kind now. Or was that a jab?

A cold rain pelted. The oversexed couple in the "Take Time Off" sign were misted over, their come-hither glances obscured in gloom. As Avi took the entrance ramp to the interstate, Meena received a call from the school. Something about lesson plans. She told the caller they could video chat from Delhi. She started texting people. The rain worsened, and he had to drive more slowly. A series of trucks passed, boxing them into the right lane.

Why was she interpreting his actions in the worst possible light, cutting him no slack? Couldn't she tell he cared about her and their marriage, but had just been overwhelmed? She didn't seem to understand what running for office and helping his family entailed. Was it his fault he had to fulfill his duties? But maybe this wasn't about him. Maybe she was still fixated on Peter and seeking an excuse to leave. If it wasn't the birthmark treatment and the miscarriage, it would have been something else.

He drove by a tow truck operator attaching chains to a stalled car. He sped past the old glass factory along the river. He approached the long-term lot, the car rental turnoff, finally the sign for the departures ramp.

What if she and Peter reconnected, somehow? Or Vishali introduced her to another guy, some rich industrialist? Then his marriage, which just last week seemed so solid, so real, would fade away, a foggy memory from a road trip taken long ago.

He felt the urge to say something sympathetic, to demonstrate how much he cared. "Sure you're up for a long flight, right now, in this condition, I mean, after all you've been through?"

"I'm stronger than you think, Avi."

Is that how she wanted it? Couldn't she tell he was trying?

"Meena, I didn't want you to treat the birthmark. It's like you're blaming me for everything. It's not like you're easy to trust, either, by the way."

"I'm not the one who sent his mother to ask his wife not to work."

"I didn't do that, Meena, and I told you I'm fine with you working." Why was she making things up? "As long as we're talking about our problems, at least I'm not the one haunted by my ex," he said.

She looked at him with a hardened expression, ready for a fight, then turned away. When she returned her gaze to him, she didn't seem angry anymore. Her eyes were red.

"Look, Meena. We both have regrets, but we can turn it around."

Her head swayed ambiguously.

"Avi, everything here feels like loss to me, right now. I need to get away. There's nothing more to say."

At the doors, she said there was no need to park, just drop her off curbside. He didn't fight for the right to escort her in. After he helped unload the suitcases onto the skycap's trolley, they hugged tentatively, warily.

"I'm sorry, Meena," he said.

"I know. I may not be in contact for a while." She walked into the terminal.

He felt empty. It was that old sensation, with him since childhood, of never getting to his destination, like playing baseball and running out an infield hit, running and running, never reaching first base.

Returning home, he went up to their bedroom. He threw bed pillows into the reading chair and started punching. He was angry at Meena's mother and sister for luring his wife away. He scorned the Punjabi 5 for their stupid wedding presents and bad pronunciation.

He resented his parents' indebtedness to Rav Uncle. He despised Jim Vinson's bigotry. He was just lashing out, really punching himself, but it was easier to hit others than identify what to smash inside.

Chapter Nine

VISHALI'S DRIVER, a young man in a safari shirt and brown slacks, held the door, and Meena slid into the black SUV. The driver announced the availability of mineral water, though two large bottles were on the tray at her nose. The driver was aiming at posh service, but his thick Punjabi accent betrayed him. The car smelled like newly unwrapped shower curtains.

She leaned her head against the glass. Seeking slumber and forgetting, she had taken a sleeping pill on the last flight. The medicated hangover, plus jet lag, had led her to wander, zombie-like, through the arrivals terminal, where the brown-and-beige carpets swayed murkily. The giant sculptures of white hands doing the mudras in the immigration hall had extended enigmatic greetings. The evergreen trees with funnel-shaped flowers, which they were now driving past, appeared man-made, like stage props. In the arid median strip, drooping bushes looked ready to succumb to the heat. She remembered her last trip here, her father's body, under a white sheet, seeming to quiver as it was wheeled into the cremation ghat.

It was now well past dawn, the city's dirty sun hanging low. She dozed off but then woke as the car came to a stop at a light. The streets were already busy, lorries and three-wheelers honking. A gaunt man in a brown sweater pushed a fruit cart. Despite the car's thick, tinted windows, she could smell the city's soot and dust, the acrid waste, cooking kilns from the slums. As they approached Ring Road, traffic stalled. A car had slammed into the road divider. A mob of police officers in khakis and berets directed traffic, arguing with irritated motorists and distributing grave looks.

As they sat, waiting for the traffic to move, Meena started to feel sorry for herself. What if she had needed to go north, not south, on the way to the hospital during the miscarriage, and got stuck in that traffic jam? She might have bled and bled. What if she'd known the impact of a misshapen uterus? Would she have had more fun, luxuriating in nice hotels and expensive dates, instead of marrying Avi? She'd thought a traditional marriage, and her own soaring spirits as she stood before that sacred fire, foretold safety, shelter, a home. They did not. Just as her father's strong convictions were no proof of health. Her own plans, yet her unreceptive organ. Avi's showy toast, his weak back. The world appeared, it did not promise. How could people? How could marriage?

She felt the ping of a specific absence, as if she'd forgotten something in Southgate. Mentally, she scanned her belongings, her dresses and shoes and books, the vase, her various documents, but couldn't identify it. She checked her phone, told her mother and sister she was on her way. Avi had texted, he hoped she had a good trip, he was sorry. She didn't respond.

Why was she given to self-pity? Was it her serious, belabored personality? She remembered the priest's playful homage to the planets and asteroids at the wedding. He'd managed to be serious and mischievous at once. He made their wedding a jaunty theater of solidarity, like offhand solemnity, performative cosmology. She should be like that, airier, more whimsical. Maybe she could learn a thing or two from her sister's fancies, her effervescence, even her fashion sense. Why not? Here in Delhi she could look up old friends, go to clubs.

The driver braked. They idled again. The cars around them stopped, too. It still surprised her that Delhi drivers now observed red lights. In the car to her left, a young woman held the steering wheel while a man in the passenger seat, probably her husband, chewed paan leaves. Juice dribbled down his chin. His wife wiped it with her fingers.

Meena's strongest impressions of the city were from primary school, when her family spent half a year in a north Delhi neighborhood. Back then, cows wandered the dusty roads. After school, Meena and Vishali, friendless and bored, would watch the beasts flick flies and shower their dung. Meena would run at them, throwing sticks and staring into the cows' dumb, imperturbable eyes. The bovine attitude terrified her, one sensation to the next, day upon day, year upon year.

"Excuse me, Madame's Sister," said the driver, smiling at her through the rearview mirror. "Madame Vishali told me you are married? Pardon my interruption, if Madame desires to be resting?"

That didn't take long. Could there be a society more preoccupied with the marital status of young women?

"Yes, I'm married," she said. There was no point in explaining the complicated truth, which might invite gossip. "And you?"

"No, no, not me, money before marriage. I am poor man still. Madame says you are the true Indian in the family. Arranged marriage! You have the true Indian values!"

She hated this routine. People like the driver, and even sophisticated types who should know better, romanticized women abroad, managed their foreignness and their supposedly exotic sexuality by turning them into goddesses.

"Indian values are changing. More women are driving," she said.

"Women drivers, yes. But who is cooking, then? What is your husband eating, Madame Sister? Is he all by himself? No one is cooking for him?"

"He's probably at McDonalds."

"Chicken Maharaja Macs!" the driver said, taking his hands off the wheel to rub his stomach. "Very tasty. But when I am married, wife's cooking should be enough."

The driver eased around a dozen cars wedged into the tight alleyway as they approached Vishali and Andrew's place, a blue and white four-story structure with a large front lawn and a courtyard. She recalled its roof-deck view of the old Islamic arch across the park. The driver opened the gate, then pulled in between her sister's fancy cars. A sign above the side entrance announced the yoga studio: *Vishali's Vinyasa*. The driver helped her unload. Then he asked if she might find him a wife in America, preferably a Sikh girl, slim and educated, but not too educated. Meena gave him a bland smile.

A teenage boy in flip-flops, a new servant Meena didn't recognize, wandered out to instruct the driver on his next errand. The teenager explained to Meena that Madame Vishali had been waiting but had now run out and would be back shortly. He carried Meena's luggage up the side staircase to the third floor. A queen bed on a modern box frame, not the low-to-ground bed Meena remembered from her last visit, took up most of the guest room. There were fresh hydrangeas and hypericums on the desk. Some snacks Vishali must have left. The room smelled of jasmine, perhaps incense wafting up from the yoga studio.

Meena brushed her teeth, pulled the blinds, and lay down to nap. It would be evening in Southgate. Avi was probably mulling over what her departure meant for his campaign. She lay in bed and listened to the ceiling fan. Despite her exhaustion, sleep didn't come. She heard a man hawking eggs out on the street. Then the vegetable seller calling. After a while, the fruit vendor. She rose and ate the crackers and papaya on the desk. She got into bed again, but kept tossing and turning. The jewelry seller announced his arrival. The cobbler. She grabbed a magazine on the side table and scanned listings of upcoming events in Delhi. If she couldn't fall asleep tonight, she would eventually hear the night watchman making his rounds, loudly clearing his throat, expectorating, thumping his stave, that high-pitched whistle, the wolfish moans.

HANDS CLAPPING. Someone rousing her. Meena's slumber lifted sluggishly, like the sleep of anesthesia. She rubbed her face. Vishali, wearing an elegant blue salwar kameez, was at the edge of the bed. Meena sat up and hugged her sister.

"My dear," Vishali said, "so, so good to hold you. I'm sorry for everything. We have so much to talk about, but I decided to let you sleep. Mummy is waiting at the Tex-Mex restaurant. Why don't you get ready."

Meena washed her face and changed into a turquoise cotton salwar. She brushed her hair and put on some makeup. She sipped the mango juice a servant must have left. In the carport, Mr. Maharaja Mac held the door for her. Once they were buckled in, Vishali explained that Andrew had gone to Japan again and wouldn't be joining them. He sent his love. Meena said Andrew seemed like a good husband for Vishali, the perfect mix of adventure and stability. "Isn't he? Somehow, I got lucky," Vishali said.

The decor at the restaurant was a hodgepodge: large sombreros hanging on hooks in the entryway, photographs of rajas hunting tigers, exposed vents, that trendy combination of imperial nostalgia and urban swank. Their mother, wearing an elegant black kaftan, two large tribal rings on each hand, kissed Meena on both cheeks, then hugged her, exclaiming, "We poor women."

At the adjacent table, a large-bellied man with henna sideburns, gesticulating to his scowling wife, noticed their mother's dramatic presence and looked up. Across the room, a pair of businessmen, maybe Scots, had pushed aside their plates to lay out engineering specs and were arguing about a flyover on the road to Agra. Three women, perhaps journalists, passed around a camera. Out the window, Meena saw a tiny pond, leaves and twigs floating in boggy water.

Their mother poured from a pitcher of margaritas and toasted "to my daughters, and to all single men, in possession of good fortunes or not." A waiter in jeans and a Che Guevara t-shirt took their orders.

Their mother said, "I had four miscarriages, did I tell you? They are no fun. And your marriage, well, don't beat yourself up. One must move on with life. Delhi is not so cosmopolitan, but compared to Southgate, it will seem like London. Have fun. Go out. Of course, your father never understood. He and I were like a paratha, two sides folded into each other, greased and heated by society."

"Munu, did you hear there is a new club in CP?" Vishali said. "Floor-to-ceiling video effects, total celeb scene, Shah Rukh Khan was there last week! It's going to be so much fun to have you here!"

"That sounds great," Meena said, though she didn't like the women Vishali went clubbing with, mostly in their late twenties or early thirties, almost all married. It's tragic to go clubbing after the age of thirty, she read in a magazine once. Maybe Meena could look up her former colleagues in town. Many were still single, as far as she knew.

Their mother was saying something to Vishali about another Bollywood figure passing through, and Meena checked her phone, wondering if Avi had written again. Instead, she saw a text from Peter: *Contact info for colleagues in Delhi? Your brother-in-law? Will be in Delhi soon. Want to expand my network.*

For real? She wasn't superstitious, but it had to mean something that she and Peter were crossing paths just as her marriage was in trouble. She wanted to see him, if for no other reason than to remember how it felt to be single. Or maybe her father was right, and her heart was just jumpy. If only she knew what to do with her surplus affection.

"What is it, some bad news, then?" their mother said. She must have seen the shock on Meena's face.

"Oh nothing, at the school I was teaching at, some teacher fell off a ladder." It felt bad to lie to her mother. She smiled, put away her phone, and their mother resumed her conversation about the movie star.

When Peter said he loved her, she had wanted to believe it, even though she knew he was lying. Now she wondered if there was any difference between love and longing. Maybe craving and desire, and the desire to be desired, which was romance, were just different kinds of love.

The waiter brought the appetizers, chicken tortilla soup and chips and salsa, as well as their three chicken burritos.

"At least you have options, Munu," their mother said, dunking a chip into the cilantro salsa, "not like your father and me."

But everyone had options. Her parents found their freedoms inside marriage—her father's unnecessary business trips, her mother's exaggerated illnesses, extra visits to family members, the purposeful accumulation of chores and distractions, who knows what in their private imaginings. Their mother had developed a series of bright lines and strategies. To defend her space, she had adopted the mindset of marital warfare. Was that what Meena now needed, a killer instinct?

"I'll get over this," she said to her mother, though she didn't feel enthusiastic. Maybe it was jet lag.

"Don't be upset, Munu, you will indeed get through," their mother said. "I raised the two of you to be strong. Now, I would love a smoke with this salsa, but for that one must step outside, I'm instructed. Blasted Supreme Court rules. Anyway, Meena, you must enjoy life now. Have a nice long rest. The driver can take you around. Go shopping. See some sights. Meet people. Enjoy. This is the life," she said, twisting her hand in the air, the cigarette ensconced in her fingers.

WHEN MEENA gave Peter Andrew's contact details, she told him that she, too, was in Delhi, and a couple days later they made plans to meet for coffee. They communicated as if this was a catch-up meeting between work colleagues, but Peter would be thinking of it as a date, because for him everything was a date. Though maybe he'd changed.

And maybe she was the one imagining a date now. How would she respond if he propositioned her? Anticipating Peter's arrival in Delhi grew into a constant, low-level anxiety. She couldn't stop recalling the way he devoured shrimp and lobster, carelessly throwing shells onto the concrete floor of that restaurant in Rio.

To distract herself, she started to meet up with ex-colleagues who frequented VIP tables at the best clubs. They were acquaintances more than friends, people to whom Meena didn't need to explain her situation. Early evenings, the women assembled in a posh South Delhi flat to drink wine, put on makeup, and pack their essentials (eyeliner, lipstick, tissues, and phones) into small purses. The clubs were packed, a handful of expats and throngs of Indians, mostly put-together young professionals from tech or business. She liked the eclectic music, medleys of EDM, disco, garage, Bollywood, and Afro pop. One night, a man wearing a half-unbuttoned satin shirt got too close, and she had to push him away. Another night a fellow in a kaftan and John Lennon glasses struck up a conversation about India as the next great superpower. She told him she just wanted to dance. When the clubs were about to close, two hundred pairs of arms reached up at once, and people screamed at the LED hearts flashing red and blue, wishing the night could go on.

During the afternoons, Meena had lunch with her mother or sister when they were free and passed the time idly when they weren't. She connected with a childhood friend now working in Delhi, and the two of them spent a lovely afternoon, bright and sunny, not too hot, wandering about Humayun's Tomb before getting dosas. With a former colleague, she took in the stunning Anish Kapoor exhibition at the National Museum of Modern Art. She shopped for fabrics in Greater Kailash and bargain jewelry at the central market in Lajpat Nagar, where she walked past the site of their family's old apartment, now converted into Value Mart Men's Store. She and a friend from Barnard went to a Hauz Khas gallery exhibiting abstract oils, which were garish, but she enjoyed the pistachio ice cream at the medieval pavilions near the water tank, and wished she could take a photo of a young couple making out in the shadows of the ruins.

It was a nice stretch, aimless and restful. She was sleeping more than ten hours a night, lazily waking in the late morning, or even in the early afternoon after club nights. Her body felt better, the cramping as well as its memory now fading.

After a while, though, she started to feel itchy. What exactly was she was doing in Delhi? What did her future hold? She had hoped going out, acting single, might provide clairvoyance. If she revisited her state of mind before her marriage, maybe she could reimagine it all, understand what her options had been, and embrace them again, openheartedly. But despite the clubs and the happy afternoons, these days felt different. It was as if she was playacting. Not only did that globe-trotting lifestyle from years ago—all those expensive dinners in dozens of capital cities, the drinks and the lounges, all the possibilities of a supposedly wide-open world—seem artificial, she also kept thinking about the child she lost, as well as the kids left behind at her school. Even though the happy months in Southgate had amounted to the briefest summer, she couldn't shake those hopes.

Seeing Peter would be a test, a meter reading of her heart. If he flirted, she knew she might reciprocate. That was her nature. And if she enjoyed it, that meant what? It was a coffee, but she worried over her outfit as if it were an evening out. She settled on jeans and an olive top, with a loose shawl. She wore yellow-gold hoop earrings. She applied lipstick and blush.

Mr. Maharaja Mac drove her to the coffee shop. As they trundled past a neighborhood park, fighting traffic, she saw teams of kids playing cricket. Meena watched a boy, maybe eight years old, his hair tied up in a cute knot, clobber a half-volley. His pals jumped, dancing, celebrating the boundary, but the boy stood still. He closed his eyes. He prayed. It was a moment. She could see it becoming the boy's happiest memory, morning cricket with friends, the lavish and unburdened hours, kismet, the memory of childhood gratitude.

Inside the café, she passed tall white bookshelves, a row of white computer screens, and two young baristas in orange aprons. She spotted Peter. He had already seen her, his bright blue eyes alert to her arrival. He wore blue jeans, a lavender shirt beneath a black blazer. His professorial attire, rather than his business outfit. Had he chosen it for her sake? He stood, leaned forward, and placed his arm lightly on her back. His lips brushed against her cheek, and hers grazed his stubble. He wore the same musky cologne, which she'd noticed, and succumbed to, when she helped with his slides in that hotel ballroom in Michigan. He draped her shawl on her chair, which he had pulled out, gallantly. He certainly was more gracious than Avi.

"Meena," he smiled and stared at her. "Have you taken up Pilates?"

"No. Why?"

"Your gait is more fluid than I remember. Something about the way your shoulders and hips swayed when you came over."

"It's been a while, Peter. You look fit, as ever."

She'd forgotten how little he was. Not slight, but still some six inches shorter than Avi. Did she expect him to be tall because she first saw him onstage, his image reproduced on multiple monitors? He had a wide face. She still found him attractive, but she had forgotten how his close crop exaggerated a large forehead. She had once suggested a different hairstyle, but he said this cut made him feel productive, disciplined.

"Thanks. Nice earrings," he said. "Didn't I buy those for you?"

His eyes moved from her ears to her chest. Her feet twitched.

"Not these . . . not for me. Anyway, what a coincidence. What brings you to Delhi?"

"Consulting with the Ministry of Finance. Made a presentation to the PM yesterday. They're interested in a long-term engagement with my team. How about you? What brings you here?"

"Visiting my family."

"Well, it's good timing, actually. Meena, any chance of enticing you to rejoin our team? We need people with your skills."

"I'm now working as a school counselor and teacher at a charter school."

"Your brother-in-law told me. If you ever want to rejoin the larger world, keep us in mind. You shouldn't waste your talents. One does more good by working at scale."

He always talked about working at scale, as if it were the main virtue. He was handsome, but she wasn't feeling the old extravagant attraction. Not much attraction at all, actually. And she didn't want to be his assistant again. She felt closer to an equal. She had her own experiences and perspectives now. Her belly felt still, her inner waters less tidal, not spilling over in his presence.

"So what are you working on?" she asked.

"They want us to look at geographic clustering and export zones. That's right in our wheelhouse."

He talked like he was selling a product. Had he always, and she just hadn't noticed? She had worked with him to make people's lives better. Perhaps she mistook his marketing strategies for values.

"How's Sarah? How are your kids?" She wasn't sure why she asked. This used to be a no-go zone. They would pretend he didn't have a family.

"Fine, fine, thank you. I heard from your brother-in-law that you married a local politician in Ohio. Aadi?"

"Avi."

"And an arranged marriage, I heard. How the hell was that? I never would've guessed, for you."

His question had an edge. Was she now a source of amusement for him?

"It's good, but surprising, in some ways."

"Marriage is indeed one of the knottiest institutions ever invented. It makes central banking seem like arithmetic."

Andrew wouldn't have told him about her issues with Avi, she didn't think. He must be referencing his own affairs.

"I saw you're writing with Nicolette, is that right?" she asked. She meant to poke him, and his look indicated he sensed her intent.

"Arranged marriage, huh?" he said, ignoring the question about Nicolette. "Have you ever considered that arranged marriage resembles central planning? I don't see how you can control people's preferences for love."

"Are you trying to embarrass me, Peter?"

"Not at all, not at all. Sorry. I meant it when I said I'd welcome you back on the team."

In addition to their mutual wariness, she was experiencing a curious unfamiliarity. She once believed the two of them recognized one another from the start, a feeling of having known one another before, as if something inside her that needed to surface emerged in his presence. Had it been circumstantial, an accident of time and place? All she felt now was vigilance, defensiveness. Maybe that's what jealousy curdled into.

"Thanks, Peter. It's kind of you to offer. I'm inclined not to, but I'll think about it."

They chatted about colleagues and conferences, the people he'd met here and there, the best restaurants and clubs.

"Meena, there's a street art exhibit you might like. I'm in Bangkok and Seoul the rest of this week. But the week after, maybe? Or I can take you by the club and we can play tennis?"

He bore into her. His raw desires were of a piece, durably packaged, with his raw ambitions. Those shrimp shells. The scraps left behind.

She didn't want to go on a date with him, but she also feared aimlessness, and loneliness, here in Delhi. If she decided to stay in Delhi for a while, she'd need to earn some money, and Peter's connections wouldn't hurt. Avi, of course, would be envious of Peter, the way he jetted around, made presentations, did deals.

"Yeah, maybe," she said. "Let's see what the week looks like. But it won't be a date, Peter."

"As you wish. Call it what you like."

Chapter Ten

THE LOCAL PAPER, owned by the Vinsons, printed glowing endorsements of Jim's farmland preservation plan and called Avi's real estate development agenda "the work of an outsider" who won't keep his vows. Jim published an op-ed asking, "Shouldn't a guy choose his policy priorities with his whole being, to have and to hold, to love and to cherish?"

It was as if Jim and his allies knew Meena had left Avi and had no qualms about targeting insults at his vulnerabilities, like heat-seeking missiles. He wasn't sure he had the stomach to withstand so much disparagement. And inflict it in return.

But then, even more provocatively, Jim staged a rally at a field that backed onto Avi's subdivision. Avi could hear the shouts and cheers from his back patio. One half-wit cattle rancher said Jim was "uniquely special in a way that's super hard to explain."

Clowns. They actually deserved whatever abuse Avi could muster. If someone hurts you, don't you hit back? Otherwise, you are perceived to be weak, and encourage further attack, in this dog-eat-dog world. There's a reason for the survival instinct. Diplomats steal secrets, spy, and launch cyber strikes in pursuit of the national interest, as part of the job. No one believes misconduct on behalf of your people is wrong.

Meena would probably counsel him to keep it chill, but she wasn't here.

And things were turning in his favor. Southgate High School administrators, mortified by Jim's behavior, were about to remove his plaque from the school's Wall of Fame. The Southgate Lions Club was considering whether to withdraw its support of Jim and endorse Avi. Before going all the way, however, the Lions invited Avi to address assembled members and distinguished guests at the annual, all-town luncheon. It would be a high-profile event, and it could trigger more endorsements. With Jim's momentum flagging, it could be the whole ballgame.

With the help of his volunteers, Avi reached out to the state associations—the Tamils, Gujaratis, Bengalis, Slovaks, Poles, Catholics, Methodists, Hispanics, African Americans, everyone he could think of—and invited them to the Lions Club speech. Avi called his high school, college, and law school friends. Rav Uncle invited the treasurer at the Rotary, a golfing buddy who worked at the basilica, and the manager of the Exxon off the interstate.

At the Curry-in-a-Hurry in the food court, and with Kohli's help, Avi revamped the closing remarks of his stump speech, emphasizing that Southgate had to move on, look to the future, not get bogged down in memories of old glory. Writing fueled his anger, and he couldn't resist extravagant allusions to Jim's affair and his "bovine preoccupations" (aka the daughter of the owner of Ohio Cattle). Wordsmithing turned out to be an enjoyable distraction from Meena's departure.

The Lions Club building, up near the interstate, between the hospital and Speedy Car Wash, resembled a small lodge in a state park. Concrete floors and exposed pine rafters. Fake stone walls made of a milky joint compound. A floor-to-ceiling brick hearth, nonfunctional, in front of which the Lions had set the podium and the mic. No air con. The organizers drew the louvered windows to keep out the late afternoon sun, but the place remained hot, as it was unseasonably warm for late September.

It was packed. Various club officers, in their red and yellow vests, sweat seeping through the armpits of their shirts, took up the front two rows. The club president, Avi's old high school counselor, was a short, squat man with eczematous skin who sported a white tuxedo top and red bow tie. Behind them were batches of businessmen in polos and businesswomen in blouses. The Punjabi 5, Avi's many invitees, and his campaign volunteers were scattered around. He'd publicized the event so widely that, hopefully, the Lions could see the power of the South Asian community.

Bob, eager for his ice cream shop franchise once his friend won, introduced Avi to the audience as "my dharma chum." Avi started by talking about the disputed ambulance arrangement, his sales tax proposal, and his stance on patrol car coverage. Then he discussed the implications of rezoning Washington Woods as commercial. There would be new infrastructure. Retail. He talked about the business opportunities. Local investing and local consuming. Moving beyond agriculture. Integrating into the world economy. Generating value and resources that could be used to help the needy. And yet the importance of traditional values. Make in Southgate. His vision was perhaps different from the factories of yore, and the verdant fields, but so promising. A mall with a pizzeria, a taco stand, a community center, and an ice cream parlor. Maybe even a smartphone store and a yoga studio. He adopted hushed tones for his closing remarks:

> I know about ghosts. In my parents' old neighborhood in the mother country, there are stone palaces. Courtyards, once the playgrounds of kings and princesses, are now homes for goats and chickens, wandering cows, and trash. Ghostly memories of former glory. Sadly, if my opponent has his way, Southgate may be headed there. Closed factories and boarded-up homes. Drugs and despair. Nothing but memories for sustenance.
>
> We won't ever be a sexy town. We'll keep our old-fash-

ioned values. We want a solid arrangement, a marriage, not dangerous liaisons. My opponent's policies are nothing but short-term flings. He wants to grease the economy with quick fixes. Lubricate for his own pleasure. He thinks he's a cowboy lassoing a bull. But ask yourself who he really is. Might he be feeding us cock-and-bull stories while pursuing his own personal cash cow? It's time for change in Southgate. Change is possible. But we have to command it. We have to will it.

The audience clapped. Someone wolf whistled. Those allusions and accusations sounded worse read aloud. Jim's people, if in the audience, might take umbrage. Avi tapped the lectern nervously.

"So you're saying you don't lubricate?" a guy shouted. The pot-bellied man laughed and looked left and right, at his buddies. Avi scowled and started to respond, but one of the boys in back was running to the standing mic.

"Excuse me, excuse me, may I ask a question?"

The boy pulled back his hoodie. He was dark-skinned, South Asian. That was a relief.

"I would like to share my story. My parents took me to our home village to visit my grandfather, who they said was sick, but as soon as I arrived, they stole my mobile, my passport, and my credit cards. It was a trap."

The room quieted. People were listening with interest. But why was this relevant?

"The relatives told me they knew I was gay. They found a village girl for me. She would cure me of my sexual perversion. I said no. I'm truly gay. But I had to marry her. Otherwise, I had no way of returning to Ohio. They forced me. When we came home, I told the girl the full story. She left me. Now my family has disowned me."

What the hell? Avi thought of saying arranged marriage can be for gay people, too, it's about your outlook, not about sexual orientation, but a clamor was rising, and he wasn't sure whether that comment would inflame or douse the ruckus. What had he been thinking, inviting all these strangers?

A woman from the posse in back stood and said, in a piercing voice, "They made me marry my cousin. They locked me into a room with him. They fed us one chapati a day until we agreed!"

A girl dressed in bright clothing, with a painted face, said, "They bought me. They trafficked me! They treat us like goats!"

Someone shouted, "Avinash Sehrawat collected illegal campaign contributions at his own wedding," and the posse started hissing.

This was a flipping setup.

"Stop child marriage. Stop forced marriage. Stop arranged marriage!" The youths in back were chanting in unison.

Chaos erupted. Shouting. Several people ran to the podium. Was Rav Uncle going take charge? Avi saw Rav Uncle shooing people, as though they were flies, and arguing with the guy in the hoodie. Avi's father remained seated in his chair in back, shaking his head, staring down. Peeku dropped his bowl of potato chips, and Chrissy, next to him, started picking up the chips, one by one. Rav Uncle bellowed, "He's not saying you must have arranged marriage. It is option! You do not understand! Giving jewels to a donkey is as stupid as giving eunuch to a woman!"

The businessmen in front leaned back and looked around, seemingly enjoying the spectacle. The club president dimmed the lights and, in an effort to restore order, asked his fellow officers to join him in singing the club anthem, "We Serve." As the heavyset men in red and yellow vests belted out the song, people started to file out.

A few of the businessmen stopped by to say thanks, and a couple of Tamils came over to commiserate ("Crazy politics in this town, like back home"), but most people simply left, laughing and shaking their heads. Embarrassed, Avi pumped the president's flaky hand, then headed out.

Jim must have rounded up these people! Wild-card radicals from

Cleveland or Columbus or someplace. Of course arranged marriage was complicated, and could be abused, but why throw out the baby with the bathwater? Maybe he shouldn't have let himself become a symbol by arguing that Diwali should be a school holiday and letting Rav Uncle go on and on at the wedding. But it was impossible to turn back now. Losing to Jim this way would be humiliating.

In the parking lot, Rav Uncle, Chrissy, and Avi's parents surrounded Peeku, who looked upset, his lips tight, clearly holding it in.

"Then what do I tell my girlfriend?" Peeku said.

"I know it's confusing, Peeku," Avi's mother said. "Don't let those people bother you. Everything about dating is so confusing these days. You see, confusion arises because we Hindu Punjabis do not have our own land. Our homeland is divided between India and Pakistan. So we wander like rolling stones—Multan, Dehradun, Delhi, Southgate, one place then another. We are flustered. But arranged marriage is better, Peeku, you understand. You need a girl who will understand your values."

"Time for action," Rav Uncle said. "Peeku, son, you must meet a few girls. Try it. Look at some options. You will be happy. Trust me. Avi, this is your assignment. Look into some girls, for Peeku. Now."

The idea of arranging Peeku's marriage felt disconcerting after hearing those stories of people being coerced, kidnapped, trafficked. But arranged marriage, as an institution, was a big tent. The fact that some employers somewhere exploit their workers doesn't mean you have to quit your own job. He could help Peeku find a solid girl, someone who actually liked and appreciated Peeku's goofy sweetness. Socially awkward people, like Peeku, for whom relationships were challenging but who couldn't understand why they kept failing at love, could benefit from arranged marriage. Finding Peeku a match was a little paternalistic, but so what? And, Avi thought, it might be an opportunity to exhibit his own discernment and generosity. People like seeing friends helping friends. Meena might appreciate it, too.

AT THE VETERANS PARK football field, Avi had Peeku run a slant. Peeku made a difficult, over-the-shoulder catch and spiked the ball proudly. This was an opportune moment. Avi asked Peeku to provide stats for an imaginary NFL trading card. Peeku listed his height and weight, how much he bench pressed, his 40-yard dash time, and his birthday. Avi probed Peeku about his main goals, apart from football. A big, happy family living in a good apartment, maybe even a house one day, Peeku said. What was Peeku's motto? Peeku thought for a moment, stroked his chin, and said, "Be yourself, dude." Avi could fudge Peeku's income and job title, and Chrissy and Rav Uncle would have details on caste, subcaste, and zodiac. The challenge was the section of the matrimonial ad about the kind of girl Peeku was pursuing—who might be Peeku's type and who was out of the question.

"Imagine you were so rich and famous you could marry anybody. Who would it be?" Avi asked.

"I'm into Sheela," Peeku said.

"I know. Just imagine."

"Sheela and I are going to get together."

"You've barely spoken to her! Come on, man, just try. Anyone in the whole world."

"Angelina Jolie."

"What about an Indian girl?"

"Avi, I'm not having an arranged marriage! I already said so." Peeku kicked the ball thirty yards. He punched his left palm and glared at Avi.

"Peeku, come on, man. Wouldn't it be nice to have someone to help you with the hard stuff? She could cook dinner, maybe pay the bills. We'll get you someone cute, trustworthy, loving."

"Do I have to? I don't know!" Peeku started running around the field to let off steam.

Rav Uncle wanted a nearby girl, someone he could inspect, so Avi placed an ad in the online matrimonial section of *Buckeye Masala*.

The plan was for Avi to meet the girls, rank them, and present a summary memo to Rav Uncle, who would do callbacks and finalize the short list.

Sharma predicted there would be more than twenty offers, given Rav Uncle's renown in East Central Ohio. A week after placing the ad, only three families had responded. The Punjabi 5 were puzzled, but Avi wondered if local families knew Rav Uncle only too well.

Avi arranged to meet the first girl, a Punjabi living in the Columbus suburbs, at the Starbucks where he and Meena first met. He sat at the same narrow table, by the window. That day, Meena had worn that gorgeous olive lehenga, matching her hazel eyes. When his leg had accidentally brushed hers, she hadn't pulled away. A sad, beautiful memory.

Peeku's potential bride showed up wearing a bindi and a traditional necklace. She had soft tresses. She seemed very nice, and Avi thought this could be promising. Then the girl expressed interest in Rav Uncle's assets, Peeku's earning potential, and the size of Peeku's house. Avi explained that although Peeku worked in retail at Sears, Rav Uncle could easily support the family. The girl said, "Sears? Oh, I see," and left a few minutes later.

The second girl, another Punjabi, insisted on sitting on the other side of the café so her father could watch them through his binoculars, from the parking lot. She said she had two offers already, both from handsome MBAs. When she pulled out a notebook, flipping through pages and pages about other suitors before coming to a clean sheet, Avi realized this one wouldn't work, either.

Avi convinced Rav Uncle to let him bring Peeku to meet the third girl straight off. This last one, the daughter of two Sikh doctors, seemed ultra-competent. Her hobbies were cooking and balancing checkbooks. She was tall, and Avi worried she would tower over Peeku, but Peeku said big girls made him feel safe. He seemed to be warming to an arranged marriage.

They ordered chai lattes. Peeku asked what kind of pizza she liked, and whether she could pay taxes, since he was crummy with numbers, except football stats. Was she a Browns or Bengals fan? She said she liked mushroom pizza and the Browns, and she had a degree in accounting. Peeku gave her the thumbs-up. The girl held her own during a discussion of backup quarterbacks, and Peeku's smile grew.

This match had promise. Remembering Meena's queries on their wedding night, Avi asked the girl why she wanted an arranged marriage. The girl hesitated, frowned. She said she was sorry. She confessed to be doing this on a lark. She and her friends were curious about what kind of people were using the Hindu wedding sites these days. They drew straws, and she lost.

"I'm not in the circus, you know!" Peeku said. He pointed at her, clenching his jaw.

Avi was furious. "You shouldn't play with a guy's hopes," he said.

It occurred to him that Meena might have been doing something similar to this girl. Experimenting, seeing if she could go through with it. At least this Sikh girl came clean about her ambivalence. Meena hadn't, not even to herself.

Hearing about this fiasco, Rav Uncle rained insults on Sikhs. He also abused Avi. Why, he said, had he thought that a man who couldn't manage his own wife would be capable of arranging his son's marriage? Avi couldn't even out-campaign a drunkard like Jim Vinson.

"Your father is like a brother to me," Rav Uncle said, "but even brothers run out of patience."

That sounded like a threat. Rav Uncle could easily, if he wanted, cripple Avi's family's reputation and erode Avi's father's customer base. He could also have a word with Avi's father's Gujarati creditors, who were floating the shop. That would be disastrous. If the shop went under, his poor father might have to do car repairs himself, out of his own driveway. Could he even do that anymore, with his seven fingers?

Avi might have to help out in the garage. Put on overalls. Father-and-son grease monkeys.

He had to find a girl for Peeku. Some cute, simple-minded girl, unburdened with high expectations. Worldwide, there were probably more than a hundred million eligible Indian girls, many simple and cute, he imagined. What about some poor and pretty thing living in one of India's unfathomable, countless villages? A girl like that would kill for an American passport.

Meena had contacts. She knew Indian ways. He, by contrast, was a fake Indian, just winging it. And Meena had a soft spot for Peeku. Actually, it would be nice to have an excuse to call her. He could check in. He could find out if she missed him. Matchmaking could function as a cover story for her, too, a way to overcome her pride, talk to her husband, and plan a return.

Sitting on the back patio late one night, sipping scotch, he decided to text: *Hey Meena, I know you asked for space, but I need your help. Rav Uncle is upset Peeku isn't married. I agree Peeku would be happier with a companion. Life's too hard for him, on his own. I tried to set him up with local Indian girls. No luck. Any chance you could find him a match over there?*

He wasn't sure how soon she would write back, but she replied in minutes: *What happened with that girl he was interested in? Wasn't she in retail, too?*

Avi responded: *Kmart. Never went anywhere. The girl's family will never allow it. I'm not sure the girl likes him, has even spoken to him, or if it's all in his head. He might even be stalking her. It's a difficult situation. Would you help?*

When she didn't answer, he added: *We can do this, I mean, you and I are the arranged marriage experts, right?*

She wrote: *Ha!*

Was she being lighthearted and soft, or rueful? It was impossible to read her tone. He decided to call. He nervously pressed the dial button.

"Hello, Avi."

That sounded formal.

"Hey, how are you doing, Meena?"

"Fine."

He waited, but she didn't say more.

"So what do you think? Could you place an ad for Peeku?" he asked.

"I barely know him."

"He's not a complicated person. He needs someone basic. There must be a million girls in India who are great and who would love to come to America, right?"

He was hoping to sound jaunty. There was a frosty silence.

"It's such a responsibility," Meena said. "I don't know if I want to get entangled . . ."

"He likes you. He said to me, 'Meena, she's nice,' like a dozen times. Remember when he called you beautiful, at our housewarming?"

He guessed she would help. She was too kind a person not to, when asked.

"Avi, if I do this, it won't mean anything about us, our future. I doubt I will ever come back to Southgate. Do you understand?"

Avi's stomach fell, but he tried to sound neutral.

"This is just for Peeku. I'm not playing a trick. This isn't a bait and switch."

The night was cool. The moon was quarter crescent, and some bright star, or rising planet, glittered brilliantly in the east.

"Send me Peeku's biodata. I'll see if I have any leads. No promises."

"Thank you, Meena. And can I say . . . it's nice to hear your voice?"

"You are a loyal friend to him, Avi. It's just . . ."

"What?"

"Maybe you shouldn't be living in Southgate, either. Think about it. For your own sake."

Chapter Eleven

MEENA RECEIVED PEEKU'S BIODATA and Sharma's recommendations for the most popular matchmaking websites. She would eventually screen the would-be brides, but for now her only task, a simple one, was to input details online. Still, she hesitated. She read glossy magazines in bed, then, feeling restless, wandered to the local market, where she chose pomegranates and passion fruits for Vishali's table. She strolled into a toy store. There was a little girl, with a big, delighted expression, talking to a cuddly teddy bear.

What if Peeku really did have feelings for his Kmart pal, or was actually in love with her? Not likely. He was probably just using the notion of this girl to fend off his father's imperious demands.

She was going clubbing again tonight, so she put on makeup and changed into black pants and a green satin top. The gaggle met at her friend's flat in Vasant Vihar, kissing and hugging and calling each other "besties." Popping open a champagne bottle, one of the girls made a bet about who could get the most phone numbers from guys tonight. No one shared intimacies or talked about anything serious. You weren't supposed to spoil the fun. They had drinks at the bar, found an open spot on the floor, and made their little circle. As the evening went on, Meena found herself dancing at a distance, on the peripheries, almost by herself. Although she wasn't in the mood, or maybe because her aloofness was attractive, men kept approaching her. A guy in jeans and a black t-shirt said, "Arre yaar, you must be a parking ticket, since you have fine written all over you." She moved closer to her friends. A handsome blond guy (for the briefest moment she thought he was Peter) asked, "Did it hurt when you fell from heaven?" A posse of guys each pointed and beelined for one of the girls in her group. The one reaching her said, "My name is Surinder. I just wanted to tell you I love the way you dance." She danced with him for a few minutes, until he put his hand on her back and she had to push him away. At the end of the night, she was in last place, no phone numbers.

A couple nights later, Peter came by to take her to the street art exhibit. He wore a black blazer over a bright blue shirt, casually un-tucked, Calvin Klein jeans, his usual musky cologne. When he tried to kiss her hello, she turned to give him a light hug. The exhibition consisted of murals spaced over ten square blocks in the Lodhi area. There were stencils of sci-fi birds sticking their beaks into bright flowers, pastel rainbow sketches captioned with mysterious gothic let-tering, an array of female goddesses covering an entire three-story house, and a portrait of Punjabi sweet sellers. Peter was enthusiastic, pointing out all the symbolic references. He described the arousing qualities of the color purple. When he said street art was defiance, a blow against unwarranted government censorship of private affairs, he raised his eyebrows. He said there was so much to love in life, so many pleasures in the world.

Dropping her off, he asked, "Let me take you to the tennis club, say Saturday evening, right after I get back from Seoul?"

"I don't play," she said.

"Here, look at this." He showed her a video on his phone of him practicing his serve, wearing tennis whites and a headband.

"I practice my toss a hundred times every day," Peter said. "Serv-ing well requires consistent practice."

He sounded earnest. And trivial. Had he always?

"Funny shorts," she said, "and the bandana!"

"Really? That's Federer's brand. Does Aadi play?"

"He likes football."

"That figures, for Middle America. Arranged marriage! I still can't get over it."

Delhi wasn't lonely. She was keeping busy—lunches with her sister and mother, shopping, museums and lectures, clubbing with friends. But it felt like another of those vacations from life she once craved, pursued, then came to regret. She had believed her arrangement with Avi would resolve her aimlessness, but maybe she was too modern, too cosmopolitan and liberated, for that kind of marriage. At least for the Southgate version. Yet here she was bored with the clubbing and dating. She was getting more and more tired of her mother, too, with her anti-traditionalisms, anti-nationalisms, anti-everythings. Nothing felt right.

MEENA HAD A LATE BREAKFAST, potato paratha and yogurt, upstairs on Vishali's roof deck. It was already hot. She removed her pullover and sat down on a folding chair, then pulled over another chair to use as an ottoman. Across the park, near the ruins of the Slave Dynasty tomb, a family was playing badminton on the dusty, stony field. A child flew a kite. A couple appeared to be holding hands, furtively, on a dilapidated bench.

She checked her phone. Avi had sent pictures of Peeku. In the first, Peeku was doing a thumbs-up and throwing a football. It was reminiscent of Avi's profile picture in his marital ad. Self-flattery, having Peeku pose as he had? Or maybe it was a message for her, a sign he was still invested in their marriage. In the second photo, Peeku wore a kurta pajama and held a copy of the *Bhagavad Gita*. Rav Uncle had obviously staged that one.

What did she owe those crazy people in Southgate? To Avi, she owed decency, cordiality, the minimal courtesies afforded an ex. No more. But what about Peeku, who seemed to admire her? If he was just one of Avi's friends, she wouldn't owe him much. She barely knew him. But given who he was, and his limitations, her obligations felt larger. He was like one of her students at the school, someone who needed her.

Placing an ad for Peeku would deepen her entanglements, whatever Avi's protestations to the contrary. Spindly strings, like cobwebs, linking her back to his parents, to the Punjabi 5 and the absurd politics of Southgate, Ohio. She still turned over the conundrums, which seemed compelling, like a crossword clue she couldn't stop trying to solve. What was Avi campaigning for, really? Why had he, a guy with talents and smarts, hitched himself to that small agenda? Was Avi all about obligations, nothing more? The questions hit surprisingly hard, at stray moments. She might be brushing her teeth or combing her hair and feel their force, like a shot to the ribs. She'd have to sit and wait for the feelings to pass. She was still entwined, still married at the cellular level. Did it take longer to get a man out of one's dreams than it took to get him in?

Meena stayed up on the deck for a late lunch, thinking and considering and reading, all afternoon. Vishali had an errand to run, something about an odd credit card statement. Her mother had her bridge club meeting. Meena stayed on the deck into dusk, as the view of the ancient tomb disappeared into the smoggy sunset. When the sky turned completely dark, she went down and cuddled up in bed, letting the scents of lavender wash over her, hoping a good night's sleep would provide insight.

"Munu, will you take tea?"

A servant had come up the steps with a tray of tea and glucose biscuits. In the darkness, Meena didn't at first recognize the old lady in the white saree and the big owl glasses. As the woman got closer, setting down the tray, Meena noticed that her cheeks sagged but her forehead was smooth and unlined, with a marking of sandalwood paste from a recent temple visit.

Then Meena suddenly remembered her. There had been a child-less widow who took care of her and Vishali many years ago. She would bring them breakfast, carrying it to their bedroom on a metal tray—boiled milk with Ovaltine. She was still here, still serving.

"Hema Auntie, is it you?" Meena asked.

"Hello, child," the old servant replied in Hindustani.

Meena embraced the old lady gently, worried she might crush her. Hema Auntie found the hug awkward, and grimaced.

"I was working in Gurgaon. Your mother found me," she said. "I shouldn't work for your family."

"I'm happy to see you," Meena said. "Why do you say such a thing?"

"Your mother became a widow. They tell me your marriage is ending. I bring bad spirits to this family. How are you, child?"

"I'm okay."

"Nonsense," the old lady said. "I've been alone since my husband died. No sons, no children. I have managed. Because I am silently praying, all the time."

"You have always prayed, Hema Auntie. It's true."

"Your sister told me your husband wants you to find his friend a wife. Have you done it?"

Vishali was such a gossip.

"I don't know. Look what happened to my marriage," Meena said.

"What is the problem? Find the boy a wife. No problem."

"I wish it were so easy, for people like me."

"You are too stubborn, just like your mother," the old lady said. "For so many years, hundreds, thousands, hundreds of thousands of years, we people have been sacrificing to the gods. We are sacrificing for you, Meena. Also for your husband, for your marriage. Also, now, for your friend's marriage. Accept the sacrifices. Open your heart. Only then will you be happy. Not alone."

Hema Auntie touched Meena on the cheek. "Now you go to bed,

have rest," she said. After a moment, she added, "What would your Papa think?" She turned and slowly headed downstairs.

What would her father say? He would think it wise to find Peeku a match. The institution was especially suited to people like Peeku, he would say. On the other hand, her father had been devoted to her, his eldest daughter, and would be rooting for her happiness, whatever she chose.

She had always believed that, but now she found herself asking questions. Had her father wanted her to be happy, really? Why, then, did he counsel a modern woman into an arranged marriage? At the very least, he hadn't realized that a traditional marriage might be hard for someone like her. Nor had he anticipated a confused desi like Avi. Like Rav Uncle. Was her father's counsel to his daughter a way to get back at his wife? Maybe her father, too, had been self-interested. Planning and scheming. Shortsighted. Like Avi. Maybe there was myopia everywhere. Maybe no one knew anything.

But if her father had been wrong, if she couldn't trust him, couldn't trust her memory of him, then what? Where would she land? These thoughts were making her anxious, so she decided to go to where they had dropped his ashes into the river. She hoped to evoke his presence, maybe even speak to him. She should have gone weeks ago, when she first arrived. That would have been the dutiful thing. But she kept finding excuses. She'd been angry at him without knowing it.

She told Vishali she was going to the site near the ghat, on the river, and asked her to join. Vishali said she had errands to do, some issues too complicated to explain. Their mother had opposed the cremation ceremony even though it had been her husband's wish. Meena didn't ask her to come.

Meena arrived on the banks of the Yamuna River late in the afternoon. Smoke was rising from the cremation ghats nearby. Scents of wood burning, and of sandalwood, but mostly the stench of trash. Decay. Flocks of seagulls squawking over the water. The ancient chaos.

She remembered wrapping her father in orange. The marigolds. The holy water, the ghee. The terrible moment he was set alight. She remembered that her mind hadn't tolerated him burning, and had fled to a memory of that time they were visiting the factory in Detroit, when she was ten years old. They'd been in a rented house in the suburbs, and it had snowed overnight. Her father came in to wake her. "Meena, wake up! Look," he said. He drew the blinds. She saw a blanket of pure white snow. Her first snow. She squealed. He laughed. Their eyes met. "Magic," he said.

Now she looked out at the rusty fence, the dirty water, the men paddling fragile wooden boats. She couldn't hold back the tears. "I'm so sorry, Papa," she said. "I tried. I tried."

MEENA'S MOTHER and sister not only thought finding Peeku a match was acceptable, they insisted on joining in. Vishali said, "Andrew is being difficult, and I need a distraction." Their mother added, "If arranged marriage didn't exist, it would need to be invented for simpletons. I set aside all political and moral scruples, in this particular case."

Late in the afternoon, they met at the Turtle Café. They got a table near the balcony, overlooking the hospital and the taxi stand. Nearby, three backpackers were snacking on baked nachos. A pair of middle-aged Indian women were sipping tea and complaining about their husbands' gambling habits. No one liked Avi's draft of Peeku's profile, so as they waited for their lassis, Meena scribbled on a napkin.

"How's this?" she asked. "Simple boy, 22 years old, U.S. national, living with parents in America, seeks devoted, loyal wife."

"A good start, Munu," their mother said, "but prospective in-laws will hesitate to match their daughters with a 'simple boy'"—their mother made air quotes— "read 'idiot.' And the advert must mention the family's assets. Peeku's employment prospects are not promising, his career at Sears notwithstanding."

Their mother took a pen from her embroidered clutch, wrote on the paper placemat in her elegant, loopy handwriting, then read aloud, "Kind-hearted boy, 22 years old, U.S. national, Punjabi Hindu, living with wealthy parents in America, son of convenience-store tycoon and devoted mother, seeks devout, loyal, and very beautiful wife."

"Why 'very beautiful?'" Meena asked.

"Every man wants a beautiful spouse," their mother said.

"You two are beating around the bush," Vishali said. "We have to be explicit. The worst-case scenario is a bride accepts, arrives, is shocked when she meets Peeku, then returns home. If the poor boy is upset now, how bad will it be then?"

Vishali took a napkin from the dispenser and wrote, "Kind-hearted boy, Punjabi Hindu, rising star in retail, 22 years old, no previous marriage, U.S. national, . . ." Her sinuous handwriting used up all the space, so she grabbed another napkin. ". . . currently living with wealthy parents in America, son of a tycoon father and selfless, Indophile American mother, seeks devoted, loyal, very beautiful wife to start family and enjoy life's greatest delight—a happy marriage. Ideal girl is intelligent and industrious, with some earning potential."

"Shouldn't we add 'caste no bar, dowry unnecessary,' or words to that effect?" Meena said.

"I don't see the need, but if you insist, fine," Vishali said.

"It's rather long-winded, at this point," their mother said.

"It's perfect," Vishali said. "Mummy, you are an old bat. Sorry to be blunt. And Munu, you've lost touch with Indian sensibilities. Trust me. If it doesn't work, I take full responsibility."

If Vishali wanted to shoulder the responsibility, why not let her?

Returning home, Vishali helped Meena place the ad on the most desirable India-based websites. Vishali also sent it to her online followers and yoga students. Their mother sent it to her bridge and book clubs.

Vishali anticipated hundreds of replies, but during the next twenty-four hours, only six women sent pictures. Over dinner at Vishali's dining table—Nirula's pizza with peri peri cheese, golden corn, and capsicum—their mother said she wasn't surprised, it was a hodgepodge ad, too many cooks in the kitchen. On her phone, Vishali scrolled to a photo of a girl from Patiala with a professional-quality photo, all dolled up, lots of highlighter and blush, and said, "She will do. It doesn't really matter who she is, anyway, for someone like Peeku."

Vishali liked easy tasks, and this episode was proving hard, no longer an idyll. She obviously wanted to be done with it, but it felt premature, and irresponsible, to decide the matter this quickly. Meena pointed out that this girl was much taller than Peeku, and she seemed to have pocks on her face, which the blush might be intended to obscure. She remembered talking to Peeku at the wedding, how impressionable and innocent he had seemed. And, honestly, how simple. "We can't foist just any woman on Peeku," she said, "or him on just any woman."

"I promise you this girl is fine," Vishali said, "and didn't you say there is a rush? Not satisfied? Call Avi, then. Ask him."

Meena could feel her face go blank. Vishali said, "You want us to leave? Come, Mummy, let's give Munu some privacy, so she can call her ex."

Her sister and mother went up to the roof deck. Meena hesitated, then picked up her phone and sent Avi a link to the photo and profile. It would be late evening in Ohio. Avi answered after two rings, inhaling sharply and saying, "Hi, Meena." His gasping transported her. They were in bed, his hand on her back and his leg draped over her hips, and he was rolling left and right agitatedly. That movement, and those quiet gasps, had been his ways of requesting affection. It was shocking, and irritating, how easily the memories returned.

"Just saw it," Avi said. "What do you think?"

"Vishali likes her, but I wonder if she's too tall?" Meena said. "And . . ." She didn't know whether to mention the pockmarks, given how Avi reacted to blemishes.

"What?" Avi asked.

"You must have noticed the pockmarks."

He made a clicking, tut-tut noise. "I underestimated the difficulty of being with a woman I didn't know," he said. "That's what I was reacting to. Not your birthmark."

What was he saying? She could still feel the cream she had applied to her leg, like poisonous foam.

"Meena, just think. I didn't tell you to treat it," he said. "Did I point you to the medications? Did I even mention treatments, let alone tell you to take them?"

She could see he had a point. But so did she. Then what? Shit happened, was that all there was to say?

"What about this girl for Peeku?" she asked, wanting a change in subject.

"I wish there were other options. Hey, what if Peeku's story got some publicity? Innocent Indian American boy seeks an arranged marriage? Some angle like that? Does your sister have any journalist contacts?"

Was this about more than matchmaking for Peeku? Was Avi trying to garner renown for their marriage, the way Rav Uncle had, with that story he wrote? She suddenly felt tired. Vishali was right, this was too much work. She told Avi she had to get off the phone.

Leafing through magazines in bed, she remembered that one of her clubbing friends was a journalist. Should she call her? She didn't have to, though her father would be encouraging her to dive in. In for a penny, in for a pound, he would say. Maybe she and Avi had been badly matched, but arranged marriage *per se* wasn't wrong, whatever Peter said about her marriage the other day. Peter's incredulity had been annoyingly self-righteous. An arrangement *might* have worked for her, if not with Avi, then with another guy. Perhaps she shouldn't have chosen Avi on her own, and instead asked someone for guidance, or maybe she and Avi should've had a longer engagement, gotten to know each other better before going ahead. That might have lessened the shock.

At first, her journalist friend wasn't interested. "There are thousands of these Indian–American arrangements these days," she said. "Why is that a story?" Meena tried a different approach. She said that her sister taught yoga to a Bollywood star and that, in exchange for a story about Peeku, she could find out when the star was next coming in for a yoga lesson.

Two days later, the story appeared in the "Delhi Business" section, on the third-to-last page in the printed edition, as well as on the website. It was a profile of two sisters—Vishali's yoga studio for movie stars, expats, and Non-Resident Indians who'd moved back to India, and Meena's efforts to find Peeku a wife, both examples of India's growing global influence and the country's newfound soft power.

The story included contact details, and Meena immediately received dozens of emails, many scattershot in focus. Some people asked about Meena's availability, not Peeku's, since the story didn't mention she had a husband. A politician called Meena a miracle worker, and a housewife called her a modern-day Sita. An air-conditioner salesman sent an animation of Hanuman shooting Cupid's arrows. Wedding photographers, tent and catering services, elephant and horse providers, and priests offered their services. A wedding-site marriage broker offered Meena commissions for every client referred, finder's fees set as a percentage of the prospective grooms' salaries. A handful requested Meena's help getting an H-1 visa, bragging about their marketable skills, including reading X-rays, singing ghazals, practicing Ayurvedic medicine, and training bears. An activist demanded that

Meena advocate the continued legalization of marriage for queer Indians. A researcher requested an interview with Meena to substantiate her thesis that arranged marriage eliminated existential angst.

By midnight, over a thousand women had expressed interest in marrying Peeku, most with photos. Many of Peeku's would-be brides had blank faces. Some smiled too widely. Hundreds looked like teenagers. She deleted a photo of a woman in a towel. Fathers sent photos of all their daughters, up to twelve, and invited Peeku's family to choose whomever they liked. Astrological omens abounded. Sun, moon, Jupiter, Venus, Saturn, earth, water, air, fire. There were dowry offers of cash, TVs, an air conditioner, a refrigerator, a share of the wheat crop, silk clothes, gold, livestock, a business partnership. So much boasting about daughters who were good at housekeeping, cooking, caring for cousins, computer programming, nursing, teaching, makeup, with accompanying descriptions that made the women seem like horses: docile, simple-minded, vigorous, or sweet-tempered.

It was impossible to comprehend these people's dreams, their vast hopes and prayers. How could she possibly choose?

Perhaps because she was considering dumping all these options on Avi, an email from him, in the middle of the computer screen, caught her attention. She assumed it was yet another bride's profile, but the subject line was odd: *Does this mean anything to you?* She clicked on the attachment. It was a photograph of handwriting, a date followed by a paragraph in ungainly cursive, a journal entry: *Meena had a miscarriage. I feel so shitty. She thinks I wanted it to happen. I said some stupid things. But I don't care about a birthmark. Why would she say that? If we'd made love on our wedding night, she might have believed me when I told her the birthmark didn't matter. Of course, we didn't make love (because I couldn't?). The miscarriage is my fault in that sense, not in the way she's putting it. But maybe our wedding night ruined everything.*

It did look like his handwriting. The date, too, was just after her miscarriage. And blaming her departure on his failure to have sex on their wedding night? That seemed just simplistic enough to be his reasoning. So had he felt bad? He had stood up for her in some ways. He had seemed genuinely happy when she got her job offer, and he had supported her without hesitation, saying he'd handle his mother's expectations.

There were fresh hypericums on the desk. From Hema Auntie? Meena got up and paced around. She was starting to seem, to herself, like her mother, mindlessly furious at her father's indifference, full of outbursts. Was Avi manipulating her, right now, the way her father had forced her mother to come to Thailand? No, he wasn't. Avi was reaching out. He was apologizing.

Her phone buzzed. Avi.

"Hi," she said.

"Did we get many offers, for Peeku?"

He sounded flat, guarded. Maybe he was waiting for her reaction to the email.

"More than a thousand," she said.

Silence.

"Any thoughts how to cull them?" he asked.

"Start by getting rid of the teenagers."

"Makes sense."

Silence.

"Avi, I saw your email."

He said nothing, waiting. The silence between them felt more fragile than usual, softer.

"You weren't relieved that I had a miscarriage?" she asked.

"I can be an idiot. But no, I didn't feel that way. Not at all."

She thought she heard his teeth chatter.

"What's that?" she asked.

"Sorry. It's cold here. The furnace is out." He made a shivering noise. "So have you been dating, in Delhi?"

An awkward transition. The question had been on his mind, and he was blurting it out.

"Peter was here. They weren't dates, though."

Did she tell him that to be candid and forthcoming, or to hurt him? She wasn't sure.

"I made mistakes, Meena. But maybe we both did."

This was an apology. But she wasn't ready. She might never be.

"I will get back to you on Peeku. Good night, Avi."

MEENA WOKE EARLY, feeling restless. The night watchman was still marking a cadence with his walking stick. She made herself tea and took her phone, laptop, and a blanket up to the roof deck. It was still dark, sunlight just ghosting the haze, the air smoky. In the park, three men squatted around a fire, warming themselves. Roosting mynah birds were twee-tweeing, guarding their ficuses against the crows.

She scrolled through pages of ads. It was like one of those documentaries about migratory birds. Flocks and flocks of young Indian women. They seemed to be homing in on one wish: Protect me. They didn't want what she had sought in her marriage—not only protection but also a measure of recognition. For many of these women, these girls, marriage would be another step in the forced march. After years sweeping stoops, collecting water from community faucets, and washing the men's plates, they were ready to abandon parents and sisters, cousins and friends, all that delighted and burdened them. And their families, pursuing relief from the misfortune of bearing a daughter, would be pleased to send their girls to a foreign land, to whichever hungry man.

She had chosen traditional marriage because she believed she could be happy with any decent guy. It was naive, but that had been the theory. She had distrusted herself. She hadn't believed in her own powers of discernment after her father died, and after Peter refused her. Her father had suggested an arranged marriage, recommended it. The time felt right. It was that simple. But she had managed the process herself, to an unusual extent. Although she had let go of *whom* she would marry, she retained control over *when* and *how*. Many of these girls had no say over anything. An imperious father, jealous mother, or greedy uncle had dismantled the possibility of personal fulfillment. In the photos, many of these girls looked naive, ingenuous, and unsophisticated, yet still hopeful, appearing to believe that their elders, and the thousand-year-old traditions, actually cared about love.

She would consider only applicants who, like her, pursued a marriage on their own initiative. Which ones were those? She adopted ad hoc criteria: at least twenty years old, a high school education, basic competence, indications of a go-getting personality. At the same time, for Peeku's sake, she would avoid women who seemed either domineering or cosmopolitan.

Meena read profiles all morning, afternoon, and into the evening. Servants brought her breakfast, lunch, lemon water, tea, snacks, dinner, and more tea. She managed to narrow the pool to two hundred fifty-two women. Still far too many to send Avi. When Hema Auntie brought up more tea and glucose biscuits late in the evening, Meena asked, "Hema Auntie, how do I make the best choice for my friend, among hundreds of women?"

Putting down her tray, the old lady looked at a picture of Peeku on Meena's computer. She noticed his birthday. She looked at photos of Rav Uncle and Chrissy. Hema Auntie looked up at the evening sky. Nothing but dusty haze.

"For this boy Peeku, the lord of the tithi is Jupiter, aspected by Venus," Hema Auntie said. "He should have an older spouse. Someone with life experience. Also, my child, the heavens say you need a home." She touched Meena on the forehead. "I am tired," she said.

The next morning, Meena called Avi to discuss the options.

"If we can't decide," Avi said, "maybe your servant's idea makes sense? Astrology is like flipping a coin. Whom you marry is kind of random, anyway."

"I bet Rav Uncle would appreciate an astrological fit," she said.

"He's actually not all that religious. He doesn't care as long as the biographical criteria are met. The rest is my job, he says, if I'm so smart, the next Kissinger."

Those expectations, mentioned in his yearbook, must have been a curse for Avi.

"Is that who you want to be? Are you the next Kissinger?"

"It's just township trustee, obviously."

"Do you think Kissinger ever sweated through his shirt and forgot his wife's name on TV?"

Silence. He seemed to be reflecting.

"I thought I already apologized for that one."

"Would you agree to bomb countries, sponsor coups?"

"No, but I'd push to be strong, for my community's sake. It's a jungle out there."

"Do you feel strong, right now?"

"To be honest, I don't get how guys like Kissinger, and Rav Uncle, just take and take. Life must be easier if you don't care."

Had he just said he was different from Rav Uncle? That couldn't have been easy for him to admit. He sounded different. Still, it was one thing to denigrate Rav Uncle in a private phone call, another to stand up to the man.

Using Hema Auntie's criteria, as well as her own intuition, Meena narrowed the marriage possibilities to three women. They seemed indistinguishable, all with smiling faces, short like Peeku. They all possessed medium chestnut complexions, made references to duty and family in their write-ups, were between twenty and twenty-four years old, put touches of henna in their hair, and had families seemingly on the sidelines of the decision. Each also had some astrological consonance. There was an accountant from Ludhiana, a woman from Gorakhpur who ran a business selling health biscuits to pregnant mothers, and a call-center worker from Lucknow.

Vishali, their mother, and Avi joined Meena for the video interviews. Vishali and their mother preferred the biscuit seller, but Avi found her too earnest and humorless. Avi said Peeku would much prefer someone playful. The call-center woman, Rani, was talkative, her eyes twinkled, and Avi liked the joke she shared: *It's a funny business. We women are taught not to talk to strangers, but then after marriage we're supposed to share a bed with one.*

Avi said he would take Rani's picture and bio to Peeku and report back to them shortly. An hour passed. Then two. Three. Finally, Avi wrote, "Sorry for the delay, campaign trouble. Anyway, Peeku says Rani is a hot mama. Rav Uncle is fine with her, too. I've already started working on Rani's visa. Thank you so much, Meena."

Was Peeku genuinely excited? She hoped so. Despite Avi's assertion about astrology, happiness in traditional marriage wasn't just a coin flip. To the extent arranged marriage made any sense, it was about a state of mind. Perhaps Peeku now believed that the world, which his family and ancestors were responsible for, was good. It was fundamentally trustworthy. Growing up, Meena had moved around too much. Perhaps that was why, when she blundered into her marriage with Avi, she had been, as Avi suggested, distrustful from day one.

Chapter Twelve

PEEKU FLOUNCED across the stage, glasses askew under his crown of flowers. He was obviously anxious, and Avi offered a fist bump for reassurance, which Peeku enthusiastically returned. A handful of jasmine petals fell into Avi's lap.

"Want to save these?" Avi asked, putting the petals into Peeku's pocket. Supposedly, jasmine petals could be an aphrodisiac.

"Quiet! Start screen share and recording," Rav Uncle said.

Avi toggled, and the sixty-five-inch flat-panel TV, which had been wheeled up to the main stage, split into thirds: Rani, in a red saree, henna on her hands and arms, alongside some family members, in Lucknow; Peeku and Avi, their parents, and the rest of the Punjabi 5, here at the Southgate Hindu Temple; and Meena, Vishali, and their mother in Vishali's posh home in New Delhi.

It had been Avi's idea to hold an unofficial, informal Vedic ceremony, via video, to lift Peeku's spirits and maintain the couple's marital momentum. It would also establish their intent to marry, which Avi's law school buddy, an official in the U.S. Consulate in New Delhi, had said would expedite Rani's visa processing. Rav Uncle agreed, saying a religious ceremony would lock things in before the "caller girl" changed her mind.

The priest had installed the bowl of ghee and sacred fire in the same exact spot as for Avi and Meena's ceremony. Forty rows of banquet chairs, from another recent wedding, spanned the largely vacant room. The Punjabi 5 and families sat near the stage. A cord ran from the notebook computer in Avi's lap to the big TV.

On screen, Meena was in a close-fitting purple anarkali, and wearing mascara. Had she dressed up for him, partly? They hadn't been to many formal events together. He tried but failed to recall what she wore for the housewarming ceremony. Had he been that checked out, during their brief marriage?

"Peeku, any words for Rani, your future wife?" asked Chrissy.

"Hey, Rani. I'm Peeku. I'm gonna be your husband, I guess. Thanks for taking a chance on me. We're supposed to consume the marriage, you know, for the wisa? Avi says we can do that later."

"He means consummate," Avi said. "We were talking, Rani, about how a K-1—you know, the fiancée visa—requires documenting the couple's good-faith intentions."

"Of course, Peeku, sweetheart," Rani said, blowing him a kiss over the screen. Grinning, Peeku caught the kiss like a pass hitting him on the numbers. Rav Uncle, slapping Peeku on the back, said, "Good one!"

Peeku seemed to have moved on from his Kmart girl. He seemed to be trusting in this arrangement. Avi's trust hadn't been as authentic. He had been cocky, he now saw. As though his wedding had been about him, his looks, his achievements, his future leadership of the community. He chose Meena not only because she could make him happy, maybe not primarily, but because she represented the kind of girl he could attract—beautiful, cosmopolitan, accomplished. She was proof of his value, his receipts. In a good marriage, the bride's and groom's worth depended on the meanings they assigned to one another. If only he'd understood.

The priest was asking Peeku and Rani to repeat lines in Sanskrit, a few words at a time. Neither knew the phrases. Rani looked puzzled and amused, her palms raised. The priest invited Peeku to place a garland of marigolds around Chrissy, who was acting as Rani's stand-in from across the oceans. Likewise, Rani placed a garland around a little girl who, in Lucknow, was playing Peeku's role. But the girl took the garland off, shook her head, and pulled at Rani.

"No, not now!" Rani said over the monitor. "Sorry, my niece wants to play pachisi; I call her my niece, her mother in Chicago is my friend." Rani's English wasn't bad, but she pronounced Chicago like "chick-a-go."

The priest instructed Peeku and Chrissy to walk around the sacred fire and invited Rani and the little girl to circle their own imaginary flame. He had the couples take turns leading. He spoke about loyalty and passion, using the same blessings and explanations as he had at Avi and Meena's wedding.

"Peeku and Rani, repeat after me," the priest said, and Rani and Peeku repeated the words. "We have walked the steps. Let us give each other pleasure in all seasons. Let the earth be honey-sweet for us. Let the days, the nights, be honey-sweet for us."

Honey-sweet, pleasurable, warm. Like a working shower?

"That's it, lovebirds. From the Vedic point of view, Peeku and Rani, you are married now," the priest said. "Avi will be finalizing the immigration papers and legal necessities."

"I can't wait to meet you in person, Peeku," Rani said. "Where should we go for our honeymoon?"

Peeku looked at Chrissy, who gestured encouragingly.

"Atwood Lake cabins?" Peeku said. "They've got motorboats!"

"That would be lovely, Peeku," Rani said.

Rani seemed to be smirking, her almond-shaped eyes alert and mobile, darting around the screen, as if ready to share an inside joke with anyone who was game. She was no shrinking violet, that's for sure. Probably a good sign, as Peeku needed a forceful partner, someone who could take charge. Peeku might overlook this side of Rani, these signs of subtle mischief, but Avi for one was eagerly anticipating having her around.

Everyone clapped and congratulated the newlyweds. Rani lifted her hand, effectively high-fiving everyone on screen. Meena's mother and Vishali threw handfuls of confetti, which seemed over the top, and, on the screen, it was hard to tell if their expressions were ironic or sincere. Avi stood in front of the laptop camera and gave an enthusiastic wave goodbye, which Meena politely returned.

Rav Uncle said, "You see, Peeku, life has twists and turns, but ultimately it's fine, so long one does not behave like muttonhead."

As people were walking out, Peeku grabbed Avi. "I'm supposed to be happy," Peeku said, "but I'm still thinking about Sheela. Maybe because Rani isn't here yet. It's hard to wait for your wife. How do you do it, man?"

Avi's stomach dropped. "Marriage is gonna be great, man, trust me," he said.

At home, Avi poured a scotch and stared at the foyer table where Meena had once placed her Chinese vase. He prepared for an upcoming speech, read the sports magazines, then poured himself another drink. He and Meena had worked well together in finding Peeku a bride. But did that mean anything at all, at this point? It was after midnight. Meena would certainly be awake. He called.

"We did it, you and me, we did it!" he said, trying to evoke the feeling of teamwork.

"How does Peeku seem?" Meena asked.

"Good, good, though a little confused. It happened fast."

"Rani seems sharp. She'll handle the complicated things, if that's what you guys think Peeku needs."

"I hope so, but, to be honest, I'm having a funny feeling," Avi said. "Do you think we did right by him, pushing Peeku into an arranged marriage? He was talking about Sheela, just now."

Meena made a sharp sound. "What the fuck, Avi? Really. Do you know how many hours, days, I spent arranging this marriage? Why did you ask me to help you if you weren't sure?"

"No, it's fine. These are just my anxieties talking."

"What do you mean, funny feeling?"

"I don't know, just that maybe we . . . pushed too hard. Too fast."

"*We* pushed him into this? I just did as you asked. You do realize, don't you, that if this marriage isn't right for Peeku, he's going to be miserable. For his whole life. But I suppose this is what you do. Avi just goes with the flow. Traditional marriage, politics, whatever the community wants."

"That's not fair, Meena. I believe in arranged marriage for Peeku. He's into girls, he wants to get married, but he doesn't know how to date. They said he was scaring that girl at Kmart. That's why I screened potential brides for him. I've been guiding Peeku through this process, holding his hand."

"Holding his hand or pulling him into a ditch?"

"I'm nervous about Peeku settling in, that's all. There could be a transition period, as he gets to know Rani. An adjustment. Like for us."

"Is that what you think I'm doing here? Adjusting? I'm not living in Southgate again. I told you. Do you understand? You have no spine, Avi. You're like a doormat."

Her words bore into him, scratches on slate. But he didn't want to inflame her further. He let the silence linger, distracting himself with the sound of traffic, distant engines gunning up, fading away.

"I do have a spine. You don't know me yet, Meena," he said. "I'll keep you posted."

He considered asking her to double-check the status of Rani's fiancée visa at the Consulate in New Delhi but didn't want to upset her further. Peeku and Rani would be happy. He knew what he was doing. She would see.

AVI HELPED Chrissy choose a new rug. He helped install a soundproof door for Peeku's and Rani's apartment in the basement of Rav Uncle's mansion. He drove Peeku and Chrissy to Patel Brothers to stock Rani's kitchenette with flour, clarified butter, lentils, vegetables, and spices, as well as henna powder for the housewarming ceremony. He continued to oversee Rani's travel arrangements and expedited her visa formalities.

He told Meena everything he was doing. He wanted to reassure her that he was committed to Peeku's arranged marriage. He wanted her to see that he *did* have a backbone. He hoped she could see that he *was* someone with bedrock beliefs, clear values. But Meena's texts betrayed no appreciation, her responses generally a word or two— *okay* or *got it*—or even just emojis.

Rani's plane ticket, which Rav Uncle had purchased, had her landing in Pittsburgh at 3 a.m. Rav Uncle asked Avi to take Peeku to the airport and keep him company. Rav Uncle and Chrissy would drive there separately. Avi's father suggested they wash Avi's car, for good luck, before heading out. As he and his father soaped and hosed down the Oldsmobile, the cold October breeze misted over Avi's face, droplets and suds sprinkling onto his white oxford. Looking mischievous, Avi's father pointed his nozzle at Saturn, bright emblem in the starlit sky. Wet vapors cascaded down on them both, like a cleansing. Avi's father held him, their first embrace since Avi's wedding night, and he patted his son's forehead with his good hand.

"Soon you will take another trip to the airport," he said, "to bring home Meena."

"Hope so, Dad," Avi replied. He hadn't told his parents that Meena was reconsidering their marriage, that she might not return to Southgate.

Near midnight, Avi pulled into Rav Uncle's place, rows of lights running around the long circular driveway, like tea lamps on Diwali.

Peeku, in a suit and tie, was waiting outside, holding a bouquet of roses in one hand and warming his other hand against his lips.

"What's going to happen?" Peeku said as he set the flowers on the floorboard.

"Marriage is a journey," Avi said. "Ups and downs. But mostly ups."

As they merged onto the interstate, Peeku was gritting his teeth and staring at the roses at his feet.

"I mean tonight. What's going to happen tonight?" Peeku asked.

Taking one hand off the steering wheel, Avi punched his friend lightly.

"It's easy," Avi said. "Kiss her. Touch the insides of her thighs. It just happens. Don't worry."

"I know *that*," Peeku said, sounding peeved.

Peeku was asking about love, not sex. Of course he was. Why had Avi not understood his friend's question? Where did his folly, these assumptions, come from? From his traditional marriage? Or maybe from being his mother's golden child, the lacquer and glaze, which now felt as stiff as a cicada's exoskeleton.

He found a spot on the main level of the parking garage, just as Rav Uncle and Chrissy were getting out of the Mercedes. Chrissy asked Avi to snap a picture of Peeku standing tall, holding the red roses, and pointing at the airport sign.

"We need a beautiful girl, after all this bullshit," Rav Uncle grumbled, the plural suggesting that he, too, was getting a young beauty. It seemed odd to put it that way, but perhaps it was the language of joint effort, the way Avi's parents had said "We got into Ohio State" as Avi opened the envelope with the admissions letter. Of course, for Rav Uncle, joint effort would entail joint ownership, expectations and rules, a marriage with strings attached. Those funny feelings were rising up, again, in his stomach. Should he tell Peeku he was worried?

But what was the point now, after the ceremony, after the visa formalities, not to mention after all the work Meena had put in? He couldn't do that. Instead, he vowed to do everything in his power to support Peeku's marriage.

They walked to baggage claim and started scanning for Rani, anxiously scrutinizing each arriving passenger. A throng assembled as the luggage conveyor belt whirred, coughing up bags from the Seattle flight. Luggage from Frankfurt, Rani's connecting airport, started to mingle in. Peeku noticed an Indian woman examining tags on a suitcase and ran over to greet her. She stared. It wasn't Rani. Peeku then approached a woman peering into the bowels of the conveyor. He waved. She waved back awkwardly.

"Peeku, stop creeping up on strange girls," Rav Uncle said.

"One of them could be my wife."

A woman in tight blue jeans and a turtleneck passed, chitchatting on her phone, and Peeku gestured again. She ignored him. Nearby was a little girl in a denim jacket with a Hello Kitty carry-on. She held a photograph.

"What?" Chrissy said, pointing. "That's a picture of Peeku." It was the photo of Peeku from the wedding ad.

"Hey, that's me!" said Peeku, brightening. "What the heck?"

Rav Uncle snatched the photo from the girl. "Where did you get this?"

The girl backed away. Rav Uncle grabbed her shoulders. "I asked where you got this picture. Answer me! Some mischief?"

The girl wriggled, appearing frightened. She opened her mouth, closed it. Extending a hand toward Avi, she said, "Sir?"

"It's the niece," Chrissy said.

This was Rani's friend's daughter, the one in Lucknow who received the garlands on Peeku's behalf during the wedding, the one who wanted to play pachisi.

"Where is your auntie?" Avi asked.

The niece looked scared, her eyes enormous.

A woman in a pink blouse, pulling a roller board, walked by, her husband and teenage son trailing behind.

"Maybe Rani is in the bathroom," Avi said. "I'll text."

Rani responded immediately: *Was trying to message you earlier, but no signal. Immigration trouble! I'm still in Frankfurt. They wouldn't let me board the U.S. flight. Something about the K-1. Glad you found her. I was panicked! They are making me put my phone away. Will come on next flight tomorrow.*

Avi passed around his phone for everyone to read.

"Fucking bullshit!" Rav Uncle shouted, the words echoing in the terminal, eliciting stares.

They all looked at one another, and watched each other realize, at the same moment, that there would be no meeting of the newlyweds tonight. No celebration. But also, this didn't make any sense—why was the niece standing here alone, with Peeku's photo?

"Hey, girl, where are you supposed to go?" Chrissy asked the girl. The girl's eyes remained glazed. Maybe her English was bad.

"She's too scared to talk," Chrissy said. "Poor thing. How did she arrive from Frankfurt on her own?"

"How? She stuck her arse in the airplane seat, that's how," Rav Uncle said. "So you fucked up the wisa, huh, Avinash?"

"I don't understand," Avi said. "If she has Peeku's picture, it looks like she was intended to arrive alone."

Rav Uncle's fleshy face went still. "Rani is a fraudster! A homewrecker! Where is she?" The passenger terminal was emptying out.

"I don't think we can jump to conclusions," Avi said. "She said the girl's mother is in Chicago. Maybe Rani is taking her to her mother. Maybe they were supposed to take a bus from here."

"What is the picture for?" Chrissy asked.

"Maybe Rani gave the girl the photo in case they got separated," Avi said. "Rani strikes me as a careful planner."

"Oh yes, a careful planner. Unlike you!" Rav Uncle said.

He'd done all he could. Why was Rav Uncle always so mad?

The girl, looking bewildered, said, "Uncle?" and reached for Peeku.

Peeku started to clasp her hand, then stopped, confused. The girl raised her arms, signaling a desire to be picked up. Peeku lifted her up. He started walking toward the exits, one arm clasped around the girl and the other holding the flowers for Rani. The girl, tired and fearful, her black eyes furtive, hung her head over Peeku's shoulder. She wore a nose stud. When she yawned, her teeth looked startlingly white against her dark features.

"Put her down, Peeku," Rav Uncle said. "We have nothing to do with this girl."

Peeku set the girl onto the floor. He threw his bouquet into the trash.

"You arranged it, Avi. You deal with it." Rav Uncle pointed at the niece. "Who knows if her wisa is walid. I do not want immigration police coming to my house. You take her."

Was Rav Uncle worried about an investigation into the illegals on his payroll? Avi barely spoke Hindi. What was he supposed to do with a little girl from Lucknow?

"Don't you think she'd be happier with you guys?" Avi said. "You speak Hindi. And there'd be a woman in the house." He gestured at Chrissy.

"No illegals in my house," Rav Uncle said.

Rav Uncle stalked into the parking garage and got into his car. Shaking her head, Chrissy slid into the backseat. Peeku opened the passenger door, mumbling something like, "My whole life, my whole life . . ." Rav Uncle drove off, leaving Avi and the girl behind.

It was nearly four in the morning. Maybe Avi's mother would know what to do. He called, but no one answered. There was no one in the parking garage. Even the rental car desks were vacant. He was alone with this strange girl.

"Let's go," he said.

She lowered her gaze. "Sir."

Avi put her in back and strapped her in. Was a girl this age, maybe ten years old, supposed to use a car seat? Leaving the lot, he chose the automated exit, rather than the lane with a parking attendant, so no one would see him driving a girl not safely secured. If Rav Uncle was right, he was potentially taking home an illegal alien. Could you get in trouble for that? If you wanted to turn her in, did you call the police, child protective services, or Homeland Security? The interstate was dark, just the occasional headlights indicating an oncoming car around the bend. What if a cop pulled him over? That could make the local headlines. *Township Trustee Candidate Arranges Immigration Scam.* He drove ten miles under the speed limit.

Who could give him advice? It would be embarrassing to share the news with Meena. He had messed up his own marriage. Now he had messed up Peeku's, too. She would say that he had no one but himself to blame. That he shouldn't have gone along with Rav Uncle's scheme. She would be right.

HE SET UP the pull-out bed in Meena's office for the girl. As he inserted pillows into cases and stretched the sheets, she leaned against the wall and watched, her brow furrowed, trying to remain vigilant, despite the hour.

"Time for bed," Avi said.

"Where you sleep?" she asked.

Would a girl this age be more worried about sleeping alone, or having a man in her room?

"In my room," Avi said, pointing across the hallway.

The girl wagged her head approvingly. She went to her Hello

Kitty luggage and removed a stuffed bear. It was a dirty animal, its pink fur frayed and worn, exposed stitching on the left arm.

"What's his name?" Avi asked, trying to sound friendly.

"My bear." She looked at him warily.

"Don't worry," Avi said.

"Sir buy new bear?"

"Buy you another bear? Okay, I guess."

She got into bed and put her head under the pillow. He turned out the lights and retreated into the hallway, leaving the door open so he could peer around the doorjamb. She put her head on top of the pillow, then pulled the blanket up to her chin.

She would be asleep for a few hours at least. The sun was coming up.

Quietly, he carried the Hello Kitty roller downstairs and emptied its contents. A few pairs of jeans, blouses, a winter coat. Undergarments. A hairbrush. There was a Hindi comic book about the superhero goddess Devi, who brandished a flaming sword. Crayons. Drawings of airplanes, elephants, and boats. Cadbury chocolate wrappers. A pink pillow with a Valentine's heart. The photo of Peeku. Several black scarves. Her boarding pass. There was no onward ticket, no boarding pass for any flight to Chicago to see her mother. Her Indian passport indicated her name was Leela Chowdury, she was nine years old, her place of birth "unknown" and father "unknown." She had a K-2 visa.

A K-2 meant Rani had passed Leela off as her daughter, somehow. But on the video screen, Rani had said Leela was like her niece. Was Rav Uncle right, then, that Rani was a liar, and had duped them?

If so, Rani might not respond to another text. But then why had she texted Avi from the airport? He tried again: *What's going on? You aren't really in Frankfurt, are you?* To his surprise, she replied in moments: *Please take good care of Leela. We had no choice.*

Setting up his phone to record, he dialed Rani's number. It might be illegal to record calls secretly in Ohio, but who cared.

"Rani, this is Avi. Would you tell me what's going on? Where are you? I don't believe you're having visa trouble in Frankfurt."

"Peeku is nice man, but he didn't want to marry me. His father is scary. I didn't like him."

Avi could hear traffic in the background. A siren. Rani sounded short of breath, like she was walking in a hurry.

"That sounds like a police car in America, not Germany. You are lying."

"Please understand. Leela and I worked in a big house in Lucknow. The master was brutal. He abused us. It was my tenth house. Leela's sixth. We had to get out. I had to get a K-1 to get Leela her K-2. She's a good girl. She has no family. I can't care for her on the run. You are a good person. I can tell. I trust you to do what's right for her."

"You used us! What about Peeku? Don't you care about what you did to him?"

"You won't hear from me again. I am throwing away this phone. She was like my little sister, and you are a good man."

That was it, then. Disappearing had been the plan all along. Rani's arrangement was not with Peeku but with someone else, paid for maybe with gold, stolen cash, her friend's cattle, who knows. Or maybe Rani would pay now, and work as a nanny or housemaid, or worse. She was probably somewhere in Pennsylvania or Ohio. Maybe she was headed to Canada, claiming to be a refugee.

Rani's smirk on screen, on the wedding day, hadn't been sweetness. She had been laughing at the clueless Southgaters.

Steps. Leela was coming down the stairs. He hurried to the foyer to repack her things, but it was too late. She was staring at her possessions dumped on the floor. She indicated for him to stay back, then picked up a black scarf, which she tied carefully around her hair. She threw the rest of her things into the bag. She was moving slowly, shaking her head, appearing chastened, sad. After she finished repacking, she went to the foot of the stairs and sat on her haunches. She stared at the floor. The demeanor of inferiority. Shame. She had the haunted look of a servant, which apparently she was. Suddenly, Avi realized that the scarf covering her hair wasn't just a scarf.

"Leela, are you Muslim?"

She said she was. She ran up the steps with her luggage.

He was housing a runaway Muslim servant from Lucknow. What a fool he'd been. He hadn't known the first thing about arranged marriage yet chose one. Then arranged one. He hadn't known anything about India, not really, despite visiting once as a kid, yet he'd been trying to act like an Indian leader. He'd been wearing a foreign costume, the empty sleeves fluttering. Due to a longing to enlarge his puny life. So much inscrutability at his own wedding, plates of ripe fruit no one ate. Being an impostor gets you into a mess, especially if you don't even know you are one.

What was he supposed to do with Leela? He wished the girl would disappear. He wanted to go back in time, to his wedding day, and give a normal toast. He wanted to erase that video of him sweating on TV. He wanted to be in the hospital when Meena had her miscarriage. He fell asleep on the couch.

THERE WAS KIDDIE MUSIC, *boing-boing* sound effects. Leela must have turned on the TV while he slept. It was *Tom and Jerry*. He checked his watch. He'd slept for only an hour, which meant she slept for just a couple. She was sitting on her haunches two feet from the TV in the corner of the living room. Tom the cat was running to the door with a bouquet and an engagement ring for his girlfriend Toodles. When the bouquet exploded in the girlfriend's face, Jerry the rodent, smug and smarmy, laughed. What a stupid show.

"You want breakfast?" Avi called out.

The girl looked over at him, her expression blank. She'd had too much TV and too little sleep. She smacked her dry lips. He should have offered her water last night. He should get her something to drink and eat.

He leaned forward to stand, extending his legs. His right leg started to spasm. His buttocks throbbed. His sacral region burned.

"Shit. Fuck!"

He fell back onto the couch. He flexed his legs to try to control the flaring cramps. He closed his eyes, breathed in and out, hoping he could manage the pain. He had fallen asleep on his stomach, a position that strained his back. Usually, he managed to avoid sleeping that way, but he must have been too tired to notice. It could be bad. How to deal with it? He couldn't send Leela to Chrissy because Rav Uncle would be angry. Who knew what he'd do. He might actually call child protective services, sending Leela into legal peril.

"Water?"

Leela was holding his NFL Hall of Fame mug. She must have gone to the kitchen and returned with it. The TV was off.

"Thank you. I was going to offer you water," Avi said. "You have some, too. And there is cereal in the cupboard next to the sink, milk's in the refrigerator."

She waited patiently until he took a sip. She appeared relieved to have something to do. He handed the mug back to her.

"Leave it here on the table, please," he said.

She went to the kitchen. He heard her fill a glass with water. She opened the refrigerator, perhaps searching for milk. The cupboard banged, banged again. Maybe she couldn't reach high enough. He tried getting up to go help, but his legs wouldn't move. There was the sound of a chair being dragged. The cupboard opening again. Silverware sounds. Sipping and crunching.

When she returned to the living room, she squatted in the corner, ignoring the love seat.

Leela was like Lakshman, a servant at Avi's grandparents' home, in west Delhi, who cooked meals, swept dusty rooms, served the family warm chapatis, and slept on a floor mat in the kitchen next to the canisters of propane, where cockroaches ran free. Lakshman, who never attended school, was supposed to entertain Avi, and with the neighborhood boys they played cricket or pitthu, a game in which you threw a tennis ball at a pile of flat, polished stones, until Avi's grandmother would call out, "Come home, Lakshman, make chapatis, don't be so lazy!"

Did Leela believe she was his servant? Was that why she reached for his hand first, at the airport, calling him "Sir"? She was now inspecting the many Hindu statuettes on the coffee table. They were ornaments to him, but to her, they might indicate the nature of authority in this house.

"Leela, please go upstairs to the room with the bookshelves and folders," Avi said. "Bring me the computer on the desk. Also bring me the phone." After she returned with the items, he said, "Now you go upstairs. Stay in your room until you fall asleep." She said, "Yes, Sir," and went up.

Rav Uncle called, but Avi ignored it. Rav Uncle called back, repeatedly. This was not the time. He had to start researching.

One website said that U visas, for noncitizens who were victims of serious crimes, allowed unaccompanied minors to reside in the United States for up to four years, but the children had to testify in criminal proceedings. What would constitute a criminal case here? American authorities couldn't bring domestic violence charges against the abusive owner of the Lucknow house, they would have no jurisdiction, but they could probably charge Rani with kidnapping. That could be wrenching for Leela, who would be compelled to turn on her friend, her near-sister.

The T visa for victims of trafficking included an exemption for children unable or unwilling to cooperate with criminal investigations, but it still seemed to require opening a criminal case. Authorities would have to charge someone with trafficking, probably Rani again. It seemed wrong to charge a woman escaping abuse, and helping a friend do the same, with trafficking.

Perhaps there were other angles. But the Violence Against Women Act applied to children or spouses of U.S. citizens. India wasn't on the list of countries for immigrants eligible for temporary protected status. Cancellation of removal for non-lawful permanent residents stipulated the immigrant to have been in the country for ten years. Deferred action for childhood arrivals required residence since 2007.

Was there was no means for a child escaping servitude to receive asylum? A lawyer at an immigrant justice center in Chicago explained over the phone that unaccompanied minors had no right to legal counsel. At the moment, the center had a waiting list of three months. Maybe Avi would need to represent Leela himself.

Avi watched online videos of squalid border police jails. Special immigrant juvenile status could be a possibility. It would make Leela a dependent of the court, which would make a best-interests-of-the-child finding. Who knew where that might lead, given the arbitrariness, and the political ambitions, of the judges Avi knew in Southgate.

Avi found this research interesting, a compelling and worthwhile legal puzzle. It felt more purposeful than his usual legal tasks—documenting small business partnerships, tax work, municipal IT outsourcing.

Tired and bleary-eyed, he slept on the couch in the afternoon, taking care to stay on his back. When he woke, Leela was again watching cartoons, the ragged stuffed bear in her lap.

"Leela, turn off the TV and come here," Avi said.

She jumped up immediately, perhaps accustomed to odd requests from masters.

"Tell me, was Rani nice to you?"

"Rani is nice," she said. She paused, then added, "Where is Madame?"

Did she mean Meena? Maybe she had noticed the wedding picture in Meena's study, where she was sleeping. Of course a little girl would be wondering about the lady of the house, hoping not to have to live alone with a strange man.

"She's in India," Avi said. "Did you like India, or is America better?"

"Rani says American chocolates good."

"Do you want to stay here, or go back to Lucknow?"

She shrugged.

"Where do your parents live?"

She frowned.

"Are you hungry?" he asked, bringing his fingers to his mouth.

"Chocolate?"

Avi told her where to find chocolate bars in the pantry. He asked her to bring him peanuts, another mug of water, the container of ibuprofen, and the bottle of Johnnie Walker Black, which he hoped would relax his back. He asked for the TV remote. Drained and wasted, but too wired to sleep, he watched with her as Oscar the Grouch sang about trash on Sesame Street. Leela ate two chocolate bars, and Avi nursed his scotch.

THE DOORBELL RANG, and it kept ringing, ten times in a row. Someone was pounding angrily on the front door. It had to be Rav Uncle.

Pushing against the armrest for leverage, gingerly swinging his legs to the floor, Avi warily rose from the couch. He told Leela to go up to her room. He wanted her out of sight. He didn't want her to experience Rav Uncle's livid bluster, which could be unnerving.

For balance, Avi rested an arm on the wall as he opened the door.

"Is Peeku here?" Rav Uncle asked.

"No."

"He's not upstairs?"

"He's not here."

Rav Uncle stared. "Then?"

"Why are you looking at me like that?"

"You didn't answer the phone. I called so many times."

"I hurt my back again, and I couldn't reach my phone," Avi said, then added, "sorry."

Rav Uncle peered over Avi's shoulder and scanned the living room, his gaze landing on Leela's comic book.

"Peeku has disappeared," Rav Uncle said. "He took no toothbrush, no pajamas. He didn't take his football. Not even his phone. He doesn't drive. Chrissy is worried something happened. Something very bad."

"You mean . . . ?" Avi said, afraid to finish the sentence. Peeku had looked despondent at the airport. Had he gone and hurt himself?

"I reported Peeku missing to the police." Rav Uncle's lips seemed to tremble. He never looked like this, so vulnerable.

"Have you called the hospitals?" Avi said.

"Will you?"

Avi called St. Luke's, asking whether a confused young Indian man had been spotted recently anywhere in the hospital, including the ER, or if there were reports of an Indian man engaging in self-harm. They had no information they could share. No news at Beauville Hospital, either. Nor the hospitals in Columbus. No reports at the Southgate bus depot of a young Indian man acting agitated or buying a ticket. Peeku's boss at Sears said she was saddened to hear of the boy's disappearance, as he was such a fine associate.

"The bitch ruined my life!"

Rav Uncle's tender moments had passed, and his natural glare was returning. Perspiration started to form under Avi's arms, across his belly.

"I spoke to her," Avi said. "Your instincts were right. Rani admitted she used us. Her plan was to disappear in America. She asked me to care for the girl. Her name is Leela. She's an orphan. She's scared. I'm trying to determine the best path forward, legally."

"The bitch Rani could be kidnapping my son. Luring him," Rav Uncle snapped. "Where is the girl? She must know the plan. Is she upstairs?"

Rav Uncle would terrify Leela.

"Let's leave her alone," Avi said. "She's afraid."

"So what if she's scared! My son is in trouble! She has food, a bed. She has nothing to complain about."

"She's in a foreign country," Avi said. "She and Rani were escaping a terrible situation, an oppressive boss in Lucknow. I suspect they were mistreated. Sometimes servants in India aren't respected."

"What do you know about India? What, you are talking about human rights, is it? Another hypocritical American! Let me talk to the girl. She can tell us what Rani was doing. I am calling immigration police."

The immigration authorities might detain Leela in a cell until a juvenile court could schedule a hearing. Who knew how long that could take.

"Leela is feeling sick, actually," Avi lied. "It's a stomach bug. Stinky." He pursed his lips. GI tract issues disgusted Rav Uncle.

"So what? This is emergency."

"The girl doesn't know anything. She's not in touch with Rani. Trust me, Uncle. Let's leave her alone."

"Police have methods."

He needed to slow this down.

"Do you remember that Jim Vinson's brother is in law enforcement?" Avi said. "If we involve the police, he could leak the story. Do we want voters to hear about our involvement in an immigration scam a couple weeks before the election?"

Rav Uncle scowled. "Immigration police are different . . . ," he started to say, then paused, confused, seeming to realize he might not be making sense. Rav Uncle had probably latched onto this idea that Rani was luring Peeku, and that Leela knew about it, because the idea that Peeku had gone away to hurt himself was inconceivable. And terrifying.

Appearing chastened, Rav Uncle turned to leave.

"It will be okay, we will find your son," Avi said, patting his shoulder.

It was quiet upstairs. Maybe Leela was finally sleeping off her journey. Avi needed coffee. Reaching for the filter, he looked at his fingers. He did not remember ever touching Rav Uncle, not that way. Sympathetically. He'd expected muscle, but the man's shoulder felt bony.

There were two problems now. Leela's presence, Peeku's absence, both stemming from his mistakes, from thinking he could arrange his life the way Rav Uncle organized the community. It was like Avi had been offered a suit that looked good on another man, and he put it on without checking the fit. Then, doubling down, he hung the suit on Peeku. Avi had been taken with externals—clothing, green salwars, marriage ads, CVs, his speeches, a glittering diamond ring, political office. Honors, ethnicities, and ceremonies. He wasn't alone. Meena had admired the customs, too, though maybe she was now reconsidering.

Could Meena help with this situation, with Leela? She was more Indian than he was, had known more servants, had conversed with and likely understood them. And she liked Peeku. Maybe she could even intuit what might have happened to him. He called her.

Right away, he heard firecrackers, maybe early Diwali celebrations. She must be outside, perhaps on Vishali's roof deck. He explained that Rani had never showed up, had gone AWOL, that it had been an operation. She was probably rendezvousing with contacts in Pennsylvania, Ohio, Canada, or Mexico, who knew. He told her about Leela and Rani's escape from the abusive master in Lucknow, how Rav Uncle wanted to turn Leela over to the police, and how he refused. He didn't know how best to protect Leela, but he had ideas, based on his legal research. He told her Peeku had run away, and they were scared what might have happened to him.

"You told Rav Uncle not to turn Leela over to the police?" Meena said.

He explained that Rav Uncle had the police put out a missing persons alert but, on Avi's insistence, hadn't yet disclosed Rani's plot, for fear of its impact on the election. Also, if Rav Uncle called the immigration authorities, as he was threatening to, they would probably detain the girl, so Avi had fibbed, claiming Leela was sick, and argued that the police might circulate rumors about Avi's and Rav Uncle's involvement in an immigration scam, messing up the campaign.

"You lied to Rav Uncle?" Meena asked.

"I guess so," Avi said.

"Is Leela scared? She must be. All alone with you."

"I'm that scary?"

"I mean with a stranger. Should I talk to her?"

"If she's awake. Let me check."

Holding the banister, he climbed one step at a time. Leela was sitting on the bed, putting on her headscarf. There were pillow creases on her cheeks.

"Madame wants to talk to you on video," he said, holding the phone in front of her.

On the phone screen, Meena smiled, projecting warmth. The girl's eyes widened.

"Hi, Leela," Meena said. "How are you? I'm Meena."

The girl stared blankly.

"Aren't you going to say anything?" Meena asked. When Leela didn't reply, Meena winked and made a funny face. That also got no response. Meena pulled her shawl over her head. She took it off, on again, off again, like peekaboo. Leela furrowed her brow. Meena tied the shawl around her hair, perhaps so that they would resemble each other. Leela's expression brightened, and the edge of her mouth quivered.

Meena spoke in Hindi, words he couldn't quite understand, something about her mommy and daddy and a game. Leela smiled and replied, also in Hindi. They started talking. He had no idea what they were saying. After ten minutes, Leela handed the phone back and put her head on the pillow.

He wandered slowly down the staircase.

"Do you know anything about her family?" Meena asked.

"Her passport lists her father and birthplace as unknown. Rani said Leela doesn't have a family."

After a moment, Meena asked, "Suppose she ends up with child protective services. What would happen?"

"I suspect she'd be detained until they can schedule a hearing," Avi said. "Days, weeks, months, it's hard to say. She wouldn't have legal representation, unless I represented her. They could return her to India."

"To the house she worked at?"

"I hope not. But they could deport her. Some judges just want to clear their dockets."

He paused, gathering himself for the next question.

"Meena, is there any chance you would come back? To help me. My back is out. Again. It's killing me, to be honest."

She said nothing.

"I'm just so worried," he said. "About this girl. About Peeku. I could use your help."

Silence.

"Maybe," Meena finally said, "but let me think about it. If I did come back to help, it would be as your friend."

"Really? That would be great."

The next morning, Avi located a juvenile court, two hours away, willing to grant Leela an emergency hearing. The clerk of the court instructed Avi to bring evidence that: a) Leela could not be reunited with her parents, and b) it was not in Leela's interest to be sent back to India. All Avi had were the recording of his call with Rani, Leela's passport stating that her father and birthplace were unknown, and the girl's own words, assuming she would talk to the judge. The clerk said that if Avi could establish those facts, Leela could become a dependent of the court, and the judge might even grant Avi temporary, emergency custodianship of the girl, at least until a social worker could visit Avi's home and conduct an overall assessment, allowing the court to make a final determination. But, the clerk said, this judge was a stickler, and he had a nose for "foreign funny business."

Avi tried to explain all this to Leela. She understood just enough to become frightened. She looked overwhelmed, so he had Meena call her and explain it in Hindi. It was still unclear whether Leela grasped what was happening.

Avi told her she could go to court in hijab but to wear some American clothes, too, if she had any. The afternoon of the hearing, Leela emerged from her room in jeans, sneakers, and a t-shirt, once sparkling green, now tattered, that read: *Kiss Me, I'm Drunk, Or Irish, Or Whatever*. Second- and thirdhand markets in India sold the oddest leftovers.

On the way to the hearing, Avi stopped at a discount store and bought Leela six plain pink t-shirts. They fit her fairly well. Maybe he wasn't utterly incompetent at this kind of thing. If only he had had someone to advise him how to dress at that eighth-grade party, and not wear that "Cool Jazz" shirt with the garish pictures of Bourbon Street. That shirt, the father-and-son matching carnations, and the whole damn party probably came off, to all the middle-schoolers, as foreign funny business.

Chapter Thirteen

THE NIGHT was smoky and cold. Neighbors had dangled golden lights along their walls for Diwali. Tea lamps lit up courtyards. Kids were setting off firecrackers. In Ohio, it would nearly be Halloween, the last leaves falling, pumpkins glowing, sheet ghosts swaying on elm limbs.

"Did you ask Andrew about the funny credit card charges?" Meena said, pulling her woolen shawl to her neck. Vishali was at the edge of the deck, leaning over the balustrade.

"He says the phone is for some top-secret deal with the Chinese, to avoid surveillance. The flowers are some business thing, too." Vishali grabbed her scarf as it swirled in the wind. She had spent days tracking down the unusual charges, worried they were signs Andrew was having an affair.

"I used to be jealous of Peter's wife. Actually, of all his women," Meena said. "Jealousy eats at you."

"You're saying the issue is my jealousy and not his behavior? Why do you always take his side?" Vishali turned to face Meena.

"Shalu . . ." Meena paused, trying to find her words. "Love is blind, therefore so is jealousy. That's all I'm saying."

"Is that the arranged marriage point of view?"

Why was her sister treating everyone like an enemy?

"Just breathe, that's all," Meena said. "Marriage needs holding on, but also letting go, sometimes. Some clarity, but also some mistiness."

There was more to say. Vishali was her own worst enemy right now. She craved constant companionship. That's why she was always flirting, pursuing someone to adore and be adored by, a presence to hold tight in her mind as she fell asleep. Like a stuffed animal. Even a shadow puppet. Vishali had romances with shadows.

Meena, too, had fallen for silhouettes. Images. The wedding finery, betel nuts and flowers, the old magnificent powers. Perhaps to purify herself after her affair with Peter. Reconstitute after her father's death. Total purity and wholeness weren't possible, but she had needed to believe they were. If she was pure, it suggested others were not. Avi was not. Maybe, as she was leaving Southgate, she had painted Avi black because she had needed to see herself all in white, after the miscarriage. He was right, of course, that she had been responsible for checking the safety of her medications, not him. Had he actually told her to shrink her birthmark, or had she imagined it?

"I thought I had a happy marriage," Vishali said, "unlike you, unlike Mummy. But maybe all three of us are losers."

"Shalu, Andrew is a good enough guy." Meena got up to hug her sister, but Vishali kept her distance. "You're so romantic. People love that. Andrew loves that. But a touch of realism wouldn't hurt. He didn't have an affair, but even if he did, it wouldn't necessarily be the end."

"You're only saying that because you had an affair yourself, with Peter."

Her sister could be right. Before Avi, Meena had already experienced a bad marriage, though from the outside. Maybe she was willing to forgive Andrew because she'd seen marital blunders, betrayals, up close.

Was Avi just blundering, too, in his own way?

"It surprises me you're going back," Vishali said.

"It's for the little girl, Leela."

"You're not going to stay there, are you? You've seen too much of the world to live in that town."

"They've filled my position at the NoMad School, but the priest offered me a job at his other school in Pittsburgh."

"Then what? You'll settle in Pittsburgh?"

There was no good way to phrase what had been running through her mind. She had better just say it, even if her sister was offended or didn't understand.

"I can't stay in Delhi. It's been great to be with you and Mummy, I love you both, but there are too many complicated memories here. And I want to work with kids. I can do that in Pittsburgh, at least for a while. Long-term, I don't know, we'll see."

"Are you sure about this?"

"Getting married, I leaped too quickly. I believed in Papa's advice. Then, coming here, I was sure he was wrong. I'll go slow now, one step at a time."

Vishali looked down at the streets below. "I was jealous of your relationship with Papa."

Meena reached for Vishali's hand. She was glad they were sisters.

"He leaned on me," Meena said. "Because he and Mummy had a lonely marriage. But I wish I'd resisted more. It might have been better for me, for all of us. I'm sorry, Shalu."

"Maybe I lucked out, in a way. The burden of their marriage didn't fall on me."

"To be honest, I've been jealous of your marriage to Andrew." She hadn't fully appreciated, until this moment, how her certitude about traditional marriage might have been the mirror image of her sister's embrace of romantic love.

"Want him? He's yours."

"Come on, Shalu!"

"I should have been kinder, more supportive, when you married

Avi. I will miss you, dear." Vishali grabbed her. It felt good, her sister holding her tight. They always found their way, despite their differences.

"Andrew is supposed to call. I've got to go down, okay?"

"Be open to him, dear sister," Meena said as Vishali descended.

Was Vishali right that Meena always took Andrew's side? Why was she prepared to believe what Andrew was saying but just a few weeks back had doubted Avi had any good intentions at all? Avi was her husband, and he had disappointed her personally, so there was that. Andrew was successful, poised and square-jawed. Like Peter. So there was that, too. And Andrew was white and Christian, governed by laws and commandments. Maybe it was because he wasn't one of their own, an Indian with a transmigrating, shape-changing soul. Perhaps matched skin tones encouraged unwarranted assumptions to go unchecked. Avi hadn't understood himself. Maybe he still didn't. But their misunderstandings stemmed from her, too, her suspicions. Maybe trust required seeing a partner from a distance, not too close. Otherwise, you tended to look around and beyond, too far ahead, imagining too many possibilities, as her father once put it.

She went down and started packing. She stuffed her carry-on with her laptop, a book to read, and scarves and lehengas she had purchased for Leela during an excursion to Khan Market. In a pair of new suitcases, she packed clothes, the picture of her family, two posters from the National Museum of Modern Art exhibition, snacks and sweets, and the Chinese vase.

Peter had invited her to a dinner at the Taj Hotel and a business meeting with his top lieutenants. She had replied: *Heading back to Ohio, mini-crisis, thanks so much, can't make it.* He wished her good luck with "that Ohio crisis" and said there would always be a spot for her on the team. Two of Meena's clubbing girlfriends were being transferred elsewhere in Asia, and they had all gone out for a goodbye happy hour, taking selfies and making grand plans to meet in Paris,

Rome, or Prague, one day. Now, after packing, Meena went one-by-one to Mr. Chicken Maharaja Mac (the driver's name was Ved), the cook, the house helpers, and all the rest of Vishali's servants, leaving each an envelope stuffed with rupees. The tradition was suspect, gifts compensating for the lack of rights, but she couldn't provide the latter.

It felt unreal to be leaving again. The people here already felt airier. Even her mother and sister. Where she was going didn't seem real, either, Avi least of all, though she would shortly be in his house. Avi seemed more mysterious now than on her wedding day, when she barely knew him.

Just before departing for the airport, Meena brought a tray of warm milk and glucose biscuits to Hema Auntie. The family's old domestic was settling into her bed in her tiny room.

"What silliness. Why are you doing this?" Hema Auntie said.

"I wanted to serve you, for once," Meena said.

"You go home to husband now. It is good decision, my child. The gods will take care of you both. You and I meet again in the next life."

Meena left an envelope on the bedside table and gently hugged the frail woman, who awkwardly patted Meena on the back.

Vishali and their mother rode with Meena to the airport. A porter, his teeth blighted red from betel nuts, took Meena's luggage. Her family walked her to the terminal, as they had in so many airports across the continents. Those memories elicited clairvoyance, and Meena knew Vishali was about to offer her flowers. It was a single long-stem rose.

"Good luck, dear," her sister said. The rose was white, the petals just opening, fragrant. "Good luck to us both, actually."

"I'm rooting for you and Andrew," Meena said, touching her sister on the cheek. Meena sensed their mother had something for her, too.

"He would've wanted you to have this," their mother said. It was a wristwatch from her father's vintage collection, black band, honey face set on rose gold, roman numerals. The watch fit Meena's wrist perfectly.

"It has an alarm. Set it, so you know when to get the hell out of there," their mother said, shaking her head and searching for a cigarette.

They hugged goodbye. Meena cleared immigration and security. Inside the terminal, she found two empty chairs in what passed for a quiet corner of the airport. She video-called Avi. He was holding onto the linoleum countertop in the kitchen, looking uncomfortable. Leela was eating cereal at the kitchen table.

"The hearing went well," Avi said. "They'll send a social worker to check this place out, but all is okay for now. Leela, look, Madame is calling."

The girl stood, took the phone.

"As-salamu alaykum," Meena said. She continued, in Hindi, "I'm flying back. Do you want a comic book, or maybe sweets from the airport shops?"

"Toffee?" Leela said.

"Toffee, then," Meena said.

Still sitting in front of her laptop screen, Meena took a blue scarf from her carry-on. She placed it on her head, leaving one short and one long end free in front. She grasped the longer end and pulled it tightly from the bottom of her chin to one side, circled it around the top of her head, and brought it back down. Using a pin with a yellow smiley face, bought for this purpose, she secured the scarf.

"Look, hijab," Meena said. "I bought more scarves." She took out the red, green, yellow, orange, and white scarves to show her.

"Dress-up," said Leela, smiling, turning her palms up, and glancing back at Avi with a look that said, I can't believe this. Avi returned her warm expression, which Leela noticed and appreciated, Meena could tell. Avi and Leela seemed to have developed an understanding.

Perhaps that's how it was. Now and then, unexpectedly, one could reach people.

THE TAXI PASSED the basilica and the billboards. It wasn't that late, but the stores in Southgate were already closed, even the gas stations. Never a soul on these sidewalks, the wide empty streets. The office parks and the lawns were tame, lifeless, and, Meena knew without opening the car windows, scentless.

Meanwhile, it would be early morning in Delhi, fishmongers and kebabwalas assembling pungent meats, unshowered rickshaw drivers grimacing in the cold air of daybreak.

As the taxi approached Avi's house, she found herself worrying about how he would greet her. An embrace, a kiss? He'd probably reach for her bag, despite his bad back, which would be dumb, but he often couldn't help himself. After he threw out his back in April, she'd cooked, cleaned, organized, doing everything she could for her marriage. Now his well-being seemed secondary. She was here for Leela. Avi was apparently doing well by her, satisfying the juvenile court judge, but she could tell Leela was uncomfortable, even scared, around him. He didn't speak her language. Sometimes he didn't have the right touch. It might be a good idea to let him present Leela with the toffees, to build their relationship. Actually, no. She'd already told Leela she'd buy toffees in the Delhi airport. Plus, she wanted to give them, to see Leela light up. Despite all her losses, the girl smiled easily.

They arrived at Avi's house. The driver took out her suitcases. Avi emerged in khakis and a windbreaker, waving from a few feet away, keeping his distance. She waved back.

The night was clear and cold.

"I wish I could help you with those, but . . . ," he said, putting a hand onto his back.

"No, no, I'm fine. Take care of yourself," Meena said. "Where is she?"

"Sleeping upstairs."

She gave him a careful hug, pushing aside her pashmina shawl to get her arms around him. He seemed tense, moved stiffly. As he held onto her, his muscles relaxed.

"Thanks for the hug," he said.

The living room looked both familiar and strange. The statuettes of the Hindu deities were gone. There were children's magazines on the coffee table. And juice boxes. Avi sat on the couch, and Meena took the love seat.

"Is she out for the night?" she asked.

"Probably, though sometimes she gets up for cereal."

"Do you give it to her?"

"Of course." He furrowed his brow.

"Sorry. It's an adjustment, imagining you with a child."

"Tell me what I should expect, Meena." He pursed his lips, looked at her searchingly.

She knew the answer, but was hesitating. Her habitual self-doubt, when it came to expressing what she wanted.

"I'm here for her," she said.

"Of course," Avi said, crossing his arms. He rested his head back on the couch. "Meena, I want to apologize for saying you were merely adjusting, when you were in Delhi. I know you were in pain, and upset at me, and I understand why. I was afraid you would date someone like Peter over there, and I wanted to pretend that nothing was wrong between us."

It sounded valedictory. He seemed sad their relationship might be ending, perhaps before it even began. It was ridiculous that he still worried about Peter. The man now seemed a joke. Maybe he'd served a function, in the first months of their marriage, as the vehicle of her resistance, for her intuition that something was wrong. Now Peter was just that guy in the bandana.

"I saw Peter in Delhi. I told you, right?" she said.

He looked worried. "How did you connect with . . . ?"

"We were in touch. From the early days, right after the wedding. I'm sorry, Avi. I shouldn't have. It probably feels like a betrayal, to you. It was a betrayal. I was confused. I wasn't sure what I had gotten into. If it's any consolation, I didn't like what I saw of him. At all."

"I felt you holding back, early on. So I wasn't making it up."

"You weren't." She paused, then decided to say more. "I want to say something else, too. You were not, are not, to blame for my miscarriage. You didn't tell me to get rid of the birthmark. I just needed someone to blame."

"I wanted that child," Avi said. He looked pained.

"I do need to ask something, Avi," Meena continued. "If you felt bad about the miscarriage, why did you say were you relieved?"

"I wish I could have those words back. That was a stupid thing to say. I'm sorry. I was under pressure from the campaign."

"I learned something else at the hospital. I have a misshapen uterus, which means I might not be able to carry any baby to term."

If she looked at him, at anyone, she'd lose it, so she turned her head. Why was she even bringing this up? To emphasize that the miscarriage was inevitable, neither his fault nor hers? That for her, their traditional marriage had always been doomed?

He got up from the couch and came over to the love seat, bringing a box of tissues.

"I'm so sorry, Meena. That must have been terrible to hear. And to hear alone."

"It was, it is, hard. Such a mistake."

"What?"

"How we married," she said. Avi exhaled, and looked upset, but she had to keep going. "I fell for what my father wanted. I thought a traditional marriage was safety. Insta-family. All done. You know? When you weren't there for me in the hospital, Avi, I saw something."

"I'm so sorry, I wish . . ."

"I'm not blaming you. I saw something about myself. I fell for a fantasy, though I didn't know it. It wasn't real."

His face lit with what looked like understanding. "I get it. I really do."

"Tell me."

"I had this idea that I had a future in politics, that I would change the world, starting with Southgate," Avi said. "I fell in love with the idea of selflessness. Rescuing my parents. Speaking for the community. Being a role model to Peeku. I had this idea I could learn from Rav Uncle, then supersede him as a leader. Win this election and the next one, but with better values."

He kicked the bottom of the love seat.

"I was thinking about you, Avi," she said, "a lot. You are a good man. Kind, decent, smart. It doesn't matter if people elect you. You don't need reflected light. You are the sun. Not the moon."

He stared at her. They sat in silence.

"I'm glad we're talking, Avi. I worried we wouldn't be able to speak at all."

"You must be tired," he said. "There's a cup of water on the bedside table upstairs." Now she noticed, among the juice boxes, Avi's water bottle and a container of ibuprofen. He was planning to sleep on the couch.

"If she wakes at 2 a.m., will she be shocked to find me up there, instead of you, in the bed?" she asked.

"She knows you're coming."

"It's not right, kicking you out of your bed."

He smiled sheepishly.

"It's okay. Go ahead and get ready. I have some papers to look over."

"Wait, what about Peeku?" Meena said. "I'm assuming you would have told me, if there was any news."

"Nothing," he said, shaking his head.

Avi was pressing his legs against the coffee table for leverage, so she helped him up.

There was a child-size toothbrush in the master bathroom. Also a hairbrush and a black scarf. In the bedroom, she saw a mini-fridge with single-serve Froot Loops boxes on top, pint-size milk cartons inside. He really had been caring for the little girl. It should have made Meena happy, but it only made her think of what they might have had.

HER CARRY-ON was at the foot of the bed. Avi must have brought it up, bad back and all. She must have slept heavily. If Leela came in during the night, she hadn't noticed.

From her carry-on, Meena removed an olive-green scarf and wrapped it over her hair, smoothing it down. She rummaged in her bag and found hairpins for holding it in place. She took another scarf, gold, and wrapped it over her head and around her neck, the long end draped in a roll and covering her chest.

"Meena, are you putting yourself in hijab?" Avi said. He came in from the hallway.

"Leela likes dress-up," she said. "I wanted to have some fun with her. You can go back to whatever you were doing."

"I was writing a letter to the juvenile court, but I'm done."

Leela entered, stopping a few feet from Meena, standing at attention.

"Hello, Leela! Look," Meena said, pointing at her scarves, "do you like dress-up?" She ran Leela's fingers across her gold scarf. "Soft, isn't it?"

On an impulse, Meena leaned in to give Leela a soft hug. The girl stiffened. A mistake. A servant girl might not have been hugged for years, especially if the house in Lucknow really had been Leela's sixth, and if she had no family. But after a moment, Leela relaxed, and Meena felt the girl even begin to lean into her. Leela wasn't entirely put off by affection. Maybe Rani had hugged her.

She let go of Leela and turned back to her carry-on. "Look, more scarves," she said, switching to Hindi. "Toffee. Comic books. It's all for you." She put the entire pile of goodies into Leela's arms.

Leela brightened, and she showed her white teeth. She twirled the scarves, then dropped them. She took a toffee and looked at Avi.

"Sir, okay?" she asked, holding the toffee by the wrapper and starting to pull it off.

"Go ahead," Avi said. "You can eat breakfast later."

Leela put the toffee into her mouth.

"Here, try some of these scarves," Meena said.

The girl hesitated, glancing at Avi.

"Sir won't mind, go ahead," Meena said. "Put on this red one."

Leela didn't move. Was she ashamed to remove her scarf in front of "Sir"?

"It's dress-up, Leela. It's okay. Dress-up." In solidarity, Meena removed her own scarves, tossing her hair. "See?"

Meena removed Leela's scarf. The girl looked terrified. She grabbed the red scarf from Meena and put it around her head.

But Meena saw it. Leela had a large mole on the back of her neck. It wouldn't be obvious, probably hidden under her hair for the most part. But it was big. It clearly embarrassed her.

"Don't worry about it," Meena said, trying to sound reassuring. She repeated the phrase in Hindi, then in English. "Did you notice that mole?" she asked Avi. He looked baffled. Obviously, he hadn't.

"Do you want to see something funny?" Meena asked Leela. This was going to be a risk, as she and Leela had just met, but why not? She was following her impulses now, on principle. She stood, turned her back to Leela, and yanked up her pajama shorts. "At least your mark isn't on your butt."

"Oh god," Avi said. He raised his eyebrows, as if to say, I don't believe this.

It was ridiculous that this meaningless discoloration had become so loaded, so bewildering, to her and Avi.

Leela started laughing. "Funny, Sir?" she said.

Meena cackled, and then all of them laughed together.

"Isn't this silly?" Meena said, still exposing herself.

Leela put her finger on her chin, and Meena couldn't tell if she was thinking or pretending to think. "Yes, Madame, silly," she said.

Chapter Fourteen

Avi DREAMT a guru beckoned him upstairs, into the attic. (Was the guru Rav Uncle?) Gripping the ladder railings, Avi ascended. The guru's buttery body was settled on a cushion, his black curls beautifully combed, smooth skin like milk chocolate. (How could Rav Uncle be beautiful?) The guru flashed a knife from under his robes and said, "I will eat you, Avi."

Shaking, sounds. Leela was waking him up. His real life was returning. Leela's immigration status. Peeku's disappearance. His failed marriage.

"Madame is taking me shopping," Leela said. "She said wake you up. It is afternoon."

He'd added another pain medication, and it must have knocked him out.

After Meena and Leela left, Avi made himself coffee and a peanut butter sandwich. He spent the day filing for limited power of attorney in case Leela needed medical care, scheduling an interview for relief from removal proceedings against her, and submitting paperwork authorizing the required criminal background checks.

He called clients, then checked in with his campaign volunteers. One, a friend from Ohio State, now a manager at Fifth Third, asked for a map with the finalized poster locations. He told her he'd send it right away, but the election no longer seemed interesting. Did he care if Diwali was a school holiday? If that land parcel was rezoned?

His mother called. She said everyone was beside themselves with worry. The Punjabi 5 wives were arranging a prayer service for Peeku at the temple. When abductees were found alive, it was usually within hours.

Toward evening, as the weak November light faded, blues and reds started to incandesce on the living room couch. A kaleidoscope of color was reflecting off the glass coffee table. A police car. He braced himself for bad news about Peeku. Or was this about Leela?

He answered a knock at the front door. An officer held out his badge.

"I'm Officer Smith," the man said. "My boss wants me to inform you that harboring an illegal alien carries a sentence of up to five years in prison. You must know that, since you're an attorney admitted to practice in this state, for the time being."

For fuck's sake. Word about Leela must have gotten out. Jim, Jim's brother, or someone else in the Vinson clan, the Southgate powers that be, must have arranged this, with an eye toward the ten o'clock news. They were tempting him to do something stupid or rash.

"I don't think we've met," Avi said. "Avi Sehrawat. I'm running for township trustee."

"Yes, sir."

"Everything I'm doing is aboveboard, completely legal," Avi said, pointing, "and you can tell the Vinsons that."

The police officer, apologetic, said he was just doing as he was told. He went to his car, turned off the siren lights, and pulled away.

Meena and Leela returned. Leela gave Avi a Styrofoam container of Chinese takeout. In the kitchen, Avi poured himself a beer, nibbled the minced chicken stir-fry, and watched Meena exhibit sweaters, blouses, leggings, and lightweight hoodies, holding up each article of clothing against Leela. The girl grabbed a brimmed, ribboned hat from the shopping bag.

"It's tacky, but she wanted it," Meena said.

"You think everything in Southgate is tacky," Avi said.

"Because it is."

"Will you be needing a suitable bag to convey Leela's attire upstairs, perhaps one by Louis Vuitton?" he asked.

Meena smiled. "Guilty, as charged."

The doorbell rang again. Just once. So it wasn't Rav Uncle. And there were no cop lights. Was it his parents, who still hadn't met Leela? Meena shot Avi a worried look. She sent Leela upstairs to take a bath.

It was a couple. An olive-skinned woman, along with Peeku!

"Goddammit, everyone is beside themselves," Avi said. "Where have you been, dude?"

"We got an apartment over by the Lions Club," Peeku said. "One bedroom plus den."

"An apartment?" Avi said. "Where did you two . . . connect?"

"At Kmart, you know that."

"Wait, so this is your friend? Sheela?"

"She's my fiancée now, man!"

Peeku lifted Sheela's hand so they could see the engagement ring.

"Nice to meet you," Sheela said. She seemed nervous, or awkward, and turned her head to look back at the street.

"I saved up," Peeku said. "We stayed at the Holiday Inn for a while. I used my Christmas bonus."

Meena walked over and gave Peeku a hug. "Peeku, hi! My goodness, we've been worried. Did you say you're getting married? Congratulations!" She turned toward Sheela. "I'm sorry, I didn't get your name?" Sheela continued to look away.

"Sorry, guys," Peeku said. "Sheela gets distracted sometimes, but she's awesome. That's my friend Meena, Avi's wife."

Sheela made brief eye contact with Meena.

"Peeku, why didn't you call? WTF man, really," Avi said. "Going and disappearing like that. It made everyone crazy."

"I didn't want an arranged marriage. Sheela and I are super awesome together. My dad would've stopped us."

"You could've at least told me," Avi said.

"Tell you? You're like dad's assistant coach," Peeku said. "Sorry if I scared you guys. Hey, you two want to come over for brunch on Sunday? Be our first guests?"

Rav Uncle would be furious if they visited Peeku and Sheela. Being their first guests would normalize the engagement. But they should do it anyway. Avi glanced at Meena, who nodded.

"We'd love to come, Peeku," he said.

Peeku pumped his fist, then pointed at them both. He seemed to believe that Avi and Meena were back together again. Peeku showed off his brand-new phone, then texted the address of their new apartment. He said they had to run. Sheela's parents were expecting them for dinner.

"Wait, dinner with her parents? Weren't they mad at you?" Avi asked.

"My dad exaggerates," Peeku said. "Anyway, they're cool now." Peeku kissed Sheela on the cheek and waved bye.

Rav Uncle had said Sheela's parents were furious and ready to sue. Had it been an embellishment, even an outright lie, that Peeku couldn't manage a romance on his own and needed an arranged marriage? Perhaps it was. Why had Avi believed it?

"Are you shocked?" he asked Meena.

"Surprised," she said. "I didn't really know him, though. I feel terrible for foisting Rani on Peeku. I'm glad he had the courage to say no."

"I just thought . . . I don't know. Peeku?"

She touched his shoulder. "Are you second-guessing yourself?"

This whole plan: returning home, running for office, the quasi-arranged marriage. He thought it was his own idea. Had he been taking orders the whole time?

"I'm embarrassed," he said. "I wish I hadn't given that campaign speech at our wedding."

"You're a better man than you believe, Avi."

Upstairs, Leela was splashing in the bathtub. She was singing in Hindi. It sounded like a happy song.

AVI CALLED HIS FATHER to say Peeku was safe. He had to reveal that Peeku had stopped by, was now engaged to the Kmart girl, and the two of them were living together. His father was relieved it wasn't worse. He said he would of course inform Rav Uncle and Chrissy.

Half an hour later, the black Mercedes pulled into Avi's driveway. The doorbell sounded, many times in a row. Avi slowly walked to the door.

Through the window, Rav Uncle glared, eyes bulging, his cheeks folding into his mustache, highlighting his fleshy creases. Meena was sitting on the couch, face in her hands, seemingly afraid to watch. Nervously, Avi opened the door, then took two steps back.

"What, arranged marriage is good for you, but not my son?" Rav Uncle said.

This man was always distorting the situation. Now he was trying to create a split between Avi and Peeku. Divide, foment, pry loose. That's what Rav Uncle did. Avi felt nauseous.

"Actually, Peeku seems happy . . . ," Avi said.

"You are saying running away from home is cause for happiness? This girl will run away from him! You will see! Peeku knows nothing of the challenges in this life. I was arranging marriage to protect him! Do you know what I have done, in this life, for sake of my family?"

Rav Uncle was shouting, but he also sounded defensive. There were undertones of helplessness. Fear and distress. What did Rav Uncle fear? That Peeku might actually be happy in a relationship, one Rav Uncle had nothing to do with?

How had he not noticed Rav Uncle's insecurities before? Why

had he promoted Peeku's arranged marriage at the moment he was losing faith in his own? He had been more than an assistant coach. He had been a faker, a carnival barker. Men like Rav Uncle sniffed out fear. When they smelled an opportunity, they steamrolled.

"Protecting him, or your own authority?" Avi asked.

Rav Uncle's eyes narrowed. "Avi, little Avi, do you remember who I am? Your father's friend. I am like his brother. I am your family's benefactor!"

Rav Uncle always pursued his own interests, though he pretended to speak for the community. He was willing to turn over a scared little girl to the police, or Homeland Security, to be deported. Return her to penury. To loneliness.

"Where is my son?" Rav Uncle shouted. "Where!?" His gaze landed on Avi's pockets, as if he knew Peeku had texted his new address.

Avi's mistakes hadn't just begun when he returned to Southgate, intent on leading the community. They had started earlier. He went into corporate law seeking status. He aimed to carry around rolls of hundreds, like Rav Uncle. Avi had believed that the Southgate Punjabis should band together. They would then be powerful. He would then be powerful. But why couldn't he hold himself up? It was true Rav Uncle had leverage over Avi's father, and had used it. The sad part was that Avi hadn't bothered to resist.

"Let me give Peeku a heads-up, so he knows you're upset," Avi said.

"Give me his address! What, you won't?" Rav Uncle clenched his fists. "I will find him. I developed half the apartment buildings in this town. We'll start with buildings near the basilica. Meet me there. Fifteen minutes."

Meena, bent forward, ran her fingers through her hair, still unable to watch. Upstairs were footsteps, creaks, the sounds of Leela getting into bed.

"You don't control me," Avi said. "Nor Peeku. I will not let you force your son into any marriage he doesn't want. Leave him alone."

"Not let me? You are small man, Avinash. I am going upstairs to get that girl."

Rav Uncle stepped inside and started toward the staircase. Avi blocked him.

"If you tell Peeku to leave Sheela," Avi said, "or bribe or threaten him, I will withdraw from the campaign and concede the election. You get the rezoning of Washington Woods only if you leave Peeku alone. I am not joking. Look, my phone has the number for the board of elections. I am about to dial."

Rav Uncle stared. It seemed he was about to scream, but then, curiously, he fell quiet. "Insolence!" he finally shouted, shaking his first. "He is my son!" He slammed the door on the way out.

Avi called Peeku and left a voicemail: "Your father still wants you to have an arranged marriage. Don't answer the door. Go to the probate court with Sheela. Get a marriage license, now. Then go directly to the municipal court and get married. I will call ahead and talk to the judge. Your father won't pressure you after you're married. A divorce would embarrass him more than an elopement. Good luck."

It felt like a winter day, and Avi was on the edge of a thawing river, standing precariously. He could at any moment slip on the icy banks. It felt new not to be grabbing onto anything for safety but moving headlong, like the river itself.

FOR MEENA, it was like watching a slow-motion car accident. Impersonal violence. Impending doom.

But it had been averted. Avi averted it. He was willing to surrender the prospect of holding office, his splendid future, which had once meant everything to him, on behalf of his friend. And he protected Leela from Rav Uncle, from the authorities. Something in him was solidifying. He was always decent, kind, but now he seemed to have resolve. On Leela's behalf. A purpose could make a person brave.

At this point, the ancient traditions did not compel her, and anyway it was clear the ones in this town had been invented, not preserved. She couldn't live here, but maybe she could have a rooted life, nonetheless. Her father might not have understood it, and her mother and sister might not admire it, but the grounding of a new life was near.

She approached Avi, took his hand. She leaned into his ear and whispered, "Avi, that was amazing. You were wonderful." She kissed him on the cheek.

"I missed you," he said. He kissed her hands, then her lips. He embraced her with a firm hug. She wanted to believe in him, but it was too soon.

"Hold on," she said. "We need to talk."

He rested a hand on her hips. "About whether I should grab you here next time?"

Maybe he hadn't changed entirely.

"Avi, listen. They filled my position at the NoMad School here in Southgate," she said, "but the priest offered me a job at the sister school in Pittsburgh. I accepted."

"Really? When you said you can't live here, I thought you would be returning to India. When does the job start?"

"January, next semester. And I think . . . I think I should take Leela . . . I think I should be her guardian. She needs someone who speaks her language. She's alone in the world . . . Then after the immigration proceedings are over, I will foster her. Adopt her, if I can."

Avi's eyes rounded, his lips parted, a look of astonishment.

"Are you sure? That's a big decision."

"At the store, she tried on some running shoes and went bolting down the aisle," Meena said. "The security guard scolded her, and she started sobbing. I hugged her. She let me hold her. She needs me."

"I tried to help her. I did my best, but . . ."

"You absolutely did. You've been amazing."

"Meena, I wish the miscarriage hadn't happened," he said, "and that we had the family we wanted . . ."

"I know, but let's not talk about that," she said.

Tears welled up. He dabbed at them with his fingers.

It was terribly sad to imagine the child they lost. But it also felt good, him comforting her, and reading her thoughts. She wasn't sure how to phrase the question in her mind, or even its premise, but she asked, "Would you ever leave Southgate, Avi? I don't know what I think about us, what it would feel like to try again, whether I would even want that, but maybe after a while . . . What are you thinking?"

He took her hands. He looked at the floor. "I thought of coming to get you in Delhi. Staying there as long as it took. I couldn't just leave my parents, though. Not that abruptly. They're going through a lot, with my dad's injury, my mom's hopes for . . . a clan, I suppose. But I can imagine a life with you and Leela, maybe."

Could they actually get together again? She had felt exquisite on the marriage platform, walking around the sacred fire. It seemed as though she and Avi were beautiful, exotic flowers. Two irises. Now their relationship felt more ordinary, but also more real. And sadder. Could they become crepe myrtles, robust and transplantable? It would be like remarrying, though under different terms. Maybe second marriages were necessary, also third, fourth, and fifth ones, if a couple was lucky. Her mother and father hadn't known. They might have been happy, had they tried to renegotiate. Vishali and Andrew, too, might have a chance to rework their relationship.

"When I went away, I thought I knew you," Meena said. "Now you seem strange to me, unfamiliar. I like it, though. I feel closer as I start to see you from a little distance. It makes me seem strange to myself, too, stranger but more alive."

Avi's face twisted. He started to tear up. He looked indescribably sad.

"It's okay, Avi," she said. "We will get through. Whatever happens, we will remain friends."

He tried to nod but was visibly upset. This was too much for him. It would be better to brighten the mood. She put on an ironic yet serious look and said, "Let's use vows this time." She grabbed her phone and browsed to a picture of a deity. "Do you swear on Ganesh that you commit?"

"Commit to what?"

"To authenticity, to knowing yourself, staying in touch with your feelings, etcetera, etcetera."

He placed his left hand on her phone, raised his right hand, and closed his eyes.

"On Ganesh, I swear," he said.

"You do know that in the epics, Hindu gods are jokesters, always lying and dissembling?"

"You scam artist!" he said.

THE NIGHT before the election, Avi hardly slept, tossing and turning. His plan was to sign the rezoning papers, give the green light to the strip mall, then resign. Forget about the Diwali holiday. That would be someone else's problem. He had wanted to suspend the campaign right away, but then Rav Uncle might actually follow through on his threats and pull creditors from Avi's father's automotive garage. He might go to the authorities about Leela. The man was unpredictable. After winning, but prior to green-lighting the rezoning, Avi would demand that Rav Uncle help his father refinance. He'd take advantage of his leverage while he had it.

But that assumed he would win the election. If he lost, he'd have no power. He had to win. He'd grown indifferent to the campaign, particularly after the Lions Club fiasco, even more so after Leela's arrival. He had to get to work. Whatever the future held, there was still the now. This would be his last stand as a Southgate candidate. Probably as a candidate anywhere. At 5 a.m., he got out of bed. He went down to the basement to retrieve a mallet, a hammer, nails, and twine from his toolbox. He grabbed a handful of quarters in case he needed to feed the meters. He loaded his last campaign posters into the trunk of his car.

Jim had claimed many of the best spots, including the car wash at the interstate interchange: *Jim for the Win, A Man You Can Trust, Us Is About Us.* Avi decided to obscure the posters at the car wash with twenty of his own. That wasn't a crime. What was Jim going to do about it anyway, get a cop to knock on his door? It hadn't rained for days, and the ground was hard. Avi had to swing the mallet high overhead to drive the posters' wooden stakes into the soil. His back ached. A car slowed, probably to gawk at a man hammering in the dark. When Avi accidentally stepped off the curb, a bus driver blasted his horn.

His volunteers had already planted posters outside the basilica, staying clear of the hundred-foot "zones of reflection," designated with American flags, for election day. He drove to the elementary schools and hammered-in posters next to sidewalks near the carpool line, and around playgrounds and ball fields. Then he drove back toward the high school, past the billboards—that ever-salacious seduction and the setting sun. He liked the billboards, reminders that there were moments when everything comes alive.

At the shopping mall, he installed fifteen posters near the food court entrance. He secured some to the guardrails at the entry ramps to parking garages. He drove through the subdivisions near Veterans Park and dotted the walking paths with *Say What Sehrawat* signs. That was pointless, no one would be at the park playing ball on a day this gloomy, but what the hell. He attached a handful to parking meters outside the courthouse. He used up more at the strip malls along the state highway.

Two posters left. What about Linden Park, near his house? Only geese would be over there on a cold gray day, but if he hurried, he might be able to see clouds turn pink over the Japanese garden, which consisted of a pond, a tea leaf bed, a cramped pagoda, a weathered wood bench, and a stand of ginkgoes. He loved ginkgoes, which adapted to harsh sites and dry, poor soils. At the first hard frost, their leaves, shaped like the lungs of small beings, would fall in a golden downpour.

He made it in time for sunrise, but the fog was thick. No rosy dawn. Avi planted his last two posters on either side of the bench. That was it. That's all he had. He sat. Across the pond, a telephone pole pointed at the sun's faint disk.

He'd put so much into this campaign, his platform, his ideas, his dreams and visions. He'd speechified, shared what he had believed to be his deepest desires. So many showy words, like falling leaves. Maybe one day they would mean something.

Avi launched his mallet into the air, as high as he could. It splashed, sinking into the middle of the pond. He threw his hammer skyward, and it, too, made a satisfying burst as it split the water. He pitched a handful of nails. They hit the water like raindrops. He threw in the twine. Then he uprooted the newly planted posters and threw those in. He emptied his pockets of quarters, flicking and skipping. Did he have a wish? He twirled his last quarter into the air and thought about what to pray for. He was going to catch it, but at the last second let the coin plop, submerge.

Marrying a woman he didn't know, maybe marrying anybody, was like nurturing a lost child. He wished he had cared for Meena the way he'd cared for Leela.

Some people married for love. Others for money, or convenience. Family. Loyalty. For God and tradition. Why had he done it? He'd wanted meaning. Weightiness. Now he would let go, pursue lightness. This was better. Wherever he ended up in his life, he hoped to live near a pond, somewhere to cast away the surplus.

In his imaginings, election night consisted of rap music and bhangra, dancing and drinking, speeches and applause. Zoning board appointments, architectural drawings. A symbolic ribbon-cutting ceremony. The release of his true economic vision, Avi Sehrawat's Social Equity Thoughts (ASSETs). Conversations with job applicants. He would gracefully accept Jim's congratulatory call.

There would be no gala tonight, not with the lingering tensions around Peeku's elopement, the uncertainty over Avi's marriage, and the presence of the little Muslim runaway. Avi's mother came over in the late afternoon, commandeered the kitchen, and made samosas, onion pakoras, and vegetable cutlets. If it was a happy party, she said, she would have made chicken biryani, buttery lentils, potato eggplant, and mango cheesecake. She cooked in silence, then passed Avi the spoon, wordlessly indicating he was to stir the frying onions.

Avi could tell his mother was stewing over his marriage and over Leela, who was upstairs getting dressed with Meena.

"Then what kind of family?" his mother said, sharing anxieties mid-sentence.

She was referring both to his continuing separation from Meena and to Leela, the presence of an outsider. His family wasn't used to mixing. It wasn't until college that he realized not all Indians were Punjabi Hindus.

"I can't say yet what's going to happen, Mom," he said. "Meena and I are living separately, but we aren't divorcing. There are all kinds of families."

"Yes, those porridge mixtures." It was probably also confusing that Meena and Leela weren't helping his mother cook, jumbling her assumptions, those subtle sequences of submission and sanction, who cooked and who sat, who ate first and last, which way a person's feet pointed.

He might as well get it over with.

"Mom, listen. Meena and Leela are moving to Pittsburgh. Mohan Ji has offered her a job at his school over there. I don't want to be township trustee, I've realized. If I win, I'm going to rezone the Washington Woods parcel after I assume office in January, as my first and last official act. Then I will resign. This afternoon Rav Uncle agreed to help Dad refinance the garage. On favorable terms."

His mother took the spoon from him and stirred the onions. She wiped a tear, then made her face rigid. "You were going to be a trustee," she said.

Avi's father, who had been in the living room, walked into the kitchen. He looked serious. He must have overheard.

"I'm sorry, Dad," Avi said.

"Son, don't be silly," his father said. "Rav blusters, but he doesn't bite. I'm his elder. He won't do anything to me. You look after yourself now."

Even his father knew Rav Uncle was a paper tiger.

After the cooking was done, Avi's parents went out for a walk. The moment the front door closed, Meena and Leela came down. They both wore headscarves. Leela helped herself to a few pakoras and wandered back upstairs.

"Rav Uncle will be startled to see you in the headscarf," he said.

"I don't want her to be the only one getting funny looks," Meena said.

"Does wearing it feel weird?"

"Kind of?" Meena said. "But I don't see why people are so fixated about their identities. It's nice to have a couple of them. It's like taking off your work clothes at the end of the day and putting on your pajamas."

The Punjabi 5 and their wives showed up at 7 p.m., just as the polls were closing. One by one, the men shook Avi's hand, settled into the couches and chairs, and began looking around, expecting drinks and snacks. Meena helped Avi's mother serve appetizers. Meena had instructed Leela not to help because she didn't want her to feel like a servant. Avi brought out the beers.

When Leela came down, Rav Uncle's gaze went back and forth

between her and Meena. Meena had been right—he was unable to control his quizzical looks.

"She's still here, then?" Rav Uncle said, speaking of Leela in the third person. "Avi, your wife is going to Pittsburgh, is it? I suppose every man must find his way out of the soups he gets himself into."

The Punjabi 5 started to discuss the quality of the pho at the new Vietnamese restaurant in the food court. Kohli reported that one of the current township trustees was retiring, so another position would open up soon, and his nephew might run. That meant that even if Jim won tonight, and skewered the zoning rules, they would soon get another shot at rezoning the real estate parcel and at the Diwali holiday.

The board of elections call came at 9 p.m. Wanting to be alone, Avi went upstairs to the master bathroom and closed the door. The final tally was 2,243 votes for Jim and 1,009 for Avi. The election commissioner congratulated Avi on a good run. "It's tough to beat those damn Vinsons," he said. Avi checked the social media sites. They were saying that winning was the Vinsons' destiny, that Jim was one tough mofo, a chip off the old block.

Had he ever had a chance? Maybe the glorious visions had only been shades dancing in his head, private fairy tales. Believing so was a relief, in a strange way. He made the necessary call. Jim was celebrating, heavy metal playing in the background, and he sounded sloppy drunk. "Good run, dude," Jim said. "My family, you know, we're a bunch of hard-asses, but I'm a big-hearted guy. I'm a lover of mankind! Give to him who asks of you! Malice toward none, charity for all! Let's get a beer tomorrow, reminisce about this crappy campaign."

Avi agreed to meet Jim for happy hour. Downstairs, everyone looked expectant as he announced the results.

"Should we ask for recount?" Avi's mother said.

Rav Uncle waved off the idea. "Our time will come. Wait until next year," he said.

"Okay, okay," Avi's father said, whistling. "That's a lot of votes, son." He put both hands on Avi's shoulders, then hugged him.

Kohli raised his glass, partly to toast, partly as a way to ask for another beer. Sharma said, "A good race. We'll get them next time!" Verma said now that the race was over, at least his blood pressure would be easier to control. It felt claustrophobic, but Avi felt obliged to stay and chat for a while, nodding as Kohli described his deer problems. Verma offered to help Kohli's nephew file election papers. There was an argument about the most promising young politicians in town, centering on whether Dinesh or Suresh, both local boys and Northwestern Law School grads, was more likely to be the next Obama.

When it felt unbearable, Avi put on his winter coat and went out front. A rush of cold air hit his nostrils. Apart from the hum of traffic on Richey Road, echoing off the brick colonials, it was entirely quiet.

"It's over!" he shouted at the empty streets.

After a few minutes, Meena and Leela joined him.

"You fought hard, Avi," Meena said. She whispered in Leela's ear.

"Congratulations, Sir, on your race," Leela said to him in English, pronouncing the big word slowly but well. Then Leela laughed, a high-pitched giggle. Where had she learned to tee-hee like that?

He leaned into Meena and asked, "Is she laughing at me?"

"At you?"

"Maybe I'm imagining it."

"Maybe she is. I've had some laughs at your expense, too."

"When?"

"When you shouted my name, when we, you know. You were right on top of me, in the kitchen. You're a loud talker, sometimes."

"I was trying to make you feel special."

Avi's mother came out to say that people were putting on their coats. With Meena and Leela, he went to the door and said goodbye, making pleasantries and thanking the guests as they filed out into the clear, glittering night, keys in hand, opening doors and flashing the headlights of their frosty automobiles.

MEENA SAID she and Leela couldn't make it back for Peeku and Sheela's wedding ceremony. Leela's attachment to doing all the daily prayers complicated travel right now. Apparently, the girl's new life, all the Sponge Bob videos and Cheerios, were making her more, not less observant. The weird foods and strange words in America, all her travels and dislocations, were catching up with her. Now and again, she would cry before going to sleep, and Meena had to rub her back. Praying soothed, creating continuity with her past life.

Meena said she and Leela were learning Arabic together. They could manage a bit of the prayers, but mostly they mumble-chanted. That was enough, as Leela held dear the sounds, not the words, and would be happy afterward.

Leela's inarticulate nostalgia actually reminded Avi of the way he kept reimagining his campaign. He wished he'd started the TV interview with Meena beside him, restricted the size of the Lions Club event, left the Punjabi 5 behind on Memorial Day. It wasn't strategy. He had no desire to run for office again and was relieved to have lost. It was just that yearning, longing for his past, made him familiar to himself, even though he knew these ruminations were pure puff, the silken strands of his solitary afternoons, long hours spent figuring out what to do with himself, waiting for his feelings, and Meena's, to crystallize.

He had given up taxes and estates and was starting up a family and immigration law practice. To earn a bit of income until he could launch the new business, he scrounged up a DUI defense and a case involving a Gujarati realtor married to a local actress who wanted, post-divorce, to void the prenup. It wasn't easy shifting jobs again, having so much idle time. He couldn't shake the sense that Rav Uncle was asking if he'd thrown his pecker into the pond, too.

At the wedding, Avi squeezed into one of the banquet chairs near the front of the Southgate Hindu Temple. Peeku, on stage with Sheela, was pumping himself up, raising the roof. Avi waved, but Peeku only had eyes for the fire and for Sheela. It was an ecumenical ceremony, part Hindu, part Muslim. Mohan Ji was co-officiating with an imam. Rav Uncle hadn't wanted either, as the priest triggered memories of his son's botched arrangement, and the imam supposedly talked like a "crypto-socialist." Rav Uncle also complained about this being an unofficial ceremony, given that Peeku and Sheela were already legally married. Rav Uncle threatened not to show, but Chrissy called his bluff. She knew he wouldn't miss his son's wedding.

Over the loudspeaker, the imam explained the many eternal significations of the ceremony, mixing Urdu with heavily accented English. Sheela, her gaze cast downward, wore a simple red saree and was the picture of a demure, traditional, and beautiful wife. Peeku was recycling his outfit from the video wedding, a gold and maroon sherwani. Someone in the row behind rasped as much: "Two weddings in eight months, he won't remember which one is his wife!" The neighbor said, "Temple management must be happy, repeat customer!"

The ceremony went smoothly. The garlands, the seven steps, the chants. Also the mirror and Holy Quran. When it was over, Rav Uncle insisted on speaking from the platform, near the fire. He thanked the gods. He expressed gratitude to the Punjabi 5 for their lifelong support. He said Peeku and Sheela were following on the heels of the other successful marriages in this great community, including Asha and Ashok, Rajeev and Laxmi, and Akhil and Bittoo. Rav Uncle's decision to omit Avi's marriage to Meena was humiliating, and someone in the row behind giggled and pointed. But it was understandable, too.

As the reception began, Peeku's voice came over the loudspeaker. "Everyone, everyone, please clear the dance floor. Before Sheela and

I dance together, I'm going to do my celebration dance. Sheela, this is for you!"

Peeku ambled, arms rocking, to the makeshift dance space in the middle of the circular tables and banquet chairs. He posed under the chandeliers, appearing somber, erect, and motionless, building the anticipation, milking the crowd. Maybe he was imitating Travolta. People whooped and clapped. The DJ dropped the song, the Pointer Sisters' "Jump (For My Love)," and Peeku started shimmying his hips, gently at first, wobbling ever so slightly, but soon gyrating his butt. As the song drove forward and crescendoed, Peeku crouched and leaned forward, pretend crawling, then he was limboing. He was dhamaal hopping, doing bhangra moves. He spread his arms wide like an airplane, he sashayed backwards, prowling around the stage and grabbing an imaginary microphone, like Mick Jagger. "I'm married!" he screamed. "I love you, Sheela! Avi, do the Facenda voice!"

Avi strolled to the standing microphone and, in the tones he and Peeku used to narrate simulated football plays, the deep bass of John Facenda, the fabled announcer who spoke in the "voice of God," Avi said, "Whoa, those dance steps are right on the money. Our guy's got a ton of muscle and a one-track mind. He pulls off an electrifying, bone-rattling, come-from-behind victory!"

As the sound engineer worked out an issue with the audio, Peeku came over to high-five Avi. "Thanks, dude. Hey, did you get my dance on wee-deo?"

"It's video, not wee-deo," Avi said.

Peeku gave him a look. "Video? What the heck? Why didn't you tell me before?"

"I should have," Avi said. "I really should have."

Chrissy was milling around, waiting for Peeku to finish his conversation with Avi so she could introduce her son to a few of the honored guests. Peeku stuck up a finger, asking for a minute.

"Dude, are you gonna move to Pittsburgh?" Peeku asked.

"Maybe," Avi said. "Meena says it doesn't feel right yet. She wants to focus on Leela, but I'm worried it will take a long time for Leela to settle in, and then they will have their own life without me."

"Just show up at her house," Peeku said. "That's what I did with Sheela."

Meena and Leela were living in a row house. It apparently had a gorgeous view of the rivers, the bridges, and the big buildings downtown, though Pittsburgh weather was gloomy this time of year, the vistas gray. If he just showed up, rang the doorbell without warning, they'd be in shock. Meena might be disconcerted, Leela disoriented. It could be exciting, though. He might enjoy a surprise visit, the suspense of not knowing how they'd greet him, putting a hand over his eyes and peering into their vestibule as a bit of sunlight made itself known.

Questions and Topics for Discussion

1. *For the Blessings of Jupiter and Venus* is told in alternating points of view. What do alternating points of view do for the story? Do you relate more to Meena or Avi? Who is the hero of the book?

2. The novel contrasts the marriages of several couples—Meena and Avi, Meena's parents, Avi's parents, Vishali and Andrew, Rav Uncle and Chrissy, Peeku and Sheela, Jim and Julie. Which of these couples do you think could be happy together? Is marital happiness mostly about compatibility, romantic attraction, or your state of mind?

3. Meena's father told her that "every marriage, sooner or later, becomes an arrangement." What did he mean? Do you agree? At one point, Meena wonders whether second marriages are necessary, also third, fourth, and fifth ones, if a couple is lucky. What is she saying?

4. Toward the end, Avi decides to live near a pond, "somewhere to cast away the surplus." What is this surplus? Has he come to understand his own desires, or is he deluding himself?

5. What do you think of the parents in this novel? How do you feel about Avi's relationship to his parents, and Meena's to hers?

6. Do you think the model minority myth is connected to Avi returning home, running for office, and getting married?

7. Meena says, "I don't see why people are so fixated about their identities. It's nice to have a couple of them. It's like taking off your work clothes at the end of the day and putting on your pajamas." Do you agree? Is it useful to have more than one social identity, or is having multiple identities the same as having none?

8. Most of the novel takes place in Southgate, a small town in East Central Ohio. How do the sensibilities of the people in Southgate play into the story?

9. This story takes place at a particular moment in history when the Indian diaspora was confident of its rising power, both in India and America. Do you believe their confidence was well grounded, or were they excessively optimistic?

10. What do you think about the way the legal system treats underage asylum seekers like Leela? How has globalization affected communities like Southgate, Ohio?

11. What is the significance of the title of this book?

12. Where do you think Avi and Meena will be in five or ten years?

Acknowledgments

I may not be astrologically blessed, but I have been lucky to receive the gift of literary friendship from many wonderful people. I will always be grateful to everyone at the Washington Writers' Publishing House for believing in this book, especially Caroline Bock, Jona Colson, Suzanne Feldman, Len Kruger, and Kathleen Wheaton.

My teachers commented on drafts, taught me craft, and above all nurtured the faith that I could pull this off. Bret Anthony Johnston's embodiment of the writing life has been an inspiration. Susan Coll pointed me to the heart of this story. Susan DeFreitas was an invaluable book coach who taught me everything I know about character arc. I benefited from Amy Hempel's exacting literary instincts and Manuel Gonzalez's insightful reactions to my characters.

Friends and colleagues read early drafts and offered astute comments, including Tom Inck, Kateri Carmola, Sarah Kass, Amy Neswald, Diana England, Neel Mukherjee, Biju Rao, Bob Lang, Saurabh Dani, Elisa Moles, Emily Pease, Peggy Levay, Michael Tager, Peter Miovic, Scott Westcott, Will Carrington, and Scott Gloden, as well as Jim Wehmeyer and Barbara Burton and their book club in Seattle, and Scott Sowers and the Novels in Progress group in Washington, DC. Wendy Blattner arranged the creation of a beautiful cover. Kathy Mills provided highly skilled copy editing. I've leaned on a lot of people, so if I've left anyone off this list, please forgive me!

I treasure my writing communities, including the VQR Writers' Conference organizers and workshop participants; everyone who teaches and works at The Writer's Center in Bethesda, MD; my friends at The Inner Loop in Washington, DC; my pandemic-era short story club friends Dan Coleman, Brian Kux, and Mark Paul; and my critique group members Daniel Knowlton, Sarah Williams, Nick Manning, Tamar Shapiro, Holly Piper, Suzanne Aro, and Amy Tercek.

I'm thankful to my parents, Kul and Kamlesh Gauri, and my brother Vinny Gauri, for their unwavering support, as well as their tolerance of my sometimes vexing sensibilities. Thank you, Ayesha, for critiquing drafts and vital brainstorming, supporting my writing in a hundred ways, and making this life with me. Thank you, Yasmeen, for your artistic advice and our uplifting conversations. Thank you, Sharif, for your resilience and loyalty and family pride, in which I know I am included. Safya, your pranks are in these pages.

About the Author

Varun Gauri was born in India and raised in the American Midwest. After studying philosophy in college and public policy in graduate school, he worked for more than two decades on global poverty and human rights, publishing academic articles and books on development economics and behavioral economics. He now teaches at Princeton University and lives with his family in Bethesda, Maryland. His short fiction was nominated for a Pushcart Prize and recognized in *Best American Nonrequired Reading*. He was a Summer Writer-in-Residence at Washington, DC's The Inner Loop. This is his first novel.

Washington Writers' Publishing House is a non-profit, co-operative literary organization that has published over 100 volumes of poetry since 1975 as well as fiction and non-fiction. The press sponsors three annual competitions for writers living in DC, Maryland, and Virginia, and the winners of each category (poetry, fiction, and creative non-fiction) comprise our annual slate. In 2021, WWPH launched an online literary journal, *WWPH Writes*, to expand our mission to further the creative work of writers in our region. In 2024, WWPH launched its biennial Works in Translation series. More about the Washington Writers' Publishing House is at www.washingtonwriters.org.

Printed in the USA
CPSIA information can be obtained
at www.ICGtesting.com
CBHW020445150924
14362CB00004B/6

9 781941 551424